KATHERINE STONE

THE OTHER TWIN

MIRA

ISBN 1-55166-747-9

THE OTHER TWIN

Visit us at www.mirabooks.com

Printed in U.S.A.

THE
OTHER
TWIN

Prologue

Pacific Heights
San Francisco
January 14
Thirty-one years ago

"You're not going to *marry* her!"

"Yes, Mother, I am." Alan Forrester's expression was calm, as was his voice. He'd expected this reaction, especially from his mother—including her feigned surprise. Both Rosalind and Gavin Forrester knew perfectly well the "very important" something he wanted to discuss. "I was hoping we could have our wedding here."

Here, the Forrester family home, was a French provincial mansion that had survived every quake to rock the Bay Area for the past hundred years.

Alan sensed a different kind of tembler now, one of

emotion not earth. His mother was formidable. Well, so was he. He was her son, after all.

Rosalind was going to have her say on the subject. Fine. That was only fair. And his father would weigh in as well. But Alan believed he would prevail. Despite their patrician heritage, and the vestigial wisps of class consciousness encoded in their DNA, his parents were reasonable human beings.

"You can marry here, darling. We *want* you to. But... her?"

"Claire, Mother. Her name is Claire. And she's the only woman I'll ever want to marry."

"She's hardly a *woman,* Alan."

"She'll be twenty-one two weeks from today. On our wedding day."

Rosalind blanched, but decided against addressing the two-week time frame. Nor could she quibble with the six-year age difference, not when she and Gavin were seven years apart. And pointing out that Alan and Claire had known each other for less than three months also wouldn't work. *Her* love for Gavin had been quite literally at first sight.

But Rosalind Elizabeth Paige and Gavin Alan Forrester had been ideally matched. Atherton and Pacific Heights. Vassar and Yale. Sole heir and only heiress to fortunes in ships and trains.

Whereas Claire and Alan...

"You're a *surgeon,* Alan, at one of the best medical centers on earth. And she's a hippie, a *flower child,* with everything that implies. Marijuana. Promiscuity. LSD."

Alan had anticipated this tack. But he'd underestimated how much it would hurt. Claire wasn't a flower child, he knew, but a forgotten child, the fourth daughter born to parents hoping for a son. Eleven minutes after Claire's birth, their hope was realized. Her twin, Robbie, arrived with a triumphant squeal.

Two subsequent pregnancies yielded two more boys, and the MacKenzie family was complete. Three vivacious daughters. Three strapping sons. And Claire, the twin—the *other* twin—the runt of the gold-and-red litter, diminutive in every way. On the rare occasions when she spoke, her soft voice was lost in the din. Which didn't really matter, she'd confessed to the man she loved. She hadn't, before their love, had much to say. And except for assigned classwork, her art was hers alone. Why show her family paintings that her art teachers had already branded too pastel?

Claire's art, like Claire herself, was barely visible. Hardly there. But not—quite—*in*visible. And even that gossamer presence was too much, an awkwardness made worse by her pathetic efforts to fit in.

Claire didn't fit in. Couldn't. Never would. She knew it. Her family knew it. Everyone in Sarah's Orchard, Oregon, knew it. So it was a bittersweet blend of relief and regret that greeted the news that Claire MacKenzie had purchased a one-way bus ticket to San Francisco.

Claire could have become a flower child. Her journey brought her to a meadowland of such lost souls. But unlike so many of the drifting blossoms, the high-school dropout had a passion.

She didn't imagine selling her paintings; never even thought to try. But passersby admired the watercolors on the street artist's easel and it wasn't long before she was supporting her modest lifestyle solely through her art.

Alan wanted to tell his parents the story of the woman he loved.

One day he would.

But today it would only fuel his mother's certainty that Claire wasn't right for him. There must be something dreadfully wrong with her. Why else would her own family have so willingly let her go?

"Is she pregnant, Alan?" Gavin asked.

"Because if so," Rosalind added, "there are things that can be done."

Alan had expected a fair fight. And maybe this was fair. Maybe all was fair in the battles parents waged in what they believed to be the best interests of their child——especially when that child was, as he was, their only child.

But Alan wasn't appreciating fairness. He was exhausted, having been on call and operating for thirty-six hours straight. More compelling than his need for sleep, though, was his need for Claire.

His parents' home was an easy three-block walk from Pacific Heights Medical Center. An effortless stroll. Unless, as tonight, you forbade yourself from stopping at your own apartment—and seeing the woman you loved—en route.

Alan had done that because he was determined to have this discussion behind him, behind them all. If they could.

"Are you really saying you'd want her to abort my child? Your grandchild?"

"How can you be sure it's even yours? I mean, heaven knows how many—"

"Be very careful, Mother. You're talking about your future daughter-in-law." *Your virginal daughter-in-law.* "Claire's not pregnant. Yet."

"Oh, Alan, why her? What do you see in *her?*"

"*Claire.* And what I see in Claire is my life."

"But she's—"

"Not our kind of people? I'm beginning to think you're right. She's gracious, loving—"

"We love you, Alan!"

"I know. At least I thought I did. But if you do, you'll love Claire." Alan held his mother's gaze until she looked away, then focused on his father, one of the Bay Area's premier attorneys. "Dad?"

"Have you considered a prenuptial agreement? It's advisable, Alan. I'm sure Stuart's told you the same thing— or he will, when you tell him your plans."

Stuart Dawson and Alan Forrester had been friends since their freshman year at Stanford. And despite Stuart's impoverished, even disreputable, roots, Alan's parents had welcomed him as if a long-lost son. Yes, family mattered to Gavin and Rosalind. Generations of careful breeding offered a certain reassurance.

But a child could hardly be held accountable for the happenstance of his birth—assuming he overcame the obstacle in what Gavin and Rosalind regarded as the most acceptable way: through education. Stuart had excelled academically. Summa cum laude from Stanford. Harvard *Law Review*. He was excelling still, on track for partnership at Forrester, Grant & Sloan.

Stuart had been with Alan in Ghirardelli Square on Halloween night. He'd witnessed the moment—the magic—when Claire and Alan met, and had long since agreed to be Alan's best man.

And attorney Stuart Dawson's only advice: *Marry her soon, Alan. Don't let her go.*

"Let's not involve Stuart in this," Alan said.

"Agreed," Gavin conceded. "And the prenuptial?"

"I understand my responsibilities, Dad. And I take them very seriously."

Unresponsive, Gavin Forrester would have countered to such a reply in court.

But Gavin recognized his son's non-answer for the challenge it was. *I'm going to marry Claire. And I'm not going to ask her to sign anything but our marriage license. So trust me. Believe in me.*

Gavin and Rosalind had spent Alan's life doing just

that. Gavin's smile made it clear he had no intention of stopping now.

Gavin was on his side. But Rosalind persevered. "What about *Mariel?*"

"What about her?" Alan's innocent query was as disingenuous as his mother's pretended surprise at his marriage plans.

"What are you going to tell her?"

"That she's invited to a wedding on January twenty-eighth. If not here, then somewhere else."

"She's going to be devastated. I'm very sure she believes the two of you will reconcile one day."

"And I'm very sure she doesn't. She would've told me if she did."

Mariel Lancaster wasn't shy, especially when it came to something she wanted. And when that was a man, she was particularly clear. And confident. Mariel had also been, until two years ago, Alan's most significant romance. The liaison had delighted Rosalind. Mariel was Alan's perfect match. Main Line Philadelphia. Bryn Mawr. Stanford MBA.

"Besides," Alan said, "there's nothing *to* reconcile. Our relationship didn't work—which, as you well know, Mariel realized before I did. We're closer now than when we were dating. She'll be happy for me. Stuart will be. So will anyone who loves me—and anyone who loves me will love Claire."

"Oh, Alan."

"I love her. And, amazingly, she loves me."

"Amazingly?"

"It's amazing, I think, that the woman I want to spend my life with feels the same about spending her life with me."

Of course the street urchin would want to spend her life with Alan, Rosalind thought. Any woman would, even if her son didn't have a dime. But this Claire was a girl with nothing, and the fact of Alan's wealth, the allure of it, couldn't be discounted.

Rosalind was contemplating whether she dared to remind Alan of such an obvious truth when she was preempted by a quiet assertion from him.

"She's not a gold digger, Mother."

"I never said—"

"She's the gold."

Rosalind sighed. Elaborately. But her faint smile acknowledged her surrender. This was not a battle she would ever win. She sighed again, for emphasis, before the ultimate concession. "I guess I have a wedding to plan...."

Rosalind Forrester wouldn't have made a good poker player, not that she would've been caught dead playing poker. Still, for her son, she attempted to conceal her skepticism about the young woman who became in rapid succession his fiancée, his wife, and who in early December would give birth to his child.

Rosalind's initial efforts failed. Miserably. But it was

the thought that counted and she *was* trying. It helped that Alan was so happy and that Gavin, Stuart and Mariel were solidly in Claire's camp.

Most of all, it helped that Claire was Claire. She didn't try to curry favor with her new mother-in-law——or anyone else. Nor did the girl from Sarah's Orchard, Oregon, make what would've been painfully awkward attempts to fit into the Forresters' world. It wasn't hostility toward the rarefied echelons of high society. Or sullenness that she might never belong. Or defiance toward those who did.

Claire was none of those things. She was simply a woman in love.

Claire hadn't quite won Rosalind over——or perhaps her mother-in-law wasn't entirely aware that, in fact, she *had*——when Rosalind suggested the newlyweds move in with them. The mansion was ideal for such an arrangement, with abundant space and privacy. An entire wing would be Claire and Alan's to decorate as they chose and live in however they wished. Neither Rosalind nor Gavin need ever pass through the heavy wooden doors.

But Alan wanted to show his parents——and Stuart and Mariel——what his artist bride had created. How she'd transformed their home.

"It feels like springtime." Rosalind's appreciation was unconcealed. "Like a Mother's Day bouquet."

"Complete with cherry blossoms," Mariel embellished

as they reached the soft pink nursery. "I love it! But I thought Claire wasn't having—didn't need—any tests. Not even an ultrasound."

"She hasn't," Alan said. "Doesn't."

"So how do we know that my future godchild, *our* future godchild—" Mariel cast a glowing smile at Stuart "—is going to be a little girl?"

"We don't," Rosalind replied. "Not scientifically. But Claire's as certain there's a ballerina dancing inside her as I was that my kicking baby was a boy."

The Forrester family vacation, slated for late October at the lodge in Pebble Beach, had been scheduled before Claire realized she was pregnant. The plans didn't change with the news. In fact, additional reservations were made for the godparents-to-be.

The eventual trip to Carmel would depend on how Claire, five weeks from her due date, felt at the time.

Fine! she insisted. *Wonderful*. Her doctor agreed. Claire was the picture of health.

The party of six would make the drive in two cars, the Forresters in Gavin's Mercedes, and Mariel and Stuart—an "item" since spring—in Mariel's Jag.

The driving arrangements had to be revised when Mariel arrived at the mansion without Stuart. A crisis had developed on a pending case, she informed the others. One Stuart felt obliged to deal with in person—in Chicago. He'd taken a red-eye to the Windy City and would fly from O'Hare to Monterey the minute he'd out-lawyered the opposing counsel.

Mariel had already decided that Claire would ride with her. Insisted on it. She was in the mood, she said, for a little "girl talk."

A storm was forecast by evening. Already the heavens wept.

Inside both cars, however, was pure sunshine.

"I've never seen Alan this happy," Mariel gushed. "I doubt any surgery resident in the history of surgical residencies has ever been this happy. Maybe *no* man has!"

"Alan loves his work."

"Yes. He does. But, Claire, he loves you more."

Let Mariel be the big sister you never had, Alan had told her. She *wants* to be. Yes, she can be overbearing and has a non-negotiable preference for getting her own way. But she likes you, Claire. And with Mariel that's not always the case. "I...thank you, Mariel."

"You're welcome! Now, let's talk about the baby shower. Are you *positive* there's no one you'd like us to invite?"

Co-hostesses Rosalind and Mariel had invited all their friends, which meant that the baby-shower guest list read like, indeed *was,* a who's who of San Francisco's most influential women.

One of whom, Rosalind was explaining in the other car, was flying in from Palm Springs expressly for the party.

"No one's said no."

"That doesn't surprise me."

"You don't sound pleased, Alan. Are you worried that Claire's feeling overwhelmed?"

"A little worried."

"Has she told you she is?"

"No. In fact," he admitted, "she says it makes her feel welcome."

"She *is* welcome. *Very.*" The softness in Rosalind's voice matched her son's. "We love her, Alan. We're so grateful she's in our lives."

The conversations remained sunny even as the weather deteriorated into a fury of wind and rain. Gavin drove more cautiously than was required, or than he might normally have done. But his slower speed obliged the never particularly cautious Mariel to follow suit.

Gavin Forrester's fifty-four-year-old reflexes were excellent. As was his eyesight. He routinely won at racquetball against players half his age—Alan's age.

Gavin spotted the fawn the instant her first impulsive hoof touched the pavement. And he saw, an instant later, her anxious parents scrambling to catch up.

Gavin swerved, recovered, then glanced in the rearview mirror to confirm that the deer family, as well as Mariel and Claire, were safe.

All were.

It was only a fleeting glance, and Gavin hadn't yet resumed his pre-swerve speed, and who'd have imagined a second fawn?

She darted, too—the other twin, the forgotten fawn—desperate to reunite with the family that had forsaken her.

Gavin swerved again. Saved her, too.

The cliffside highway curved sharply at the precise moment of the second swerve, and just beyond the bend a massive oil slick gleamed bright purple on the rain-gray road. Gavin couldn't avoid it; no driver could. And the fate of his own family was irrevocably sealed.

Gavin sounded his horn in urgent warning even as the car skidded across the stain and took flight, soaring down.

Down.

Down.

"No!" Claire and Mariel cried out as they rounded the bend and saw the car flying off the cliff.

Mariel's Jaguar skidded, too, on the oil slick. But its slower speed, thanks to Gavin's warning, enabled Mariel—and the drivers of the four cars behind them—to stop.

One of the drivers left immediately, to summon help. The other three created roadblocks, to prevent further tragedy, while Claire and Mariel scrambled down to the crash site.

It was a steep descent, and a hopeful one.

No flames engulfed the metallic-blue sedan. And remarkably, the soaring vehicle had landed right-side up. Its sleek contours were damaged, of course. Badly bruised. As, both scrambling women knew, its occupants would be. Their muscles would ache with even greater stiffness tomorrow. But a Pebble Beach hot tub would soothe the unhappy muscles, as would cocktails by a blazing fire, followed by dinner in the seaside suite, in robes and slippers if they liked, then off to bed for a good night's sleep.

But there'd be no aching muscles for Alan's parents. No hot tub, no fire, no Vodka Collins and Ramos Fizz.

The driveshaft, broken on impact, had sliced through Gavin's heart. And although at first glance Rosalind appeared unconscious, but quite unscathed, what remained of the other side of her face told the horrific tale.

Gavin was dead. Rosalind was dead.

And their son? Alive, conscious and achingly aware of the saber in his father and his mother's half-face of blood. Alan was also aware of his own plight: trapped in steel, unable to move, with muscles that would never ache—but would scream, as they were screaming already, as already they were beginning to die.

Dr. Alan Forrester knew his wounds were mortal.

But he smiled at Claire from his shining blue coffin and nodded a reassuring *I'm okay.*

Alan didn't speak the reassurance, or even mouth it. He couldn't for fear of the gush of blood that would accompany even the slightest parting of his lips.

The hemorrhage was major, from his lungs, and it was ongoing, flooding his throat, again and again despite the gulping swallows he took.

Lips sealed, jaw clenched, Alan smiled through the shattered windshield at Claire. And she smiled at him, as if believing his lie—and when her placenta tore from her womb, and she knew without looking that what drenched her legs was blood, Claire lied as well.

"I'm in labor, Alan. That's the startled look you undoubtedly noticed. And yes, I admit, there's a *little* pain. But it's nothing, my love. Nothing! And it means our precious baby is on her way. The timing's perfect. You hear the sirens, don't you? Lots of paramedics, Alan, *lots,* and they're almost here. While some are getting you out of the car, others will help me deliver our baby girl. She can't wait. She wants to see her daddy *now.* You'll hold her soon. You'll hold our daughter, Alan. Our Paige Elizabeth. *Soon.*"

They'd decided on the name weeks ago and had planned to reveal it this weekend. But in the sunny car, two miles before it flew, Alan had given the baby's namesake and grandmother—formerly Rosalind Elizabeth Paige—the news.

Alan wanted Claire to know how happy Rosalind had been, how moved, how thrilled—and that she'd also been worried for the daughter-in-law she'd come to love. Shouldn't the baby be named for Claire's mother, too? Was Alan certain this was what Claire wanted?

Very certain, Alan had told his mother during those final two miles. *We're* Claire's family now.

Emotion had filled his throat then, and blood did now.

So much blood. More and more. He couldn't swallow fast enough, and he was getting weaker with each pulsing mouthful. The cracks on the windshield were beginning to blur, as was her lovely face beyond.

And yet, even in the blur and despite her courageous smile, the physician saw what Claire could not hide. The pallor, as if she was losing blood, too. And the pain, far more than the *little* she'd admitted to. And the fear. The terror.

The fright of a mother for the fate of her unborn child.

Alan was trapped. Weak. Dying.

But he closed his throat against the rising tide of blood just long enough to say the words he must.

"I love you, Claire. I *love* you."

Pacific Heights Medical Center
San Francisco
Saturday, November 2
Present day

Gweneth Angelica St. James had not, to the best of her knowledge, been inside a hospital before. Ever.

She'd most likely been born outdoors, in the lee of a sand dune or beneath a canopy of pines. Her mother hadn't abandoned her there. In late October, a newborn couldn't possibly have survived—especially since, the nuns later told her, she'd been born during a storm.

Gwen's never-known mother had been making the rain-drenched journey to St. James Convent on foot when a Good Samaritan offered her a ride. It was the Samaritan who'd presented Sister Mary Catherine with the newborn baby girl, an infant so healthy there'd been no need to take her to a hospital.

And no need for Gwen to take herself to a hospital during the thirty-one years of glorious good health since.

But definitely a reason.

Laser surgery was readily available these days. And the advances were remarkable. The Laser Clinic at Pacific Heights Medical Center offered state-of-the-art technology, and its staff was world-renowned. Gwen couldn't ask for a better place to inquire about the meticulous— tiny blood vessel by tiny blood vessel—application of laser beams to one fourth of her face.

Nor could Gwen ask for a place more likely to produce life-changing results.

All she needed to do was ask—if she dared.

Gwen tossed away the thought with a shake of her head. The issue—would she change? could she change? did she dare?—was hardly new, and today's visit was about authentic courage: the bravery of an eighty-two-year-old great-grandmother.

Louise Johansson had waged a valiant battle against cancer, and even as she was surrendering, the final victory would be hers. She was going home, to spend with her family the remaining hours, minutes, seconds her strength would allow.

Louise's granddaughter, Robyn, was a sound technician at the FOX-TV affiliate where makeup artist Gwen St. James readied the on-air anchors for their camera-friendly appearances during the dinner-hour and late-night news.

Gwen knew about Robyn's grandmother's struggle with cancer. Everyone at the station knew. But Robyn shared the most with Gwen, describing every medical twist, every emotional turn.

Robyn also shared with Gwen her gratitude to the oncologist who'd been with Louise every step of the way. Dr. Paige Forrester had kept Louise alive, with quality, for as long as Louise had wished to fight. It had been tricky at times, a careful balance between the efficacy the chemotherapeutic agents Paige needed to use and their toxicity.

But today Louise was going home, assuming her last-minute worry could be conquered. Her appearance was too frightening, she feared, for her great-grandchildren to see. She'd lost so much weight. Her skin hung like a monstrous jowl from her skeletal cheeks.

Maybe she shouldn't go home after all.

Robyn had approached Gwen for tips. Was there a way to add color without making her grandmother look like a clown—or worse, she'd added quietly, an apprentice undertaker's corpse? And was there some reverse contouring Gwen might suggest, the opposite of what she did for the station's ratings-magnet anchor, Madolyn Mitchell? A seldom-used technique of making a face look plump, not thin?

Gwen offered to do Louise's makeup. Of course. She

would have, regardless of whether she lived close to the hospital or not. As it happened, her apartment was nearby, a leisurely two-minute walk; she'd come to the hospital whenever Robyn wanted her to.

So the day's plans were made. It would be best for Louise, least tiring, if she and Gwen were alone during the makeup session between one-thirty and two, after which Robyn and Dr. Forrester—off for the weekend, but coming in to say goodbye—would appear.

No matter how the made-up Louise looked (there was only so much even Gwen could do) both grand-daughter and oncologist would encourage Louise to permit the waiting orderlies to whisk her to Robyn's pillow-laden SUV.

Gwen reached the hospital's main entrance at one-fifteen. But it was apprehension, rather than the fact that she was early, that slowed her long-legged gait. She'd never seen anyone ravaged by cancer. By any illness. Nor had she ever been with someone who knew that within hours she would die.

Gwen vowed to do what she could to make this day perfect for Louise. Whatever discomfort—or even alarm—she herself might experience would be hidden away.

Somehow.

Gwen did have something to draw on. True, it'd been sixteen years since anyone had reacted to the sight of Gweneth St. James with less than unqualified approval. But the memories of pity, even horror, were easily recalled.

The double takes had been the most difficult, when her good side had been glimpsed first and she sensed the observer's eagerness to see the rest. And when all was revealed, the dashed expectations made the shock all the more...shocking.

Well. Gwen had no inflated imaginings of the way Louise would look. Indeed, she'd spent a restless night envisioning the worst. And if the reality was worse yet, there'd be no double take of shock. No instinctive gasp of revulsion. Gwen had heard those, too.

Gwen wasn't alone as she neared the hospital. Nor was hers the only long-legged gait to suddenly slow.

The other woman hoped, perhaps, to avoid reaching the heavy glass doors at the precise moment as Gwen. To forestall the inevitable—if fleeting—interaction with a stranger?

But that wasn't it. She was quite oblivious to Gwen. To everything. She walked with her head down, lost in thought.

She was dressed in silk and cashmere, in shades of cream and sable, an ensemble of slacks, blouse, coat— and pearls. Such elegance could have taken her anywhere in this sophisticated city.

Something in her carriage said she'd be welcome... anywhere.

But she wasn't on her way to an auction at Butter-field's. Or to private showings of Tiffany gems or Pearl Moon couture. Nor was she attending a Nob Hill recital—for Guild patrons only—performed by the symphony's virtuoso cellist.

She was visiting the hospital instead. Approaching with trepidation. To say farewell to a dying grandparent, perhaps, or to a parent, a husband, a...child.

Maybe *she* was the patient. The thought came as Gwen caught a glimpse of the face framed by a stylishly cut halo of dark brown hair. The hair was thick and lustrous, but the face was thin and pale. And her dark blue eyes were troubled. Perhaps she, too, was en route to 8-North, the oncology ward.

Gwen reached the door first and held it wide.

"Oh!" the patrician voice exclaimed. "Thank you."

"You're welcome." Gwen smiled. And unaccountably ached for this stranger. *Help her,* she whispered as the elegant woman crossed the lobby and disappeared. *Someone help her.*

Please.

Someone would, Gwen decided. The journey from lobby to cancer ward was a brightly lighted passage of sparkling walls, shiny linoleum floors and smiling personnel. Its message was crystal clear.

Here was a place of life, not death.

Of hope, not despair.

Help was available for anyone with the courage to seek it—and the boldness to follow through.

Witness Louise Johansson...which Gwen was about to do.

No double take, she had vowed. No matter how ravaged Louise looked.

But Gwen couldn't completely block her surprise.

The elderly woman wasn't huddled in her bed. Indeed, as if this were a hotel, the bed had been freshly made for the day. The impression of a hotel, and a grand one at that, carried through to the furnishings. And the view.

Louise was enjoying both—the panorama of white-capped Pacific, observed from the comfort of a plush armchair situated before the window.

Louise's bathrobe was fluffy, as was the blanket draped from lap to floor.

And Louise herself? Skeletal. Cadaverous.

But her eyes twinkled, and her wasted muscles drew her chalky lips into a sassy smile.

"I look like death warmed over, don't I?"

"*No*. You look—" *so alive, too alive to be dying* "—lovely."

"Ha!"

"You do!"

"You must be Gweneth St. James, the makeup wiz. You *do* belong on the cover of *Vogue!* My word, look at your eyes. They're honest-to-goodness forget-me-not blue. And your hair. Copper! Robyn said you were model-gorgeous, and she was right."

No, she wasn't. "Well...I am Gwen, Mrs. Johansson."

"Louise! Please. Robyn also said how nice you are to *everyone*, including—no, especially—the bedraggled and forlorn. I can see she was right about that, too. I just hope you're not so nice you'll tell me I don't need any makeup."

"You don't *need* any. But I do believe I can come up with some colorful things that might be fun."

"Then by all means do! I've always been a big believer in fun."

"Great." Gwen drew a second armchair closer and sat face-to-face. "So. Let's see what colors you are today."

"Gray with just a hint of green."

"Nope. That's not what I'm seeing."

"How can you *not* be?"

Gwen smiled. "Rumor has it I have a knack for seeing colors trapped beneath the surface."

"True colors shining through? To which you give their freedom?"

"I try to."

"Where do they come from, I wonder, those true colors? The heart? The spirit? The soul?"

"I don't know," Gwen said softly. But she'd wondered, too.

"Does anyone ever come up colorless?"

Just me. "Some people are more colorful than others. You, for example. Just wait till you see the palette that's clamoring to be set free." Gwen studied Louise's face a little longer, then gave a decisive nod. "Okay, I have a plan. First we moisturize—"

"My skin's so dry."

Gwen touched the aged face. The skin was warm.

Alive. And paper-thin. Tissue paper draped on bones. "Not really. I use moisturizer on everyone. It's the best makeup glue I've found. Just close your eyes and relax... and no peeking until I'm through."

2

"Gram!" Robyn exclaimed, thirty minutes later, from the doorway. "You are *beautiful*."

"Oh, I doubt that."

"Haven't you seen yourself yet?"

"Not yet," Gwen replied, her gaze remaining on Louise as Robyn approached. "And she's been impressively restrained about not looking."

"You told me not to! And although it was hardly the case for my first seventy-nine years on the planet, since my three-year duel with cancer *compliance* has become my middle name. Isn't that so, Paige?"

"That's so," a second voice answered. A patrician voice. "And *wow*, Louise. Just wait until you see!"

"Which will happen in about ten seconds." Gwen finished her appraisal of Louise's face, then made an expert survey of Louise's hair. The snowy mane had vanished, Robyn had told her, with the chemo. But it had reappeared with exuberance…when, with equal exuberance, the cancer had returned. Gwen gathered the bountiful chaos, leaving fullness around Louise's face but lifting it off her shoulders and neck. Then, satisfied that the swept-up style was better, she plucked the clip that held her own long copper curls in a casual twist and transferred it to the chignon she'd created. "There. Very Helen Hayes. *Now* it's time to look."

As Gwen reached for the mirror in her makeup bag, she glanced at Robyn and the doctor beside her—the elegant woman for whom Gwen had held the door—who acknowledged the coincidence with a smile.

"Hi, Gwen. I'm Paige."

"Hi." *Help her. Someone help her.*

Gwen still felt the urgent plea. Why? Dr. Paige Forrester was someone who helped people herself. One of the best. And the trepidation Gwen had seen? The haunting?

Vanquished, for the moment, for Louise.

Louise was only one of many similar worries for Paige. There were additional patients on 8-North, an entire ward full, and more, perhaps, in the ICU. Even the luckiest ones, at home on this Saturday afternoon, were out of sight but far from out of mind.

But for Louise, Paige had hidden all visible worry that could—without makeup—be hidden. An abundance of concealer would be required to hide the lingering shadows of exhaustion beneath Paige's eyes.

Such fatigue was familiar to Paige's patients. In her grateful ravings about Louise's doctor, Robyn had said as much. Perhaps the shadows even offered comfort—evidence that Paige Forrester was fighting with them, for them, around the clock.

Paige was fighting now, helping now, as she encouraged a hesitant Louise to look in the mirror.

"It's well worth it, Louise."

"Okay. Here goes. Oh! Oh, *my*. I don't believe I looked this pretty on my wedding day. If only your grandfather could see me...well, maybe he will. Maybe with the moisturizer Gwen used, the makeup will last until we see each other again."

"Gram..."

Louise waved away her granddaughter's tearful concern. It was a merry wave and a jingling one. Louise's wedding rings, worn throughout her sixty-three-year marriage and during the fourteen months since her beloved's death, moved freely on her bony finger. "I feel eighteen. A bride in shades of peach and pink. Those are my colors today?"

"I think so."

"I do, too. Not only do I feel *peachy*, but also *in the pink*." Louise's blush beneath the blush Gwen had given her was glowing proof of a spirit tinted a delicate rose. "You're a marvel, Gwen."

"No, Louise, you are."

"Well. Thank you, sweet girl. Thanks to all three of you sweet girls for giving me this day." The bride's jingling hand shooed away both replies and sadness. "I've been so blessed. I've lived life to the fullest. Given it my very best shot. I can honestly say I don't have a single regret. I wish such happiness—and serenity—for all of you."

There were replies this time, a trio of whispered thank-yous, during which Louise studied Gwen's face as intently as Gwen had studied hers.

Was she searching for Gwen's colors? And seeing only colorlessness shining through? Maybe. Except, as Louise cupped Gwen's right cheek in her wedding-ring hand, she smiled. "Live life to the fullest, Gweneth St. James. And no regrets."

When her hand fell away, Louise turned to Robyn and Paige. "Ladies? I guess it's time to go."

Gwen didn't join the entourage of 8-North staff that escorted Louise to Robyn's SUV. She remained in Louise's room, in the chair by the window, her vision blurred, her heart weeping, her emotions swirled.

She had no idea how much time had passed when, from the doorway, came the quiet "Gwen?" in a now-familiar voice.

A now-welcome voice.

Gwen hadn't expected Paige to return to the ward, much less to Louise's room. She wasn't on call this weekend, Robyn had said; she was merely coming in to say goodbye.

But perhaps returning to her patient's room was part of Dr. Paige Forrester's last farewell. Perhaps she would sit in a chair by the window and embrace—as Gwen had embraced—the invisible yet shimmering spirit that still lingered. Maybe Paige could even hear, as Gwen herself imagined she was hearing, the faintest jingling of wedding rings.

And if a private memorial was something Paige always did for her patients, she was finding today's solitary ritual intruded upon by an interloper with watery eyes.

Gwen swiped at her tears as she turned. "Paige. Hi."

"Hi."

"I'd better go."

"No, Gwen, don't. Not because of me. But...may I join you?"

Paige seemed uncertain, but hopeful, as if sharing her final goodbye with Gwen was something she wanted to do.

"Of course, Paige." *Welcome.*

"Thank you." As Paige settled in Louise's chair, she said what Louise would have. "Don't be sad, Gwen. She doesn't want us to be."

But you, Dr. Forrester, are so sad. Sad wasn't a word Robyn had ever used in describing Paige Forrester. Nor was *troubled.* Or *haunted.* Robyn's Paige was always cheerful. A bright facade. A shining veneer for her patients and their families. "It's hard not to be sad."

"Yes. It is. But what a gift you gave her, Gwen."

"Not me, Paige. *You.*" But it clearly wasn't enough. Paige appeared haunted again. As if her best wasn't enough. Never enough. As if she should have tried harder. Done better. *Help her. Someone help her.* "You must be exhausted."

"A little tired. I imagine I look it. I didn't get much sleep last night."

Or the night before, Gwen thought. Or all the nights spent worrying about—and caring for—her patients. Every night. "Can you go home and crash?"

"In a while. I promised to drop by my mother's first. In—" Paige glanced at her watch "—fifty minutes."

"Promises to keep," Gwen murmured. "And miles to go?"

"No. Just three blocks."

"And from her home to yours?"

Paige's smile was weary. "The same three blocks in reverse. I'm in the condominium across the street from the main entrance. You live nearby, too, don't you?"

"Yes, but how do you—oh, Robyn."

"Robyn," Paige affirmed. "Who just happens to be a charter member of the Gwen St. James fan club."

"*And* a charter member of the Paige Forrester fan club. I do live nearby, at Belvedere Court. In fact, I may be the only tenant in the entire apartment complex who doesn't work in this hospital."

"Have you lived there long?"

"Seven years. It *is* a bit of a drive to the station. But I

travel off-peak. I go in at three and come home at midnight. Even if it wasn't a low-impact commute, I
wouldn't move. I love living in Pacific Heights. The
homes, the views, the *feel*. Don't you?"

"Oh. Yes. Of course. Although I don't appreciate it the
way I should. I'm spoiled, I guess. I grew up here. I take
views like this for granted." Paige gestured to the vista
beyond the crystal-clear glass. Leaves flew from nearby
branches. And in the distance a dancing sea cast diamonds
into the wind. "It *is* spectacular."

"Yes," Gwen said. And, she knew, Paige Forrester was
far from spoiled. As Robyn had explained, she was the
sole heiress to the "vast Forrester fortune," and "could've
gone jet-setting around the world 24/7." Instead, she
wore herself out caring for patients with cancer.

Not spoiled at all, Gwen thought in the comfortable silence that had fallen as they marveled at leaves and waves.

And, in that companionable hush, Paige had a similar
thought about Gwen—based, too, on what the talkative
Robyn had told her.

Gwen St. James *might* have been spoiled. With her
beauty and her talent, she had every reason to be. But she
wasn't. She was the most attentive, in fact, to those who
needed attention the most. "In stark contrast," to the station's "prima donna anchor," Madolyn Mitchell, who
deigned to converse with the production crew only when
she had complaints or demands.

That Gwen was more beautiful than Madolyn was beyond dispute. Gwen was also, in Robyn's opinion, more talented, a true artist—as evidenced by how *lovely* she could make the imperious Madolyn look. Madolyn was simply adept at reading a TelePrompTer.

Gwen was "incredibly easy" to talk to, genuinely interested, always discreet. Everyone confided in her. The men, the women, the anchors—Madolyn included— the crew. And all of them, Madolyn included, trusted the makeup artist absolutely.

But the confiding of problems, of anything really, was a one-way street. Well, okay, Gwen had revealed she had a boyfriend, David, she'd been with "forever." That was all anyone knew about David—except for the obvious: Gwen was so happy in David's love she had no problems to share, no worries to confide.

But, Paige realized, that wasn't true.

"It was so nice of you to confide in Louise," she said. "I'm sure she was very flattered that you did."

"I didn't confide in Louise."

"Oh! I just assumed, given what she said to you before we left, that her words had some special meaning."

No regrets. Live life to the fullest.

"They did." That was all Gwen needed to confess. Paige expected no more and was far too polite to pry. But... "It was as if she knew about my birthmark. Here. Where she touched. Everywhere she touched. The entire cheek."

"A port-wine stain?"

"Yes."

"That must've been difficult for you as a child. Laser surgery wouldn't have been an option then, and my memory is that nothing before lasers really worked and could even result in permanent scars."

"Treatment wasn't an issue for me as a child. Nor, for that matter, was the birthmark until I moved away from the convent at age thirteen."

"The convent?"

"Where my mother left me the night I was born. I don't know why she didn't want me. The birthmark, I suppose, or maybe she was just a panicked teenager who would've given her baby away regardless. I do know I was lucky she chose St. James. The nuns christened me Angelica—Angel—and said the birthmark was a blessing from God. They believed it. I believed it. As did all the other girls who attended the convent school. I wasn't more special to God than my classmates. The nuns were *quite* definite about that. But I was definitely not less special to Him, either."

"Good for the nuns."

"They were good people. I had a blissful childhood, thanks to them."

"But something happened when you were thirteen."

"Yes. But...do you really want to hear this?"

"I really do."

"Okay. Well. When the convent closed, I was given the choice of relocating with the nuns to a diocese in New

Mexico or remaining in California—and moving to San Francisco—as a ward of the state. I chose the latter."

"Even though you loved living with the nuns."

"Even though. But it was such an easy decision at the time. It would be a grand adventure, I thought, a chance to live with families and make friends with boys as well as girls. Had anyone told me new friendships wouldn't happen, that no one would want to be my friend, I'd have waved the worry away. I was *so* confident, empowered by the nuns' conviction that I was just like everyone else—and with a dark purple imprimatur from God besides. Needless to say, the world beyond the cloistered walls was a far cry from what I'd expected."

Gwen paused abruptly, as the memory of joyful innocence became swamped by the anguish that followed. She was in danger of drowning again, as she'd almost drowned then. But she had perspective now, eighteen years of it, and used it as a buoy to float atop the emotional flood until the worst of the deluge had passed.

"I've subsequently learned," she said matter-of-factly, "that virtually all living creatures make nearly irrevocable decisions about revulsion or attraction within the first fifteen seconds of seeing a potential friend or mate. It's natural to do so. Instinctual. The most efficient way to ensure that the species survives. Eventually, most human beings realize you can't necessarily tell a book by its cover. But if the cover's sufficiently off-putting, even an avid reader's unlikely to bother seeing what's inside…unless, of course, the book's recommended by someone he or she trusts."

Gwen drew a breath, exhaled, submerged herself in the still-turbulent waters of memory. "So there I was, a girl with a repulsive cover and no one around to recommend the inner me."

"*That* was difficult."

"Very. Teenage girls can be vicious. They made it painfully clear that my very presence was an assault on their sensibilities. How dare I contaminate their school? I was such an extreme horror to them that even the other outcasts—the girls who were too fat, too thin, too *wrong*—shunned me, fearing any association with me would make their own situations even worse. At first, I was just bewildered. So stunned, I suppose, that I couldn't really process what was happening. But it didn't take long, once the shock wore off, for my bewilderment to turn to anger. The nuns had lied to me, I decided. *Set me up.* Of course, the Angel they'd raised to believe in herself would've marched right up to her new classmates and explained that she wasn't a ghoul, the stain wasn't contagious, and if they were lucky she might, just might, become their friend. But that Angel was long gone. For all I knew, I *was* a ghoul. I certainly felt like one. And maybe the purple ugliness *was* contagious. Why not? Everything else the nuns had told me was false. I went through a few foster homes, and a few schools, before landing in a group home for troubled teens. I wasn't really troubled compared to my housemates. Or, I suppose I should say, compared to them I had no cause to be. I didn't acknowledge that of course, or how fortunate I was to have been raised with such love. At the time I was at war with the world."

"At the time," Paige said, "you were only thirteen and terribly hurt."

"By then I was fourteen—and hurting even more. I'm a social being and always have been. With each passing day of isolation, I felt worse. Who knows where or how I might've ended up? But in the home for troubled teens, I was saved by the most troubled girl of all. I have no idea what horrors she'd endured. They'd been hideous, I have no doubt. And sexual, considering her compulsion to make herself as undesirable as she possibly could. She craved tattoos and body piercing the way undamaged teenagers wish for clothes. Well, not exactly—her choices were more about disfigurement than fashion. Not surprisingly, she was intrigued by my birthmark. Not a caress from God, she said, but the claw mark of the Devil. She immediately intuited what I'd discovered over the past two years, that the very sight of it accomplished the only thing that mattered to her— keeping others far away. With my permission, my blessing, she painted her right cheek purple, and for a while we prowled the world as twins—including our names. She asked if I'd mind if she was Angel, too."

"She wanted to be you. To *become* you."

"No, Paige. She just wanted to be someone else. Anyone else. Any girl other than the one she was. And she loved the irony, she said, of an Angel touched by Satan. That's who she was, an ethereal creature ravaged by evil. She pretended to be tough, but was really so fragile. She wanted to reinvent herself. To be free. As, of course, I did. I'd thought about trying to conceal my birthmark with makeup. But I didn't have either the know-how or the confidence. Maybe I would've figured it out eventually. She'd learned how to do it, though. Had to. She was so pretty that even with tattoos and safety pins, men stared at her. Predatory men. I asked her to show me what she knew. She didn't want to. I realize that now. But she did—she taught me, helped me, saved me...and died of a heroin overdose several days after I'd mastered the technique."

"Her death was *not* your fault!"

Gwen had told herself that. Repeatedly. And convincingly? Not really. Never entirely.

Not at all.

But from Paige, and spoken with such passion, the assurance was a soothing balm on an open wound.

"Well," Gwen admitted. "It wasn't her first OD. But the fact remains, she helped me and I failed to help her. Maybe if I hadn't been so desperate to conceal my birthmark, and if we'd wandered around as twins for another week or two, she would've opened up to me. I don't know. I'll never know. I enrolled in a new school that spring, with a new face and a new first name. Her name. I was a hit, thanks to what Gweneth—the true Angel—had taught me. Quite a hit."

"Wasn't that good?"

"It was wonderful. But I knew I was an imposter, and the fraud bothered me...so much so that I eventually convinced myself I could have what I'd had in the convent—friends *and* truth. The classmates who'd become friends would remain friends even after the birthmark was revealed. It wouldn't matter. They wouldn't care. I celebrated my fifteenth birthday by going to the school's Halloween dance as my undisguised self. Trick, not treat."

"Your 'friends' did care."

"A lot. Too much. I reenrolled in a school I'd attended the year before. I didn't want to, but had no choice. I'd been to all the other schools available to me. As it turns out, no one recognized me as the girl with the purple cheek."

"But your hair, your eyes, *you*."

"When the birthmark's revealed, it's *all* one sees. Which isn't surprising, really, if you think about the book-cover analogy. If you're turned off by the cover art, you're unlikely to remember the title. It was an important lesson for me to learn. It made my decision to wear makeup—always—a simple one."

"A decision you kept until you had the laser surgery?"

"I haven't had it."

"The birthmark faded away?"

"Oh, no. It's still there. What's changed is the make-up. Thanks to advances in concealers—camouflage creams—a thin coating is all one needs."

"I can't believe—you're *sure* it's there?"

"Very sure." Gwen smiled, frowned, debated, decided. "Want to see?"

3

"Yes," Paige replied. "I would."

"Okay." Gwen withdrew a packet of facial wipes from her makeup satchel. She grabbed a black plastic headband, too, and swept her hair away from her face. "You're about to see what no one else has seen since that Halloween sixteen years ago."

"No one? But I thought—"

"That I have a boyfriend named David?"

"Yes." Whose love, Robyn had said, was the reason Gwen had no problems to confide. "David."

"He's a fiction, Paige. A phantom. There's never been a David...or any other man."

"But," Paige said softly, "it's easier to say there is."

"To lie. Yes. Much easier." Gwen wondered how and

why Paige had made such a discovery. For a moment, she thought Paige was going to tell her.

But Paige kept the conversation focused on Gwen.

"A port-wine stain doesn't preclude romance."

"No. Of course not—for others. But it does, it has, for me. I'd spent two years as a pariah. When I finally found a way to be accepted again, I wasn't going to jeopardize that relief for anything. Besides, at age fifteen, romance wasn't even on my radar screen."

"And since?"

"Not even a blip. I've viewed men as potential friends, not possible lovers, for such a long time I never even think of them as anything else."

"But what about how they think of you?"

"Some of my male friends have *claimed* they'd be interested in a romance. But that's a pretty safe admission, since they believe I'm hopelessly devoted to the nonexistent David. Just as it's safe for me, the imposter Gwen, to pretend I'd be interested in return. *Pretend* being the operative word. Wearing a mask is a license to pretend, to be anyone you choose and everyone you're not." *And when the mask comes off* . . . Gwen opened the packet she'd retrieved from her satchel. "Okay. Here goes."

With a few practiced swipes, the birthmark was revealed to be exactly as Gwen had forecast: a dark purple discoloration of her entire cheek.

"I'm amazed," Paige admitted.

But not horrified. Or pitying. Paige was, quite simply, interested.

So interested that she moved even closer before observing, "The skin's very smooth."

"Unusually so, as I discovered when—for reasons I do not know—I typed 'port-wine stain' into the search window at Google.com. That was four months ago. In addition to learning that laser therapy exists and works, I now know quite a bit about the birthmarks themselves. Port, the wine, may improve with age. But port-wine stains definitely do not. The skin typically becomes thick, cobbled and can be topped with blebs that rupture and bleed."

"I imagine the smoothness would make it more susceptible to laser therapy."

"I imagine so, too, since the best results are reported in children before the thickening begins."

"You imagine, but don't know? Haven't you seen anyone?"

"Not yet."

"Why—"not? Paige answered her own question before completing it. "You're worried you might be disappointed."

"Yes, but not with the outcome. I assume it would be good. I might be extremely disappointed, though, with myself—with how I adjusted to the new me. If I *could* adjust."

"You'd be the same Gwen the world sees now."

"I'd *look* the same. But the Gwen who's worn a mask ever since going maskless to a Halloween dance is as much a fiction as David."

"But you know who you are."

"Yes, Paige, I do. I'm the girl behind the mask, the one who decided sixteen years ago to spend the rest of her life in disguise. I knew how I felt when the birthmark was hidden. *Happy*. And when it was revealed, well, I'd learned that painful lesson twice. It was the right decision, too. The disguise has worked."

"You're happy," Paige said. "And have lots of friends."

"I've been very lucky. I *am* very lucky. Which makes my impulsive Google search all the more strange. My life was good, happy, *calm*. It still is, except that now the boat's been rocked. *I've* rocked it. And now... Two months ago, I began to pursue one of the ripple effects. I've decided to try to find my mother."

"That's a ripple effect of your Internet search?"

Gwen nodded. "I've wondered about her from time to time, of course, though I've never missed her, at least not consciously. I had a convent full of loving mothers. I still don't miss her, or I'm not aware of it if I do, but I *have* been worrying about her. What if she was as badly damaged—and sensitive and fragile—as the Gweneth I met in the home for troubled teens? And what if the guilt she feels about abandoning me is an ongoing torment for her? She might even feel guilty about the birthmark itself. It developed in utero, after all. It happens during the first trimester, the articles say, a developmental glitch unrelated to anything the pregnant mother does or doesn't do. But she might believe it was her fault and that she doomed me to a life as unhappy as hers."

"You want to reassure her."

"I really do. But it's pretty unlikely that I'll ever have a chance. She wasn't actually the person who left me at the convent. That was done by a Good Samaritan passerby. A woman. She met my mother, though. Spoke to her."

"So you're trying to get in touch with the passerby?"

"Not yet. Probably not ever. I'm quite sure that Sister Mary Catherine, the nun who took me in, never knew her name. But the woman might've said something to Sister Mary Catherine about my mother." Gwen shrugged. "Or not."

"You've never asked her?"

"No. It didn't matter to me when I lived with the nuns in the convent—and I haven't been in touch with any of them since I remained in California and they moved on to Santa Fe. That wasn't the plan, of course...."

She and the nuns had promised to write each other. But only the nuns kept the vow. They wrote to their Angel, and wrote and wrote, long past the time it became clear there'd be no reply. Gwen never read the letters from New Mexico. But the girl at war with the world imagined all manner of hateful replies.

Not once, though, had she put poison pen to paper. Deep down, she'd known how lucky she was to have been raised with such love. And when that knowledge came to the surface? And the birthmark was hidden away? She should've written then. Thanked them.

But she hadn't. Because she was no longer the Angel they'd known…the girl who'd lived and dared, confident and unmasked.

"Two months ago, I wrote to Sister Mary Catherine. I know the letter was received—I sent it UPS and tracked it—but so far there's been no reply."

"You will hear back, though, won't you?"

"Yes. I'm sure I will. And that in itself will be nice."

"I wonder…"

"What, Paige?"

"Whether the mother you really want to reassure isn't your birth mother but Sister Mary Catherine."

"Maybe," Gwen admitted. "I *did* reassure her, I hope, in the letter I sent." Gwen drew a breath. Then said in a rush, "This must sound so trivial to you. Not the idea of reassurances but my indecision about laser therapy. It *is* trivial compared to the real problems you see every day. And shamefully self-absorbed."

"I don't agree. It may be different, but it's definitely real. And *not* trivial. The prospect of revealing one's true self is daunting." *Terrifying.*

"Well. It's generous of you to say so. And nice of you to have listened with such interest." Which she had, as if there was absolutely nothing she'd rather be doing on this Saturday afternoon, absolutely no place else she'd rather be—or needed to be. "Oh, Paige! Look at the time! I've been babbling on and on, and you've been too polite to interrupt. But you need to go, don't you? Like about ten minutes ago?"

Paige frowned at her own wristwatch. It was unusual for her to lose track of time. Unheard of. As astonishing as her decision to join Gwen in Louise's room...and to feel so glad, and oddly grateful, that she had. "I'm fine, Gwen. I'm not late. It's only those three—short—blocks. But I suppose I'd better get going."

Even though you don't want to, Gwen thought. *Even though you're dreading it.*

But Paige was standing, righting her delicate frame against the invisible weight, about to go...and Gwen felt again the urgent wish for someone to help Paige Forrester. *Help her.*

The only available someone was Gwen.

She made the only offer she could.

"I'd better get going, too. We can walk out together."

It wasn't much of an offer. Gwen didn't expect much of a reply.

But... "That would be wonderful, Gwen. Thank you."

"I usually take the stairs down to the fourth-floor sky-bridge," Paige explained as they left Louise's room. "For exercise. If that's all right with you?"

"More than all right. I'm a stairtaker from way back."

"Great."

The stairwell was in the elevator foyer. Paige set

the pace, a brisk clip, and they were almost there when she spoke.

"Oh, no."

Paige's tone was at once annoyed, as if chastising herself for something she'd forgotten, and resigned.

"What is it, Paige?"

"I'm afraid I have to sit." She slid down the wall and onto the shining linoleum floor. *"Damn."*

Gwen knelt beside her, saw the clammy skin, the gulping breaths, the translucent pallor. "I'll get help."

"No!" Paige managed a wobbly smile. "I'm fine. Will be...fine."

"What can I do?"

"Nothing." Paige's smile collapsed and her eyes closed in concentration as she battled whatever was draining the meager amount of energy and color she had left. "It will pass."

4

It wasn't passing, had not relented even a tiny bit, during what felt like an eternity before someone spotted them and help arrived.

The foyer itself was at the intersection of two wards, Medical Oncology and Trauma Surgery, and their adjacent medical and surgical ICUs. The intensive care units were behind closed and windowless doors. But the wards were open, with excellent views of the foyer, except for the small alcove to which Paige had veered—intentionally—when she realized she had to sit and the stairwell was too far.

The alcove wasn't hidden from anyone who was getting on or off an elevator, and if it hadn't been Saturday afternoon, that traffic would have been almost constant.

It was from an arriving elevator that help eventually

appeared, in the person of a pink-coated, college-aged volunteer.

"Dr. Forrester!"

Paige opened her eyes, recognized the pre-med student who spent weekends running errands for eighth-floor patients and personnel. "Hi, Shirley. I'm okay."

"No, you're not! Dr. Ransom's on rounds in the unit."

"I don't need—"

"I'll go get him."

"Don't get Cole."

Paige's words fell on deaf ears, and vanishing ones as Shirley scampered to press the metal plate that activated the surgical ICU doors.

Paige closed her eyes again, still fighting whatever had compelled her to sit in the first place and further exhausted by the minor skirmish with the insistent Shirley.

Gwen watched both Paige and the SICU doors... which swung open in a gratifyingly short period of time.

The black-haired surgeon wore scrubs, a stethoscope and a physician's coat embroidered *Cole Ransom, M.D.* above the left breast pocket and *Department of Surgery* below.

He also wore an aura that was at once intense and calm.

"Paige," he said softly, kneeling, too.

His fingertips found the place on Paige's neck where her carotid artery signaled what needed to be known about the pace and force with which her heart was pumping blood to her brain.

But Gwen could see that wasn't enough for this surgeon. He wanted to know whatever it was that could be determined by sliding a gentle, expert hand beneath the sleeve of Paige's cashmere coat.

The blood flow to her limbs, Gwen surmised. The heartbeat measured at her wrist.

But Dr. Cole Ransom didn't so much as pause at Paige's wrist, forsaking the radial pulse in favor of something to be gleaned by reaching deeper, farther, up her forearm.

What?

Gwen couldn't imagine. But she had every confidence that he knew what he was doing, and that whatever he did was right—and best—for Paige.

Let him touch you, Paige. Let him take care of you. He cares so much.

Except, Gwen realized, Paige didn't want to be touched by Cole.

Or cared about by him.

Paige had told Shirley as much. *Don't get Cole.* But to no avail. And at the surgeon's first whisper of her name, she'd stiffened.

Now Paige's eyes opened, exhaustion trumped by resolve, and she pulled away.

"I'm *fine*, Cole."

The surgeon held up his hands in surrender. But he surrendered not an iota of his concern.

"You're not fine, Paige."

"*Yes, I am.* I bent over, stood up too quickly and became

a little light-headed, so I decided to sit down. It's not a big deal."

"It could be."

"It's not."

"If you'd rather I didn't examine you, I can find someone else."

"I don't *need* an exam. I just need about thirty more seconds of sitting right here."

"And then what?"

"Then—" it was Gwen who replied "—Paige and I will resume our walk."

Gwen was right beside him. He'd knelt, after all, right beside her. And she'd been so very aware of him. His voice, his hands, his gentle caring for Paige.

Cole Ransom's focus had been on Paige.

But surely he'd been aware of Gwen, however vaguely. He might have logically assumed she'd gotten off the elevator, perhaps with Shirley, and remained with Paige while Shirley found him.

Whatever Cole's awareness or assumption had or had not been, with Gwen's intrusion into the conversation, that awareness was now obliged to change.

He turned to her, looked at her. "And you are?"

The girl behind the mask. The outcast who'd vowed never to reveal her blemished face again.

But here she was, without her mask.

That Gwen had shown the stain to Paige, had *wanted* to, was remarkable. And to have forgotten, when she'd offered to accompany the suddenly apprehensive Paige, that it was still revealed…extraordinary.

And now as this man, this *man*, looked at her?

Excruciating.

Gwen was naked before him. Fully exposed. Grotesque and becoming more so as her cheek burned hotter, darker, bloodier beneath his appraising gaze.

Gwen couldn't tell the precise moment when Cole Ransom noticed her birthmark. His eyes, stone-calm, stone-gray, would not be read.

But Gwen knew what Cole saw. *All* he would see.

Get over it, Gwen told herself. *This is about Paige, what's happening with Paige, not you.*

What was happening with Paige, as Gwen was giving herself a mental shake, was the formulation of a reply to Cole's question.

"This is my friend," she said. "Gwen St. James."

"You saw what happened, Gwen?"

"Yes," she answered at once. But before elaborating further, she looked at Paige. The episode was passing, as Paige had said it would. The only lingering danger for Paige, Gwen decided, was posed by the surgeon himself. Whom she faced, made herself face, as she spoke the lie. "In fact, I *caused* it. I was checking to make sure I hadn't forgotten my keys. I hadn't, but when I found them, I dropped them, and Paige picked them up."

"How far are you planning to walk?"

"Not far."

"If Paige gets even the slightest bit dizzy—"

"I won't!"

"Okay." Cole smiled slightly at the clearly improving Paige.

The suddenly apologetic Paige. "I'm sorry, Cole!"

"For what?"

"Being so ungracious. I guess I'm just feeling a little embarrassed...and a lot foolish. Neither of which is an excuse."

"And no excuse is required. Don't give it another thought. Besides," Cole said, "you were right. All you needed was time."

"Well...thank you."

"You're welcome."

Cole held Paige's gaze for several uninterpretable heartbeats. Then he stood. And without looking at Gwen—why would he?—he walked away.

Still, she pulled the headband from her hair, allowing the spill of copper to veil her blemished skin.

"Thank you," Paige murmured when the doors to the SICU closed behind Cole. "He wasn't buying my story."

"I don't think he bought mine, either."

"Well." Paige shrugged. "Sometimes it's easier to lie."

"You're pregnant, aren't you? With his baby? And you don't want him to know."

"*What?* No! I'm not pregnant, and there's nothing between Cole and me. I really did feel embarrassed. Foolish. My kidneys are...on the fritz, and have been for a while. That's why I felt faint. The embarrassing, foolish thing is that I really should've gotten the hang of it by now."

"The hang of what?"

"Making sure my blood pressure doesn't drop so low that I have to sit down before I fall down."

Gwen knew nothing about malfunctioning kidneys. But she was enough of an athlete—a pretty fair athlete— to know a little about fainting. She'd never fainted herself, but she'd seen it happen, often, in the annual Bay to Breakers race. Fellow runners collapsed, their blood pressure too low, a consequence of failing to keep up their fluid intake in the sometimes sweltering heat.

"Why don't I scoot back to 8-North and find you something to drink?"

"No, Gwen. Thank you."

"You're not thirsty?"

Paige's smile was wry, and wistful. "Always. But I can only drink so much every twenty-four hours. I've had my quota until eight tonight."

"Except that you almost fainted."

"True. But it was a distribution problem, not a fluid problem. My blood pressure's low-normal to begin with, so I don't have much reserve. I was so relaxed while we were talking that blood pooled in my legs. And I forgot to pump my calf muscles before standing up. But now I have." Paige stood. "And I'm fine. See?"

Gwen stood, too. And saw. The blood that had been languishing in Paige's lower extremities was back at work. There was even a hint of pinkness in her snowy cheeks.

"And," Paige said, "I'll be fine walking to my mother's."

"I'm walking with you."

"I really *am* fine, Gwen."

"Great. I really *am* walking with you, Paige."

5

"Cole knows about your kidneys."

"Yes." With a flourish that proved her strength was restored, Paige held open a heavy exit door. Following Gwen outside, she added, "He does."

"But for some reason, you didn't want him to know what really happened today." Gwen studied her critically. "Maybe we shouldn't be talking."

"I really *can* talk and walk at the same time, and I'm happy to explain why I didn't want him to know. The fact is he has far more important things—real patients—to worry about."

"He didn't seem to mind worrying about you."

"Cole Ransom is a dedicated physician. He would've been equally concerned about a stranger."

"Are you sure?"

"About what?"

"He seemed to care about you. A lot."

"I'm sure, Gwen. That's just the kind of doctor Cole is."

"Dedicated."

"And brilliant," Paige said. "And, come to think of it, a neighbor of yours."

"He lives at Belvedere Court?"

"I think so. I haven't heard that he's moved."

"How long has he lived there?"

"Ever since he joined the faculty. A year ago this past July."

"Where was he before?"

"Dallas. Where he was rumored to be so happy with the setup that we almost didn't even try to recruit him— as much as we wanted him here."

"'We'?"

"I was one of a six-member search committee."

"Because Cole specializes in cancer surgery?"

"No. Vascular. It was simply my turn to serve on the search committee. It's one of those important but time-consuming responsibilities all the faculty shares. I was the junior member of the committee, but took my turn reading letters of recommendation and interviewing candidates. And, as I said, Cole was a reluctant candidate. *We* pursued *him*. Fortunately, he accepted our invitation to visit. Once he did, he was convinced."

"You convinced him."

"No. The facility did, the faculty did, maybe the city did. I was assigned to convince him, though. The entire committee was supposed to take him to dinner at the end of his first day. But everyone seemed to think that Cole related best to me and I'd have the best chance of convincing him if we were alone. The good news is that Cole was already convinced. He told me en route to the restaurant that he'd decided to take the job. It was a relief for me. I couldn't really see persuading Cole to do something—anything—he didn't want to do. So we just had a pleasant dinner instead."

"And you dated after he moved to San Francisco?"

"No! There's *nothing,* Gwen. Not for him, not for me. We met for lattes a few times when he first arrived. That's not a date, by the way. The hospital cafeteria has an excellent latte bar. Since then, he's been busy, I've been busy. We see each other primarily when I need his surgical expertise. He puts in the vascular access lines—lifelines—for my patients."

"So they can receive chemotherapy?"

"And parenteral nutrition, stem cell transplants, blood transfusions—whatever they need. Cole also did a major surgery on one of my patients. Her superior vena cava—one of the two large veins to the heart—had become obstructed by a tumor. She was a terrible surgical risk, and the prevailing wisdom was that she'd die on the table… which made everyone but Cole unwilling to operate. But he did operate, Gwen, and she survived—and has responded so beautifully to a new round of chemo that she's been in remission for almost twelve months."

"So he really is a brilliant vascular surgeon."

"And a brilliant trauma surgeon. He's trained in both, and committed to both. He made it clear during the recruitment process that he wanted to remain active in trauma. But until he got here, no one understood exactly what that meant. You can't be on call for both vascular and trauma, not at the same time. Each can be almost too busy by itself. The assumption had been that Cole would occasionally take trauma call and take proportionately less vascular call when he did. But for the sixteen months he's been here, he's taken full call for each."

"So he's on call twice as often?"

"As every other surgeon on staff. That's right. It's what he wants, and no one's about to tell him no. He's talented, *gifted,* pure steel under pressure. The steeliness comes in handy, since he works almost every weekend—he wants to—which is when the most emergencies roll in."

"I wonder why."

"He loves to operate. In fact, in one of the letters a colleague from Dallas wrote about him, he said that as good as Cole is with patients—and he is—he believed Cole's preference would be to spend all his time in the operating room. His patients, prepped, draped and already under anesthesia, would be wheeled in, their surgical dilemmas presented by another doctor—after which the other physician would challenge Cole to operate his way out of *this* one."

"As if Cole was a master magician," Gwen mused.

Like Houdini. Master magician...and escape artist. "I wonder why he chooses emergencies, though. Why life and death?"

"I don't know, Gwen. I really don't know Cole very well. I'm not sure anyone does. Oh. Here we are."

The mansion, cream with teal trimmings, was familiar to Gwen. She made a point of driving by it, in fact, twice a day, to and from work.

"*This* is your mother's home? And yours, too, when you were a girl? It's so...majestic, yet inviting. Cozy. I've always wondered who lived here."

"And now that you know, you should feel free to drop by. My mother's always here and she loves having visitors."

"Even ones she doesn't know?"

"Especially those. I'd really like you to meet her, Gwen, and I know she'd love to meet you—and, of course, she'd love to show you the house. I'd invite you in today..."

The unspoken *but* drifted in the autumn air. It seemed to settle, along with Paige's frowning stare, on the dark blue SUV parked in the mansion's circular drive.

"I tried reinventing myself once," Paige said. *Setting myself free.* "Being someone different."

Gwen read the lettering on the driver's side door and made a logical guess. "With Jack Logan? Of Jack Logan Building and Remodeling?"

Paige nodded. "He was a college senior at the time. Twelve years ago. And I was a sophomore."

"And?"

"Oh. My disguise? I was April. *Avril*."

"You were French?"

"No. I just pretended I was majoring in it."

"What happened when he found out?"

"He never did. Our relationship, such as it was, ended—Jack ended it—before I had a chance to confess."

"An important relationship."

"Not to him."

"But to you."

"Back then, yes. I was deluding myself as much, *more*, than I was deluding him."

"And now?"

"Now? Nothing…except that last spring, and unbeknownst to me, my mother decided to renovate. There's no reason she *would've* told me, much less who she was planning to hire. Her friends, many of whom also have historic homes, were more than happy to help her select a contractor. She met with everyone they recommended to her. But she did her own search as well, in the Yellow Pages and on the Internet. She found Jack. Liked him. Wanted him for the job."

"Not realizing you'd dated him at Stanford?"

"We didn't actually *date*. But she didn't know Jack and I had ever even met. No one did."

"Would you have objected if she'd told you she was considering him?"

"No. I would've admitted we'd known each other at

Stanford, and I would've said—her friends' skepticism notwithstanding—that my mother's instincts about him were right. He could be trusted to do the job, and do it well."

"Her friends doubted that?"

"Only because Jack was unknown to them. Unheard of. Unlike *their* contractors, who'd been in business forever, Jack had been at it for only ten years. Successful years, as it turns out." Paige paused, and when she spoke again there was apology in her voice…as if she were apologizing to Jack. "He was vetted, you see. Our family attorney, who's also a very dear friend, felt he really had no choice. The project was so huge that it would test any builder. Tempt him."

"To overcharge, you mean?"

Paige nodded. "That was Stuart's worry. Especially since, based on various personal tidbits Jack had already mentioned to my mother, it was clear that Jack had significant expenses beyond the usual business ones. He has an eleven-year-old daughter, Beth. He was awarded sole custody in the divorce. She attends Marine View Academy—it's private and pricey. She's also a gifted musician, a pianist, so there are lessons, and the piano itself, and Jack recently purchased a home within walking distance of Beth's school, which is about half a mile from here. The house is a fixer-upper, but expensive simply by virtue of being in Pacific Heights. Oh, and his parents also live with him and Beth."

"So he has lots of expenses, because of the responsibilities he's chosen to assume. I'd think it's fairly unusual—and pretty impressive?—for a father to get sole custody of a child."

"*Impressive* was the word Stuart used to describe Jack when all was said and done. He wasn't an unscrupulous builder, Stuart decided. Nor was he likely to become one. Impressive, and incorruptible."

"So Jack passed with flying colors?"

"Definitely. He also learned, in retrospect, about the investigation. Stuart told him when they finally met—in response, I gather, to a direct question from Jack."

"Was Jack upset that he'd been investigated?"

"I don't know. If so, Stuart didn't mention it."

"But *you* didn't know about the investigation."

"No. I didn't. My mother didn't either until it was over. She would've hired him anyway. I have a feeling she already had. But it became official four months ago, when she told her friends who she'd selected. That's when she also told me. Stuart's investigation had, of course, revealed the overlap between my undergraduate years at Stanford and Jack's. No one imagined, though, that our paths had ever crossed. There was no logical reason they would. And I didn't volunteer it. Nor at any time during the past four months have I picked up the phone..."

"And let Jack know that Paige and April were one and the same."

"Exactly. So here we are. The renovation begins Monday morning and is projected to last six months. I'm bound to run into him. And if he'd been anyone but Jack, I'd have made a *point* of meeting him long before now. When my mother mentioned that he and Beth—and Beth's friend Dina—were dropping by this afternoon, I said I'd drop by, too." Paige drew a breath. "It seemed like a good idea. It *is* a good idea. I need to get it over with. Besides, it's really much ado about nothing. Jack probably won't even remember me. It would be better if he didn't."

No it wouldn't, Gwen thought. *It hurts to be forgotten. To be forgettable.*

The thoughts came with emotion. Which, for the moment, Gwen held at bay—along with the other emotions of this extraordinary day. But she needed to deal with them. Soon.

"Well," Paige said. "I guess I'd better go. Thank you again, Gwen. For Louise…and for me."

Paige Forrester wasn't a hugger.

Gweneth St. James was.

Not since her convent days, however, had Gwen hugged anyone with her face scrubbed clean. And never did she recall hugging someone as delicate as Paige, who was even thinner than she looked, her elegant ensemble a camouflage of its own. And her bones felt as fragile as a bird's.

"Onward," Paige murmured as the embrace ended.

"You'll dazzle him, Paige, whether he remembers you from Stanford or not."

Paige didn't consider herself the dazzling type. But the certainty of Gwen's prediction, and Gwen's smiling confidence in her, made her feel...good. Like smiling, too. Like laughing. "Ha!"

"Mark my words, Paige. I'm known for an uncanny accuracy about such things. In fact, I wouldn't mind a follow-up...if you'd care to give it."

"I'd be happy to—grim though it might be."

"You said there's a latte bar in the hospital cafeteria?"

"There is. An excellent one."

"We could do that."

"Let's."

"Okay." Then recalling Paige's apparently rigid quota of fluids for the day, Gwen asked, "Would something less liquid be better?"

"No. A latte would be great."

I can take a sip, Paige mused. Pretend to. I need to indulge in a little make-believe with the makeup artist.

Just as, twelve years ago, she'd needed a little make-believe with a man called Jack...

6

Paige discovered the Drama Department library in spring of her freshman year. It became her preferred place to study. The lighting was good, the tables were spacious and no other pre-medical students studied there—ever.

Nor, for that matter, did many others. Drama majors, who might logically have studied in their departmental library, rarely did. All the world being a stage, they could no doubt study anywhere. In fact, the rehearsing of scenes, which was something she imagined a drama major would do, wasn't practical in a library.

There were many days and evenings when Paige was the drama library's only patron. And it wasn't simply that it was a glorious spring in Palo Alto, sunny and warm, and Lake Lagunita beckoned as the ideal place to study, or at least to take one's books.

Paige discovered, upon her return to campus in the fall of her sophomore year, that the drama library was nearly as deserted in the unseasonably drizzly autumn as it had been in the summery spring.

She had the library almost to herself until mid-October. Then, two weeks before her nineteenth birthday, *he* appeared.

He chose a separate table, a respectful distance from hers, and was removing a notebook from his knapsack when he noticed her noticing him. He smiled in greeting. And, when she didn't instantly respond, as if unsure the smile was truly for her—even though they were quite alone—he added a friendly wave.

Then he waited, watching, smiling, until she waved in reply.

And that was that. He began to study. She returned to her own studying. He left at ten-thirty. She left at eleven. The ritual was the same—the smile, the wave, the studying—the following evening, and for the six evenings after that.

There was a little more to his studying ritual. From time to time he'd take a break, stand, walk—a graceful and leisurely stretching of his long athletic legs.

Paige was so aware of him then. Aware of him always. And as he prowled the library but never invaded her space, she found herself wishing he would. *Talk to me. Please.*

And fearing he would. *No, don't! I have nothing to say. What* would *I say to someone like you?*

On their eighth evening together, Paige's wishes—and fears—were realized.

"You're not an actress."

Paige looked up into eyes that were even greener at close range. And a face more handsome. A body more powerful. And dark brown hair, as dark as hers and a similar shade, but which, she saw now, held golden glints of sunlight. Quite unlike hers.

"I'm not?"

"*Are* you?"

"No. But...how do you know?"

"Your lips don't move." *She* didn't move. Much. It was a rigid stillness. And a wary one. As if something—her head, he thought—hurt her terribly. There was occasional motion, the necessary turning of pages as she peered intensely at her class notes. And perhaps necessary, too, most necessary of all, her one-handed removal of pills from the open bottle of over-the-counter pain meds—which she swallowed down with diet soda. It was a fluid motion, the retrieval of pills and the washing down with caffeinated pop. A practiced one. A *frequent* one. "Do you have migraines?"

"What? Oh. No."

"But something hurts."

"I'm fine!"

"You take a lot of pills for someone who's fine."

"You're right. Too many." *But not enough.* "Especially since I'm much better, almost back to new."

"From?"

"Oh, you know, the most common of all campus mishaps—a collision with someone else on a bike. He was fine, by the way. And I'm fine." It was a lie. All of it. Her head throbbed. She had no bike. And the only collision was between the demands she placed on herself and what—she feared—would be the less-than-perfect outcome she'd be able to achieve.

Less than perfect...like having him, *him,* notice that she was hurting, and took so many pills. Paige should have been embarrassed. Mortified. And, of course, part of her was. But he'd seemed concerned, not critical.

He seemed, *seemed,* to care.

And she was emboldened. So bold. "Your lips don't move, either," she heard herself say. "Ergo, not an actor."

"Not an actor. I'm an engineering major. I'm Jack Logan, by the way." As she undoubtedly knew, or so he'd believed. The assumption was realism, not arrogance. He'd become a minor celebrity on campus. Okay, a major one. It was football season, after all. A welcome distraction—and passion—for much of the student body. Jack was the second-string quarterback, had been throughout his Stanford Cardinal career. He'd had some playing time in previous seasons, nothing spectacular. But this year, each time he'd been called to the huddle, the results had been dazzling. Jack was well aware that they were due to pure luck, coupled with great athletes at the receiving end of the passes he'd thrown. Even his scramble into the end-zone in the final seconds of the game against Southern Cal had been a fluke. He was an okay quarterback. The coach was right to stick with the guy who'd always been first-string. But there'd been a groundswell of support for Jack, the sort of frenzy that had a life of its own—especially as midterms drew near and the need for escape, and expression, dramatically increased. For the past two weeks, every edition of the *Stanford Daily* had carried on its front page a photograph of Jack—a different one every day—with the headline Let Jack Play! and variations thereof. And, at the games themselves, *Jack, Jack, Jack* had become the chant du jour. Last weekend, during the halftime show and on national television, the irrepressible Stanford Marching Band had spelled out his name on the field. For better or worse—worse— everyone on campus knew about Jack. Except, apparently, this girl who was not an actress. There wasn't a flicker of recognition. None. "And you are...?"

He would know her name, Paige realized. *The* name. Forrester. As in Forrester House, one of the first campus dormitories, and still one of the most popular. Or Forrester Library in the School of Law. Or Forrester Arena. Pavilion. Tower.

She'd had no idea, when she applied, that the Forrester

name would be as prominent here as in San Francisco. Yes, she'd known that her father had been a Stanford graduate. But neither of her grandparents had. And, although a tireless fund-raiser for Pacific Heights Medical Center—in Alan's memory—and a patroness of the arts in memory of Rosalind and Gavin, her mother had no association with Stanford, fund-raising or otherwise.

The contributions to Stanford had come from more distant generations. Gavin's parents. And grandparents. Gavin Forrester's railroad-magnate grandfather had, not surprisingly, been a crony of that other famous railroad pioneer, Leland Stanford himself.

"No *wonder* you got in." How often had Paige Forrester heard that since her enrollment here? Too often. All the time. As if the Forrester legacy was the only thing that mattered, and her acceptance to the notoriously competitive college had been guaranteed. As if it had nothing to do with her or all the hard work she'd done to earn the necessary SATs and grades.

It bothered her. And not just because such easy assumptions were personally insulting. It bothered her on behalf of the generations of Forresters she had never known. The buildings they'd funded, the scholarships they'd endowed, had been for the college they'd attended—and loved—and for students, less fortunate than they, who couldn't afford tuition without their help. The intent of their largesse hadn't ever been to ensure that some great-great-granddaughter would be accepted, even if academically unfit.

Paige was sensitized to the Forrester name and the comments it evoked, long before arriving at Stanford.

All her life. *Oh, darling Paige,* the society women of San Francisco would say, *we loved Rosalind so. What a grandmother she would have been to you. We were invited to the baby shower she and Mariel planned for your mother and ended up going to Rosalind's funeral instead. And Gavin's, of course. And your father's.*

What a terrible time that was. Too much even for someone as strong as Mariel. But Rosalind and Gavin had been like parents to her, far closer than her own, and she and Alan were best friends. For a while she withdrew from anything that reminded her of them—even that gorgeous Stuart Dawson.

Another woman would always take up the next part of the story. *So we all stepped in to help your mother, as Rosalind would've wanted us to. It was out of duty at first. We all admit it. But we love Claire now, as much as Rosalind did. She's simply...lovely. And such a talented artist. You must be, too. She's taught us all how to paint. And we're good! Thanks to her. I never knew I had an artistic bone in my body until she showed me.*

You're so lucky, darling Paige, a third woman would say, *to have a mother like Claire. We all feel so fortunate to have her in our lives. And, dear girl, what a comfort you must be to her. You look so much like Alan. What a wonderful reminder that must be. A wonderful reminder of a perfect love. It was, you know. And you're the child of that love.*

We all worry, one would add, frowning, *that Claire doesn't get out. We go to see her, of course. She's made the man-*

*sion feel—for all of us—like a second home. We needn't worry,
I suppose, about her reluctance to leave. The house itself is idyllic, and that's where her memories are.*

"April," Paige Forrester replied to Jack Logan. *April.*
The name came out of nowhere. Had her subconscious
been envisioning new beginnings, springtime awakenings, April showers and May flowers?

"April," Jack Logan echoed in a way that made her
shiver. "April who?"

Paige didn't hesitate. "Dawson." The last name of her father's closest friend—and the only father Paige had known.

"And your major?"

"French."

"Your lips don't move," Jack reiterated. "Impressive."

Paige Forrester's French *wasn't* impressive, at least in
its spoken form. She was simply too inhibited, too far
from an actress, to give the accent its due. But she'd taken
six years of French. Her comprehension was excellent.

"Do you speak French, Jack?"

"Not a syllable. Will you teach me?"

Bon soir, Avril, Jack said every evening when, after
football practice, he met her in the drama library.

Bon soir, Jacques, she replied. Every evening. With racing heart and soaring relief. And having put away, before
he arrived, her notes from physics, calculus and biochem.

She read French literature, every evening, after he
arrived.

At eleven, he'd walk her to the house on Greek Row where he believed she lived. The old fraternity house had become one of the many specialty living areas on campus—in this case, a residence for French majors where only French was spoken.

Bon nuit, Avril, he'd say at the front door.

Bon nuit, Jacques, she'd reply, and walk inside. Once he'd vanished into the darkness, she'd dash to her car, parked nearby, and drive to the off-campus apartment where she lived alone.

Each night they made the short walk more slowly.

Jack told her about football: the phenom status he'd undeservedly acquired; how glad he'd be when the season was over; that he'd played well enough in high school to earn an athletic scholarship, for which he was grateful; that he had no intention of playing professional ball.

In addition to *not* being that good, he'd never really liked getting tackled.

"So you're going to be an engineer."

"Not if I can help it." Jack smiled. "But it'll come in handy, I hope, in what I want to do."

"Which is?"

"Fixing up houses. Restoring old homes."

"Have you ever done that?"

"I've done pieces of it ever since I was a kid. My dad's a housepainter. I did that with him for a while. There were usually others at the job site. Carpenters, roofers, electricians, plumbers. I apprenticed. Learned. Reached the point where it was more than reasonable to get paid. I'd like to have my own company someday. And make all the pieces come together."

Jack wanted to work in San Francisco, he told her. Live there. To be close to his parents.

They were old for parents of a twenty-one-year-old college senior. Pete Logan was sixty-one. Eve was fifty-nine. Jack was their second child. Their first, a son named Jason, was born eighteen years before Jack—and died of sudden infant death syndrome when he was three months old.

"They didn't plan to have any more children."

"Because it was too sad, too hard, to lose Jason?"

"That, and, I think, they blamed themselves for Jason's death."

"But they weren't to blame!"

"No. But Jason was their innocent little baby. He depended on them to keep him safe. They've never stopped missing him. How could they? I've missed him, too."

"You have?"

"Sure. Just because we never met doesn't mean he wasn't my brother. And..."

"What, Jack?"

"I've never told anyone this. But...even before I knew about Jason, I didn't think of myself as an only child."

"And you weren't."

"No. I was, however, a surprise."

A baby, Paige thought, who'd renewed his parents'

battered lives. Just as he planned, one day, to give new life to battered homes.

There was truth, in moonlight, when Jack was talking.

And when it was Paige's turn, April's turn, there were lies.

April Dawson was everything Paige Forrester was not. Carefree. Happy-go-lucky. She hadn't the foggiest idea, she told Jack without alarm, what she was going to do after college. *Que sera sera!*

She came from Boston, she said, from a family of five children, all daughters, which was just fine with her surgeon father—he loved his girls—and her mother was like a sixth sister, they were all *that close*.

April was the baby of the family. Which was the reason, according to magazine articles she'd read, that she was so *laissez-faire*. Her oldest sister, the firstborn daughter, also fit a classic profile. Driven. Goal-oriented. Determined to achieve.

At the age of seven, this invented older sister decided to follow in the footsteps of the father she adored. She made straight As, and raced through college in just three years. She didn't graduate, merely took the classes required for medical school. Yes, it was possible to become an M.D. without ever receiving an undergraduate degree.

"But what's the point?" Jack asked the girl who, unbeknownst to him, was committed to that very same three-year plan. "What's the rush?"

"I...don't know. But that's who she is. She *pushes* herself. She's not happy-go-lucky—like me."

"And is she not happy, either?"

"Oh! No. She's happy. But I think it's been lonely for her at times."

"Are the two of you alike?"

"Quoi, Jacques? Mais non!"

Jack wanted to feed her. She needed real food, he told her gently, sustenance beyond the diet soda she drank and the pills she consumed. Yes, he'd agreed, she *had* cut back on the pills. And he was glad.

Thanksgiving neared. Jack told her his plans. Four days with his parents in their Daly City home. Paige didn't tell him hers. Four days with her mother in their mansion in Pacific Heights. She was flying home, she said, to Boston early that Wednesday.

"I'm taking you to dinner on Tuesday, then."

"You are?"

"If you say yes."

"Yes. Jack? There are some things I need to tell you."

"Tell me."

"I will. At dinner. Tuesday night."

Paige wanted to tell him everything. And maybe she would. She'd tell him the little things, of course. Her real name, her true major, why she'd had to pretend.

And, maybe, the not-so-little ones.

That she knew he'd succeed in his dream of fixing

damaged houses and making them whole, because that's how he made her feel. Whole. April *and* Paige.

Maybe he'd kiss her. *Please.* She believed, felt so sure, that he wanted to. He was being a gentleman, though. Waiting until after they'd gone on an official date.

Waiting until Tuesday.

But Tuesday never came. Not the kiss. Not the date.

When he arrived on Monday evening, she thought he'd discovered her deceit. He looked so different from the Jack she knew. Wild. Ravaged.

"I met someone last summer," he said. "At a wedding. She's pregnant, April. With my child."

Not the Jack she knew.

Another woman's Jack.

"You've been seeing her?"

"No. Just at the wedding. Just that one night."

So Jack did not, apparently, wait for a first kiss until after the first official date. When he met someone he liked and wanted, he simply made love to her.

Jack Logan hadn't wanted *her,* not even the bold and carefree April she'd become.

The man who made love whenever he wanted to was also a son who loved his parents, missed his brother, believed in family...and responsibility.

"You're going to marry her."

"Yes. I am. On Saturday. And after we're married, I won't be returning to school. April?"

"Yes?"

"Let me take you to dinner tomorrow, as we planned."

"No."

"Tonight then. Now."

"No. I have to go."

"There were some things you were going to tell me."

"They aren't important. You're going to be a father, Jack. A *dad*. You'll be a wonderful one. I know you will."

"April..."

"*Au revoir, Jacques.*"

Goodbye.

7

And now, twelve years later, Paige Forrester would be saying hello to Jack Logan. Hello *again?* Maybe. If he recognized her. Which, Paige had convinced herself, he would not.

After a final wave to Gwen from the mansion's front door, Paige let herself in. Quietly. And was relieved to find herself alone in the foyer.

She had to sit, though not so urgently as before and not for long. Just a few minutes to regroup. Prepare. She sank down on the bottom steps of the banistered staircase.

Even if Jack did recognize her, it should *not* be a major ordeal. And as for her delay in fessing up... *I thought about calling you, Jack,* she could say. Or even *Bonjour, Jacques!*

C'est Avril. Aka Paige Forrester. Quelle surprise! But I know how busy you are, your business is such a success, it seemed much ado over a brief acquaintance a lifetime ago.

Paige *might* have been able to pull off something so light and breezy. At one time. Before her kidneys had failed—no, she amended sternly, before she had failed her kidneys.

But, since then, everything was difficult. Fatigue was ever-present, unrelieved by sleep, and she was weak, thirsty, irritable.

Do better. Try harder. For a very long time, those had been the mantras of her life, the underpinnings of the cheerful facade she presented to the world. But with the havoc wreaked on her electrolytes—and her equanimity—the facade was in constant peril.

She had to guard against emotions that yearned to run amok, her frustration at the predicament she'd gotten herself into and her impatience with herself for handling it so poorly. She wasn't doing a good job of suppressing those feelings either, as her recent irritability with Cole had so amply proved.

Paige needed to be cheerful for her mother, who asked so little of her. And a smile would also be nice for Jack. And for Beth and Dina.

So. Paige pumped her calf muscles, stood without swaying, and draped her coat over the newel post.

Do better.

Try harder.

The mantras of her life weren't working. What lay ahead still felt like a monumental ordeal.

But there were other words that might work. Because of the memories that accompanied them. The feeling of not being—quite—so alone.

It felt, in fact, as if Gwen was right here, cheering her on.

You'll dazzle him, Paige.

Mark my words.

Jack wasn't in the mansion living room. Paige saw him in the garden, making an inspection of some kind. The girls could have gone with him. There were the fountains and the view. But they'd chosen, and Paige was hardly surprised, to remain inside with Claire.

For Paige, the scene in the living room was achingly familiar: other daughters chattering happily to her mother.

It was so effortless for other daughters to talk to Claire. And so effortless for Claire to be with them.

Claire Forrester should have had the mansion full of daughters—the daughters "April Dawson" had given her. She would have, Paige felt quite sure, had Alan not died.

But friends brought their daughters and granddaughters to visit Claire, and Paige's classmates flocked, too, to the Forrester home.

And did the presence of such faux daughters bother the authentic one?

Paige *was* jealous in a wishing, wistful way. She would've loved to play with Claire as easily as they did. To play at all. But she couldn't. So she was glad, truly, that her mother found others who could.

And, Paige told herself, having other girls around made her awkwardness with Claire—and Claire's with her—less obvious.

And less aching.

But that wasn't true. The discomfort between them was there, no matter how crowded the mansion was or how hard they tried.

And they did try. Both of them.

And failed.

They were artist and scientist; spring and winter, playful and rigid. Enchantress of make-believe—and practitioner of cancer therapies.

Were they also mother and daughter?

As a girl, Paige had tormented herself with the specter of a hospital mix-up. Or even an intentional exchange. Who wouldn't have preferred Claire's real daughter—in all probability a healthy newborn—to the desperately ill neonate Paige had been?

Eventually, Paige had been compelled to put that torment to rest. She was Alan Forrester's child. The father-daughter resemblance could not be denied.

"Paige!" Claire exclaimed as she spotted her in the living room archway. "I'm so glad you could make it."

Mother and daughter walked toward each other. But

they stopped, both of them, at a distance just out of reach. It was a dance perfected after years of imperfect hugs—too brief, too long, too loose, too tight.

Too frantic.

But Paige was close enough to read her mother's worry about her—how tired she looked, how thin and pale.

I'm fine, Mother! Fine, fine, fine.

Lies, lies, lies.

And more to come. As the French door to the veranda opened behind her, Paige felt the coolness of the breeze and heard the warmth of his voice.

"You must be—"

"Paige." She turned, hand extended, to the quarter-back who was now a builder. And a single father. He recognized her. At once. There was absolutely no question. *And it bothered him.* A lot. "And you must be Jack."

"Yes. I'm Jack." His hand, rough and strong, encircled hers. Then let go. "This is my daughter Beth. And Beth's friend Dina."

The girls might have been sisters, both willowy, both blond.

Dina, the older and bolder of the two, beamed as she greeted her. "Hi, Dr. Forrester."

Beth's greeting came from behind a lock of hair. "Hi, Dr. Forrester."

"Hi, Dina. Hi, Beth. Why don't you call me Paige?"

Dina did, instantly, beaming even more brightly.

But Beth cast a questioning glance at her father.

May I? Should I? Paige couldn't tell which question Beth was asking—whether she wanted permission to use the grown-up greeting, or whether she was perfectly content to address Paige from the distance of a child.

A memory came to Paige, ancient but vivid, a dinner party when she was about Beth's age. It was the usual foursome. Her family. Claire, Paige, Stuart, Mariel.

Aunt Mariel, until that dinner party, when—in the throes of putting the final touches on the second of what would be three failed marriages—Mariel announced that it was time, in her view, for Paige to drop the "Aunt."

Paige remembered her reluctance to make what felt like a quantum leap toward adulthood...and the responsibilities she knew, even then, awaited her there. But she'd honored Mariel's request, and the relationship had irrevocably changed. Become more distant.

As for the never-married man who'd been her father's best friend and like a father to Paige... To this day he was Uncle Stuart, and Paige felt as close to him, as safe with him, as she had during childhood.

"Paige is okay," Jack told his daughter. And of course it was. Jack knew his Beth, would keep her safe. "Any name Paige wants is fine."

"Hi, Paige."

"Hi, Beth. Are you really Elizabeth?"

"Yes."

"Me, too. Elizabeth's my middle name."

"And you went to Stanford, didn't you? At the same time as my dad?"

"Part of the same time."

"But you didn't know each other?"

"Actually," Paige said. "We sort of did."

Paige looked from Beth to Jack. His eyes, even greener than she remembered, glittered with a darkness she didn't want to name. But she knew what it meant. He'd remain silent for now. She could lie all she liked to the others. But soon, very soon, he expected a truthful explanation—to him.

For now, he was merely watching. And waiting.

"Your dad dated a girl I knew," she said to Beth. *A phantom named April.* "We saw each other a few times, but were never introduced. And now we have been." And now Paige was searching for a new topic—which she found emblazoned in white script on the girls' cobalt-blue sweatshirts. *Marina View Swim Team.* "Are you swimmers?"

"No. But *Larry* is." Dina cast a meaningful smile at Beth—who blushed.

"I see."

"You *could* see," Dina said. "If you came with us."

"We're en route to a swim meet," Jack explained. "Why don't you come? Both of you."

Claire didn't hesitate. "Thank you, Jack. And Dina and Beth. I'm afraid I won't be able to go this time. But I'll see you ladies on Monday after school—and any other day you'd like to visit."

"Claire..."

"I'd love having them here, Jack! I'm sure we could find a room that isn't being torn apart where they could do their homework. And I'd be thrilled to have help going through thirty years of *stuff*. And there's always cookie-baking for the crew."

"You do not need to do that."

"I know. But I want to. And with two helpers..."

To whom the idea of baking with Claire, playing with Claire, even studying with Claire obviously appealed.

Jack sighed. Smiled. "Okay." His smile vanished. "But you'll come with us, won't you, Paige?"

It was barely a question.

And she had no choice.

"Yes," she replied. "I'd love to."

8

Gwen staggered, or felt as if she did, and wondered if she, like Paige, was on the verge of fainting.

If so, like Paige, it was because her blood had congregated other than where it should have been. The pooling wouldn't be in her legs, of course. And it wasn't because, as she traveled the five blocks between the Forrester mansion and her Belvedere Court apartment, she felt relaxed.

The blood, if pooled, was in her blemished cheek— where it had rushed the instant Dr. Cole Ransom had looked her way. And far from relaxed, the emotions she'd managed until now to keep at bay were in a turmoil.

But she was almost home, and if she was smart she'd let herself into the building without pausing to scan the directory beside the locked front door.

But as long as she was fumbling with her key... There it was, he was, *Cole Ransom, Apt. 812*. Two floors up from her own apartment—603.

It seemed an odd choice, for the vascular-and-trauma maestro to rent instead of own. He could afford a penthouse condo, even in Pacific Heights. She could imagine him there, the black-haired surgeon with the stone-gray eyes, and she could imagine—

Get over it! Him, Gwen commanded herself.

To limited avail.

Cole's mailbox was labeled, as well, she noticed as she opened hers.

The contents were unsurprising. She wasn't certain why she'd stopped. Christmas catalogues. The new *Allure*. And a notice from the post office of an attempted delivery. Even that wasn't a surprise. Makeup artists regularly received samples from cosmetic companies, many of whom wanted proof the products had been delivered.

She'd sign the yellow form, and the package would appear on Monday, and, as she always did, she'd give the enclosed foundation, blush, lip gloss or mascara a fair and conscientious try.

"I usually sit there." Jack pointed to the uppermost row of wooden bleachers.

The girls had scampered off to join a cluster of other girls already seated—and saving seats for them—three rows up from the start/finish line.

No one was saving a seat for Jack in the rafters. No one else was there. The competitors' parents sat at poolside. And the other parents like Jack, whose daughters came to watch, not to swim...

There were plenty of such *daughters* in the Golden Gate Aquatic Center.

But only one such parent—Jack—whose discreet yet watchful presence, a caring presence, didn't bother Beth or her friends in the least.

"It's a bit of a hike," he admitted. "One we don't *have* to make."

"It's fine," Paige replied. *It's fine. I'm fine.* How many times—just today—had she uttered that lie? And how many more times could she say it at all?

Not many more. She was in serious trouble. Her veins were dilating with cavalier disregard for her marginal blood pressure. It was a completely normal physiologic response, of course, given the ambient warmth in this environment.

But she wasn't normal. Her kidneys weren't normal.

The humidity, too, was a problem, making it difficult for her to breathe. *Except,* Dr. Forrester reminded herself, there wasn't any physiologic reason to back that up.

Her breathlessness had to be emotional, the memory of an emotion, the feeling of drowning when her renal failure was first diagnosed. She'd been discounting the signs and symptoms until then: the weakness, the ankle swelling, the irregular heartbeats, the relentless fatigue. Do better. Try harder.

But when the excess fluid within, having nowhere else to go, had flooded her lungs... Yes, her breathlessness now was emotional. Had to be. She could breathe. Was breathing. Okay.

The nausea, however, was real. A sympathetic reaction, perhaps, between the chlorine in the dewy air and the elevated chloride levels in her blood.

"Paige?"

"It's fine, Jack. The uppermost row of bleachers is fine."

"You're sure?"

Paige set her determined sights on the rafters. "Positive," she lied and began to climb.

But the lie came true. It *was* fine, she was fine, in the rafters.

With Jack.

The vigilant father...and vigilant man.

"So what was that all about?" he wanted to know.

"The heat and humidity got to me. And the chlorine, too. But I'm better now."

"Then tell me," Jack Logan said softly, "what April Dawson was all about."

"May I tell you something else first?"

"Go ahead."

"It wasn't until *after* your meeting with Stuart that I knew anything about your renovating my mother's place——or, for that matter, about the renovation itself."

"Is that true, Paige? You really didn't know?"

"It's true." *My mother and I aren't that close, you see.*

"And if you'd known?"

"There wouldn't have been any investigation. And *of course* the job would've been yours. Did it bother you to be scrutinized so closely?"

"Not until today, when I saw you and wondered if you'd insisted on it."

"No, Jack. *No.* Please believe——"

"I do, Paige. And the answer is that it didn't bother me until today. I have no objection to Stuart's watching out for your mother's best interests. He seems like a good man."

"He is."

"And his last name is Dawson," Jack said. "The same as a girl I once knew…and who Stuart doesn't know, at least not as April."

"You asked him?"

"If he happened to be related to an April Dawson? Sure. He said he really doesn't have any family to speak of."

"No. Although he does take care of my mother. And me. He always has."

"A good man," Jack repeated.

"Yes. Very."

"Then I'm happy to have his seal of approval. And impressed, by the way, with the professionalism of his investigator's report."

"You saw it?"

"Once I got Stuart to admit it had been done, I asked him for a copy. Have you seen it, Paige?"

"Yes."

"And read it?" *As carefully as the girl in the library studied her notes?* Jack saw the answers—Yes, and *yes*—in the myriad emotions in her expressive blue eyes. "So, you know about me." *My marriage. My divorce. My finances. My family.* "Now, tell about you—beginning with April Dawson. Who is she?"

"No one, Jack. She doesn't exist."

"But we both know she did. Why?"

"Because I wanted to know what it would feel like to be someone else, without the labels."

"Labels such as Forrester?"

"Yes. And pre-med."

"When did you become April Dawson?"

"The night we first spoke." *And she died the night we said goodbye.*

"But you'd already begun studying in the drama library. Why?"

"No other pre-med students in sight. It wasn't to avoid the usual pre-med pressure—the feeling that as long as any pre-meds were studying, you should be, too. That wasn't an issue for me. I was always the last to leave. The problem was that my classmates wanted to study with me."

"Because you always set the curve?"

"No. Well, my grades were good. But the course work never came easily to me. I needed to study very hard, and I wasn't the team-studying type."

"So when you said no to studying with a group, you

felt guilty—but when you said yes, it meant spending extra hours studying on your own."

"You, too?"

"In a way. I think it was mostly that I had my fill of team endeavors on the football field."

"But the other engineering students would've wanted to study with you, wouldn't they? Because *you* always set the curve? Jack?"

He shrugged. Smiled. "I did pretty well. I'm a good test-taker."

Paige smiled, too, then narrowed her eyes. "The kind who scores perfectly on standardized tests, even when the subject is unfamiliar to him?"

"Not perfectly, but…it's pattern recognition, I think. And—this much I do know—it's simply the way my brain is wired. The ability to see a play unfolding came in handy as a quarterback, and as a builder it helps to be able to visualize the disparate pieces—and various subcontractors—working as a whole. But we're not talking about me, remember? Let's get back to you. Paige."

"You mean April."

"No," Jack said. "I mean Paige. You did have headaches, didn't you?"

"Yes. How could you tell?"

"You were so still when you studied, your head especially. It looked like it hurt. And, although you cut back, you kept taking the pills. Were they migraine headaches?"

"No. Just tension."

"Why?"

"Why was I feeling tense? Because that's who I am." *The girl behind the mask.* "I put myself under pressure. I always have. Remember April's oldest sister?"

"The firstborn daughter who pushed herself and was sometimes lonely."

"And driven. And goal-oriented."

"I remember her, Paige. Very well. She wanted to be a doctor because of her surgeon father. Your mother told me that your surgeon father was injured in a car crash the day you were born and died of his injuries five days later. Did you decide, at age seven, to follow in his footsteps?"

"Yes. But the good news is that a high-school summer spent doing oncologic research convinced me that medicine really *was* what I wanted to do. I tried, for quite a while, to make my career imitate his. In terms of locales—Stanford, UCSF, PHMC—it has."

"But you're not a surgeon."

"No. I finally gave myself permission not to be. I wasn't any good at it. Despite my artist mother and my surgeon father, I've never been good with my hands." Paige looked down at those hands, knotted in her lap. *See, Jack? This is me. Paige. Tense. Taut. There's really nothing more to know.* Paige focused beyond her lap to the youthful activity in the pool area below. "Which one is Larry?"

"The skinny kid closest to the clock."

"He doesn't look too menacing."

"He isn't. Yet. He and Beth are best friends. Have been

since second grade. The boyfriend-girlfriend spin is purely Dina's—for now."

"But you think it might happen someday?"

"I wouldn't be surprised. Happily, for the time being, Dina's teasing—she teases Larry, too—is making him as embarrassed about the idea of a romance as Beth is."

"But Dina persists, doesn't she?"

"She does. She's been a best friend, too, for the past four years."

"Even though she's quite a bit older."

"Not quite a bit. Just three months."

"A precocious three months."

"Yes. Very. That precociousness is actually pretty new. But Dina's always laid claim to the big-sister role. It just feels more authentic now. Dina's a nice girl, and Larry's a great kid, and Beth is…"

"Lovely."

"Lovely," Jack echoed with wonder, with love. "And as innocent as Dina is precocious. Which isn't to say I haven't started having flashbacks to when I was twelve, and thirteen, and fourteen. They scare the hell out of me."

"You're a wonderful father."

"Just a father, Paige."

"A—" wonderful "—father who worries."

He nodded. "Once upon a time, when Beth was very small, I told myself it was in my power to protect her from harm. I merely needed to anticipate all potential accidents and be on the lookout for the earliest signs of illness."

"Merely."

"A tall order, but not an impossible one—at least not when she was young. But she's changing, and so is the world. We made it safely through chicken pox and the threat of Reye's, but there may be smallpox, among other terrors, to contend with in the future. That's an extreme worry, of course. And becoming a teenager is worrisome enough. Cars. Boys. The natural high of growing up, the synthetic one of ecstasy."

"Beth's *not* taking ecstasy."

"No. And she says she never will. But who knows what pressures she'll face, what confusion she'll feel?"

"You'll know," Paige said. "She'll tell you."

"I hope so."

"But you're not sure? It's obvious how much she loves you, Jack. Trusts you."

"Something's confusing her now, Paige. A worry of some kind. A sadness. I'm not certain which. She's always been a serious little girl."

"A sensitive little girl."

Jack nodded again. "There've always been issues that troubled her. But before now, she's always told me when there's something she's been thinking about and is going to want to discuss. Then, when she's finished mulling it over on her own, we do."

"What kind of issues trouble her?"

"Oh, you know, just the impossible ones, the imponderables of life. It's the answer, more than the question, she wants to discuss. She's usually formulated an answer by the time we talk. Such as the reason people hurt each other——she's decided it's because *they* hurt. And the reason dogs don't live as long as humans is so there'll be humans around to love them all their lives. A dog would be sadder than a human if its owner died first."

"Oh, Jack."

"I want to hear them all, Paige. Every worry, every sadness, every thought. Until now, I was pretty sure I had."

"And you think there's something bothering her?"

"Yes."

"You could ask her."

"I probably will. Even though I could argue that she should be allowed a little privacy. A secret here and there. I tell myself, without much conviction, that it's permissible on occasion to be sad. She can't be happy every second of her life, even if that's what her father wants for her."

Happy, Paige mused. And safe. If any father could give such gifts to his daughter, it was Jack. After all, it was because of Jack that *she'd* felt so happy.

Jack, who'd also done his best to save her.

9

"You were right about the pills, Jack." Paige broke the silence which, for the time it took eight teenage boys to race the length of the Olympic-sized pool, had been filled by the sounds of splashing. And cheering. "I was taking way too many."

"Weren't they just over-the-counter headache meds?"

"Yes. Over-the-counter headache meds washed down with diet colas."

"Talk."

"My kidneys are damaged. It's called analgesic nephropathy, and it's caused by long-term excessive use of pain meds."

"Over-the-counter pills," Jack repeated.

"Yes."

"Which ones?"

"That's where the issue becomes both confusing and contentious. For every seemingly definitive article, you can find rebuttals. Admittedly, methodology is a problem. You obviously can't design a study in which you give patients more than the recommended dose of a drug in the hope of determining whether renal damage will occur. So the information that's available is retrospective only. A patient with newly diagnosed renal disease is asked to recollect which over-the-counter meds he——or, more typically, *she*——took, and how much of each, how often, and whether it was in combination with other drugs."

Paige shook her head. "Sorry!"

"For what?"

"I feel like I'm giving you a lecture."

"And I feel like I'm being told things I want to hear. I'm with you so far, Paige. If anything comes up that I don't understand, I'll ask."

"Okay. The first cases were described almost fifty years ago. The pain med was phenacetin and was taken off the market as a result. But its major metabolite was, is, acetaminophen."

"Tylenol."

Paige nodded. "Tylenol."

"I'm aware of liver damage caused by Tylenol."

"Yes. Both in an overdose setting, and——especially in association with daily alcohol consumption——in recommended doses as well. The data's clear."

"Unlike the kidney damage data."

"Yes. And there are other reasons, too, for being cautious about implicating Tylenol—or any single pain med for that matter—in renal disease. It's well-documented that most patients with chronic pain take a *variety* of painkillers. I know I certainly did. The data, such as it is, suggests it may be the combination of different drugs that causes the harm. Caffeine may be a factor, as well. You remember all those diet sodas I drank along with the pills."

"You're not blaming yourself."

"There's no one else *to* blame. I had to know that taking all those pills couldn't be good for me. And even if I didn't know, the labeling on the bottles was clear. Then as now, over-the-counter pain meds are to be used only for temporary—meaning a few days—pain relief. And far from the handfuls of round-the-clock pills I used to take, the recommended daily doses are really quite small. I routinely exceeded both dose and duration. That's probably the case for most, perhaps all, patients with analgesic nephropathy. Too many pills, day in and day out."

"But you had headaches day in and day out."

"I *made* myself have them. And sometimes, many times, I'd take the pills even when my head wasn't really hurting, when I worried that I might get a headache and had studying to do."

"Do you have headaches now?"

"Sometimes."

"And?"

"They go away."

"You make them go away." *Will them away.*

"Yes."

"Can you make the analgesic nephropathy go away?"

"No. The damage is irreversible."

"So what do you do about that?"

"Manage it—badly, if you're me."

"I can't believe you're a bad patient."

"No, well, I definitely try not to be. I certainly have a new appreciation for what normally functioning kidneys do. They're quite remarkable. You can feed them protein, calcium, potassium—and fluids galore—and they adapt. My best efforts can't come close to maintaining such a balance."

"Your mother doesn't know, does she?"

"About my less-than-perfect kidneys? No."

"Why not?"

"Why worry her?"

"Because you're her daughter. It's her job to worry… and her joy."

"Spoken like a true parent."

"A parent who worries that his daughter will hide something from him—for fear of worrying him. Something he really needs to know."

"It's complicated with my mother."

"Spoken like a true daughter. Are you referring to her agoraphobia?"

"She told you about it?"

"She really had no choice. It's traditional for builders to send clients to showrooms all over town. Your mother was up-front about her reluctance to leave her home."

"She actually used the word *agoraphobia?*"

"She did, and even defined it for me as the desire to avoid anxiety-provoking situations——which occur, she says, if she takes so much as a single step outside the mansion."

"But you invited her to the swim meet."

"I thought if she was with you, the girls and maybe even me, she might feel less anxious. I assume she'd *like* to be able to go out."

"I'm not so sure."

"Because there's something more, isn't there? Something I'm missing. I'm not surprised. I've been having trouble imagining what in the outside world would cause Claire Forrester to feel anxious in any way. Certainly not crowds or strangers or even the unforeseen. At her insistence, I've brought my various subcontractors to meet her with almost no advance notice. Not only has she greeted every one as if she'd been expecting him, but it was as if he was a long-lost brother, as well. She's looking forward to six months of construction, she says—claims it feels festive—and I'm

fully convinced she really wants Beth and Dina under-
foot."

"She does, Jack. Absolutely. She'll love having the girls
there. And the work crews. The more the merrier."

"So it's great for the world to come to her, but she's
reluctant—even fearful—to venture into it herself?"

"That's exactly right. You're not missing anything."

"I'm missing the *why,* Paige. Do you know?"

"I think so. It's not the outside world that frightens her.
It's being away from her home. She's afraid of what she
might miss, *who* she might miss, while she's gone."

"Who?"

"My father."

"Your father," Jack repeated. "Who died when you
were five days old."

"Yes. And there's no doubt that he died. She was with
him, watched him. There's no miraculous happily-ever-
after for her, for them. He's not about to awaken from a
thirty-one-year coma, nor has he been wandering the
planet in an amnesic haze. He's dead. She knows he's
dead. But she's waiting for him, Jack. She's been waiting, all these years, for a ghost."

"She knows her," Dina asserted for the zillionth time.
"Definitely."

"You think so?"

"I know so, Beth. Who do you think the girl was that
your dad was dating? Your *mother,* of course. Dr. For-

rester——Paige——knows her. You've seen how seriously they've been talking. Paige was friends with your mother, and that's probably why *your* first name is the same as *her* middle name. This is so great, Beth. This is how you can find out."

10

Larry placed first in the individual medley, anchored his team to a third-place finish in the hundred-meter relay, and came in second in the fifty-meter freestyle.

The IM—individual medley—triumph was a surprise. A boy from Bayside held the regional record and was predicted to win. The team-relay third was also a better-than-expected result. Thanks to Larry. Marina View Academy had been dead last when he'd dived into the pool.

The biggest surprise and apparently an unpleasant one, however, was Larry's second-place finish in the fifty-meter freestyle, his signature event. Indeed, judging by his father's reaction, the loss was a disaster of monumental proportions.

"We could kill him," Paige said as she and Jack witnessed the harangue from the rafters. They couldn't hear the words. Didn't need to. The man's body language was eloquent.

"We could," Jack agreed. "I've been tempted many times."

"Have you spoken to him?"

"Sure. Only once in the heat of the moment—with no success—and at various other times over the past four years. He's reasonable then. Rational. Acknowledges that he goes overboard and vows never to do it again. Then... this. The good news is that with each passing day, Larry gets closer to recognizing that the problem is entirely his father's. He's not quite there, but in the meantime, Beth admires him for simply diving into the pool, and Dina's casting him as a heartthrob."

"You're a supporter of his, too."

"You bet. I'm going to ask him to join us for dinner. 'Us' meaning you, too."

"Oh. I..."

"The girls and I talked about the Wharf, but we can go anywhere you like. There must be menus that are best for you."

"Bits and pieces of any menu, really."

"Great. But?"

But maybe Forrester mother and daughter had something in common after all: a tendency toward phobias. If so, it was just a small similarity—the tendency, not the phobia itself.

Nephrophobia, Paige's affliction could be called. The fear of all things renal...now that the remarkable kidneys had been destroyed.

Breathlessness was a worry. The consequences of excess fluid drowning her lungs. Even the memory of such gasping caused fear. And there was fainting to worry about, and nausea, weakness, thirst. And having to be so careful about what she ate that the girls and Larry would surely wonder what was wrong with her.

There was a different kind of breathlessness, too. Another kind of memory. Fearsome? Yes.

And wondrous. The way she'd felt, twelve years ago, with Jack...and the way she was feeling *now.*

Paige wanted to curl into his arms and murmur to the strong and steady heart beating in his chest, *Hold me, protect me, make everything go away.*

But everything was within *her.* The pressure, the drive, the doing better and trying harder that had led, amidst all the successes, to poisoning her kidneys.

All of which Jack knew.

Nonetheless he was looking at her as if she'd be more than welcome to curl into his arms. He seemed to be saying he'd protect her—maybe they'd protect each other—and all the bad things would be banished.

"Paige?"

"I'd like to, Jack. I'd...love to. But could we make it another time? I think I should go home now and get some sleep."

"Okay. And yes. We can make it another time. Anytime."

And, they both vowed in silence, *we will.*

The moon glowed yellow during its ascent, a wintry pastel that sparkled in the cold night air.

But as the hour grew later, the night darker and deeper, the light from the heavens turned bloody. Parents of small children, and even the father of an eleven-year-old girl, were grateful the lunar hemorrhage waited until the littlest innocents were asleep.

This was not a moon that children should see.

That *anyone* should see, the majority of San Franciscans would have said.

Once seen, however, the disturbing light was impossible to ignore. Only those with other duties turned away from its unholy glow. Newsroom personnel, in particular, were obliged to focus elsewhere. Their late-night viewers—and Sunday-morning readers—would expect a scientific explanation of the celestial event. And some, perhaps, would expect comparable precision when it came to defining the exact shade of lunar red to be named in the front-page headline.

Once in a Crimson Moon.

Once in a Cinnabar Moon.

Once in a Vermilion Moon.

Most would ultimately conclude that the accuracy of the color didn't matter. *Once* was the essential word.

Readers and viewers wanted to be assured this blood-hued moon was a phenomenon they'd be unlikely ever again to see.

Claire Forrester wished she'd never before seen such a moon. But she had. On this date, November second. At this time, midnight. Thirty-one years ago.

The date, the time, her Alan died.

Claire made no attempt, then or now, to name the color. Colors, for now as then the artist saw two, red and purple, the same hated purple, the oil-slick purple, that had caused so much blood to spill.

I love you, Claire. I love you.

Alan had lost consciousness, never to regain it, after whispering those final words. Claire fainted seconds later. But she'd heard his words, seen his love...and the blood that gushed from his mouth after speaking them.

She'd known in those seconds that he would die, and that he wouldn't let her die with him. Die at all. His words, their force and their fury, had echoed in her brain, giving her strength, making her fight....

Claire awakened in the hospital in Monterey. Her husband was in one ICU, her infant daughter in the other. For five days and nights, Claire divided her time between the two, never torn yet always torn, fearful of what might befall one while she was with the other...yet knowing, thanks to Mariel's presence, that neither Alan nor Paige was ever truly alone.

And when Stuart arrived at last from snowed-in O'Hare, he too kept watch at the loved ones' bedsides.

Mariel and Stuart could have kept the separate vigils then. They offered to, so Claire could sleep, at least lie down. She wouldn't rest, of course, not even for a minute. She was so healthy compared to her family. Yes, she'd lost some blood. Quite a bit. And she was groggy from the anesthetic she'd received, and at times confused.

But she wasn't in a coma, as Alan was. Nor were her muscles crushed, her spine shattered, her lungs hemorrhaging. And unlike her baby girl, Claire wasn't jaundiced, wasn't intubated, wasn't struggling to survive.

Alan and Paige were dying. Would die. The prognosis for both father and daughter was that explicit. That grave.

But Claire lied to them both.

"Wait till you see her, Alan. She's *so* beautiful. She looks just like you, my love. *Exactly* like you."

"Wait till you see your daddy, Paige. Wait till he holds you. He loves you so much. We both do. We're going to spend forever loving you."

On this night, thirty-one years ago, Claire's lies had stopped.

They had to.

Alan was gone.

And the blood-and-purple moon had glowered in the stark black sky...as, tonight, it was glowering anew.

When the mansion phone sounded, Claire knew with relief, with gratitude, who it would be.

11

"**Y**ou're looking at it, too," Claire greeted her midnight caller, the man who—thirty-one years ago—had finally made it from snowy Chicago to stormy Monterey. Stuart had been at her side then, helping her survive the impossible. And Alan's best friend had been at her side, figuratively and often literally, ever since. "The moon. Stuart?"

"I'm looking at it."

"What do you suppose it means?"

"Nothing, Claire. Not a damned thing. But if you're interested in a meteorological theory, the prevailing one seems to be that the cold, clear weather we've been having has created an inversion layer that's trapping an unusual amount of smog."

"But there wasn't any smog in Monterey during those

five days. And it had been raining, hadn't it, until that night?"

Those five days, Stuart echoed in silence. *Until that night.*

Never in all their years—decades—of talking to each other had he and Claire so much as alluded to the last five days and final night of Alan's life. They'd talked about Alan, of course. The happy times, the magical love. But not about those few days, when so much had been lost. Why would they? There was nothing to discuss, no memories to retrieve. Stuart had been there. Claire had been there. Detailed remembrance was carved indelibly in their hearts.

Or so Stuart had always thought. "Don't you remember?" he asked.

"That it was raining? Yes, I guess I do. But the more I try to remember, the more blurry everything becomes."

"Why are you trying to remember?" *Why don't you— why can't you—let yourself forget?*

"Because there's something I *should* remember, Stuart. I see glimpses of it, flashes of clarity, but I can't quite bring the entire picture into focus. And I need to."

"How long have you been trying?"

"Oh, I don't know. Since sometime this spring, I suppose."

It was the answer Stuart had expected and dreaded, and it confirmed what had become painfully clear in recent months. Claire's decision to renovate the mansion, a decision she'd shared with him that spring, was not an indication that she was getting on with her life. Not that she'd ever said it was. And, in point of fact, she'd used the term "renovation" in its purest sense: to restore to the condition of being new...as good as new, in this case, as the last time the Forrester family home had been lovingly restored from foundation to rooftop—not long before her wedding to Alan.

Renovation didn't promise change. And now, as further evidence that she was polishing the past, not creating a shiny new future, was the revelation that her search for a missing memory coincided with her decision to renovate the mansion.

Hating that truth, but helping her as he always did, Stuart said, "Tell me what you see in the flashes of clarity."

"I'm wandering in the rain. It's dark. Cold. It's the night of the crash, I think. Or the following night. One of those two nights, definitely. You're still in Chicago. You haven't yet arrived."

"How do you know that?"

"Because," she said softly, "if you'd been in Monterey you'd have been with me. In the memory I'm very much alone. And desperate."

You're still very much alone, my Claire. I would be with you now, if only you'd let me. "If you were wandering in the rain, you wouldn't have been with either Alan or Paige. You would've felt desperate to be with them."

"But I know I'm *not* with them, and that's not why I'm so desperate. It's all right with them that I've gone away.

They know there's something I have to do. They want me to. They," she repeated quietly. "My dying husband, my critically ill baby. It sounds like a dream, doesn't it? A nightmare. But it feels so real, Stuart. Did anyone ever tell you I'd left the hospital?"

"No. But I can imagine your taking a wrong turn. The hospital was a maze. You might have gone through an exit door by mistake. What does Mariel say?"

"I haven't asked her. And I'm not going to. Talking about that time with Mariel would be too difficult for both of us."

"Would you like me to ask her?"

"No. Thank you."

"Then how are you going to resolve this?"

"By making the memory become clear."

"And if you can't?"

"Then I'll be forced to acknowledge that it's not real and I was hallucinating. That's the most likely scenario, anyway, that it's a figment of postpartum psychosis."

"What?"

"Haven't you wondered, Stuart?"

"Never. You were despondent, Claire. Grieving. We all were."

"But I was also postpartum. And if I crossed the line from sanity to psychosis, my symptoms would've been virtually impossible to detect. Very little was expected of me. I was a zombie, floating through the motions."

"That's not true. You were right there, Claire, fighting with all your heart for Alan and for Paige."

"For Alan, maybe. But after he died and Paige was transferred to the neonatal ICU up here..."

"You were with her, Claire, every minute, *every second*, touching her, talking to her, comforting her."

"I didn't succeed in comforting her, though, did I?"

"Of course you did."

"No. If I had, she'd have come to me for comfort once she was old enough to make the choice. And, as we both know, she never has. Why would she? I wasn't a trustworthy sanctuary for her. I'd had my chance, when she was inside me, but without a thought for her safety I scrambled down the embankment to Alan."

"That didn't cause the placental abruption."

"So everyone says. But how do they know? All that really matters is what effect the torn placenta had on Paige. And that we do know. One moment she was protected, secure, and the next she was fighting for her life."

"But she survived."

"No thanks to me, Stuart. If the paramedics hadn't arrived when they did and gotten me to the hospital in Monterey in time for her to be delivered there, not on a hillside... And even then, she was so ill, so *fragile*."

"She was five weeks premature."

"And she needed those five weeks. Desperately. Might have had them—"

"Her premature delivery was *not* your fault. Paige loves you, Claire."

"And I love her, Stuart. You know I do. But you also

know, we all know, that Paige and I have never been close. And if you'd seen her today when she dropped by to meet Jack and the girls... She looked so exhausted, Stuart. She needed a safe haven *so much*. But she knew it wasn't me. She's *worse* when she's with me, tense and wary, and trying so hard to be the perfect daughter. I've wondered if her drive to be perfect is another consequence of my failure to nurture her during those first few months."

"Paige's drive has nothing to do with you, Claire, or, for that matter, with nurture of any kind. It's nature, pure and simple, an inheritance from Alan that's even more striking than her looks."

"Alan wasn't a perfectionist, Stuart! And he didn't drive himself like Paige does."

"Yes, he did. More so, by the way, than Paige ever has. And *that*—Paige's softness, her loveliness—is thanks to you. Just as you made Alan softer. Happier, too. Claire? This is crazy."

"Exactly."

"You're the most *not* crazy person I know."

"Except—" Claire stopped with a gasp of pain. It was becoming familiar, and ever more frequent, the burning within. Her gasp, the intake of air, only fueled the flames.

"Claire?"

"Except," she said on an exhalation, suffocating the fire in her stomach, trying to, "that I never leave my home. You, Paige, Mariel, my other friends, have spent the past few decades tiptoeing around that little problem of mine."

Not decades, Stuart thought. It might've been that long since Claire started to *feel* that way, wishing never to leave. But she had for the little girl who needed her mother with her, at a school event or on a trip to the library, or at a birthday party for a classmate. Stuart had often accompanied them, and he'd loved doing it. Until he caught a glimpse of the panic Claire had managed to hide for years.

It was a fleeting glimpse, and an anguished realization. Just as Claire wasn't a sanctuary for her daughter, he wasn't a sanctuary for Claire—not when she left the sanctuary that mattered most, the home she'd shared with Alan.

As far as Stuart knew, and he *did* know, Claire hadn't left the mansion since Paige's highest-honors graduation from medical school.

And now Claire was restoring that home to the way it had been when Alan was alive, its paint fresh, its floors gleaming, its invisible skeleton fortified against decay.

She'd admitted to one blurred memory, and maybe there were others that had faded—and she needed them bright again.

"Claire?"

"Stuart?"

"May I take you to brunch tomorrow? At the Top of the Mark?"

"You really think I could do that?"

"I know you could." *If you want it——me——badly enough.
If you want any life at all beyond your fading memories of
Alan.* "I'll pick you up at ten."

"Oh, Stuart." The fire seared. "I can't."

"Oh, Claire," he said gently, smiling for her even as he,
too, was scorched with pain. "I know."

Gweneth St. James had never seen a cinnabar moon.
But there'd been one, she knew, shining above the convent a few nights after she arrived. Sister Mary Catherine had told her about the moon, and that it had been
a sign. Celestial proof her birthmark was a blessing
from God.

Gwen was online at midnight, unaware of the moon,
as she'd been online—and oblivious—since nine. The
five hours before had been spent reflecting on the events
and emotions of the afternoon, from her initial encounter
with Paige at the heavy glass door until their hug——and
promise to meet for lattes.

Two hours——that was all it had been.

During that time she'd met the lively, dying Louise.
Don't die. Please don't die.

And the lovely, haunted Paige. *Help her. Someone help
her.* She'd confided secrets to Paige she'd never shared before, then wiped away her mask. And when Gweneth St.
James was fully exposed, there he'd been.

Cole.

Let him touch you, Paige. Let him care about you. He cares so much.

Paige clearly thought she'd been wrong about Cole's feelings. And most likely it was true. The detached observer who was usually so good at reading the hearts of others had not been present in the elevator foyer. Perhaps Gwen's own heart had been involved.

Quite possibly, she'd been wearing it on her cheek.

Cole's concern for Paige was undoubtedly just what Paige had said it was: the reaction of a dedicated physician. His voice would have been as soft, his talented hands as gentle, had he discovered, crumpled on the shiny linoleum, a stranger with a massive birthmark.

It was at that point, when Gwen found herself wishing she was the one who'd collapsed, that she abandoned her retrospective of the afternoon, booted up her computer and engaged in a far more productive enterprise.

She began at Google.com with a search for "kidneys on the fritz"——on the off-chance that there was, in medicine, such a thing. There wasn't.

"Kidneys" and "not working" yielded thousands of hits, however, and she'd been visiting the myriad Web sites ever since.

Gwen now knew why Paige was always thirsty and why she took the stairs for exercise, no matter how exhausted she was. Gwen also knew why, when they'd hugged, Paige's body was so ravaged, her bones so frail.

Gwen believed she knew *what* Cole wanted to touch

when he reached beneath Paige's cashmere sleeve, but not *why*. The elusive *why* might well be right in front her. But Gwen's concentration splintered at the memory of the surgeon's hands. Even her computer screen was blushing!

Bleeding.

Gwen spun in the direction of crimson light.

The port-wine moon.

And saw in the distance the gleaming purple bay... and, almost close enough to touch, the silhouette of the medical center shimmering red.

Cole Ransom didn't see the moon, not at midnight, or at any other time. He was operating from moonrise to moonset.

His first patient, an angry teenager, had slammed his fist through a plate glass window. The boy would have died on the scene had not his little sister tied a shoelace as tight as she could above the bleeding site.

The teen's brachial artery was severed. But he'd reached the hospital alive, and what presented to the vascular surgeon was an easy repair.

Cole's second patient was a seventy-two-year-old retired airplane mechanic whose abdominal aorta had ruptured. It took all night to save him, to stem the bleed, then resect the aneurysm, then sew in its place the man-made graft.

So Cole never saw the moon. He would have hated it if he had.

Because it would have reminded him of a birthmark seen earlier in the day? A blemish that marred the beauty of an otherwise exquisite face?

No. The birthmark didn't mar her beauty. Or her courage. She'd faced him with such courage, fierce in her protectiveness of Paige despite her discomfort...because of him.

Cole regretted the discomfort he'd caused her. But the port-wine moon would have tripped a different memory entirely, one of ugliness, not beauty. Of cowardice, not courage.

Cole would've seen the moon as a hemorrhage too massive to control, its splatters, like crimson moonbeams, everywhere: the floor, the walls, the ceiling.

The white satin comforter on the four-poster bed.

The moon would have reminded Cole of that carnage.

Not that he needed reminding.

Ever.

Louise Johansson didn't see the moon, either. But she would have thought it beautiful. It would have recalled springtime fuchsia baskets she'd loved, and the joy of watching hummingbirds feast on the floral ambrosia.

Louise was asleep at midnight.

Dreaming, smiling.

She didn't awaken at dawn, as throughout her eighty-two years she so often had, to witness the moon's gentle descent from the sky. Louise never awakened at all.

But the moon, at dawn, was Louise's moon. A bride's moon. Peach and pink.

And it was in the glow of that bridal moon that Louise, dreaming, smiling, flew to the heavens and the man she loved.

12

Monday, November 4
Pacific Heights Medical Center

"Dr. Forrester's office. This is Alice. How may I help you?"

"My name is Gwen St. James—"

"The makeup artist."

"That's me. Paige and I talked about getting together for a latte. I was calling to see if we could find a time."

"Today?"

"That would be great if she's free. But tomorrow's fine, or the next day—whenever."

"How's this afternoon between three and four?"

"Perfect."

"I'll double-check with Paige and get back to you if it isn't going to work. Gwen?"

"Yes?"

"You know about Louise, don't you?"

"Yes. Robyn called to say that..." *Louise had died, smiling, in her sleep.* Gwen drew a calming breath. "Is Paige all right?"

"It's always difficult for her. More difficult, it seems, as time goes on."

Following her conversation with Alice, Gwen put the post-office notice, now signed, in her mailbox. Unless Paige canceled, she'd be away from her apartment when what she presumed to be the samples of new cosmetics arrived.

Paige didn't cancel. On her return from her brief errand, Gwen found a lilting message from the oncologist herself.

"I was going to call *you* about a latte. I was planning to suggest tomorrow morning, though, since I thought you'd be on your way to work by three. But you must be off today? Three's better, anyway. Deserted cafeteria, window tables galore. I'll meet you there. At three. And Gwen? Thank you for calling."

Gwen's call to Paige's office had been her third call of the morning.

The first was to the station at 6:45. Gwen knew the station manager would be in by then, and she was.

Gwen's request for two weeks off was easily granted. She had almost seven years' worth of unused vacation and sick-leave days. And both Gwen and the manager knew a makeup artist who'd be delighted to fill in, beginning today.

The primary issue, as far as the manager was concerned, was *why*. Were Gwen and David going to tie the knot? Inquiring minds, she quipped, would want to know.

Gwen denied nothing, let assumptions stand.

A Tahitian honeymoon was the station manager's last—of many—guesses before, with a laugh, Gwen said goodbye.

Gwen didn't know what, if anything, she'd reveal to her co-workers. That was one of the decisions she'd make during the coming two weeks.

She knew only that the events of Saturday had been life-changing—and she needed to change accordingly. No longer the vicarious watcher of other people's lives, the girl behind the mask had to begin living her own.

Gwen's second call was to the Laser Clinic.

The clinic receptionist was more than happy to schedule an appointment. But Gwen would need to get a hospital card—more specifically a hospital number—before the appointment itself.

It was simply a matter of dropping by Clinic Registration between now and then.

Gwen did so en route to her rendezvous with Paige. The enrollment process was so efficient she reached the cafeteria at two thirty-five. After purchasing a single-shot, decaf, whole milk latte, she settled at a window table with views of the bay.

The cafeteria was deserted, as Paige had said it would be. For PHMC employees with defined hours, the workday was nearing its close. Better to finish all pending projects and go home on time than take an afternoon coffee break and risk an unanticipated delay. Even the hospital staff with open-ended—and sometimes never-ending—hours were nowhere to be seen.

On afternoon rounds, Gwen imagined. A prelude, barring emergencies, to the time when those not on call could also go home. The physicians' rounds, in turn, explained why patients and their families, too, were on the wards.

So it was Gwen, the lavender-smocked baristas, and...Cole.

Cole.

Approaching the latte bar.

He looked tired. Exhausted. The price of magic.

Cole loves to operate, Paige had said. Such passion could explain the surgeon's taking call for vascular and trauma, as well as choosing to work when life-and-death crises were most likely to occur. But there were other explanations. A godlike arrogance, for example, the egomaniacal certainty that he could pull off whatever miracle happened to be required.

But what if Cole didn't really *like* the life-threatening emergencies for which he made himself so available? What if he *hated* them, but chose them because it was at that perilous brink of eternity that he had the most to offer and could do the most good—no matter how much torment it brought him?

Torment. Now there was an illogical notion. Cole Ransom. Gorgeous, talented, sensual...and tormented? Yes. It was what Gwen had seen on Saturday afternoon. True, she hadn't been seeing very clearly when it came to Cole. She'd read an affection for Paige that probably didn't exist.

But Gwen couldn't shake her impression of a very deep, very dark shadow of pain. And maybe *that* was the reason Cole Ransom spent as many hours as humanly possible in the operating room, not in search of torment but as a respite from it. Personal demons didn't belong in the operating room, especially when the stakes were so high.

So Cole's patients found magic, and the escape artist found peace.

Gwen looked at the man who was filling the largest available cup with steaming black coffee—sustenance for a battle-weary warrior, not nectar for a god. And an indication that despite his weekend on call and his obvious exhaustion, the surgeon was in no hurry to go home.

Gwen watched him openly. Why not? Even if he sensed her gaze and returned it, he'd have no idea who she was. Gwen St. James had been a birthmark to him on Saturday. A birthmark, period. The red-and-purple blemish was all that nature would have permitted him to see.

And the Gwen St. James he would see today? As beautiful as he was handsome, her mask in place, her hair unbound.

And so, not surprisingly, when Cole looked her way, he smiled slightly and approached. He was in pursuit of companionship. Pleasure. *Sex*. A sensual creature on the prowl for a different kind of escape.

Let him touch you. He wants to. Well, not you exactly. In fact, let's be honest: he doesn't care—about you—at all. But it could happen, tonight, with the imposter Gwen. He'd touch you, and you'd touch him, and the night's darkness would be a mask of its own. He'd never know, and you'd never forget. You can do it—do it, do it—if you dare.

"May I join you?"

Do it! Do it!...Don't you dare. Unlike the unfamiliar voice that was encouraging her to pretend with Cole Ransom as she'd never pretended with another man, the *Don't you dare* voice belonged to someone she'd once known. Angel. The Angel she *should* have been. The girl who would've stood before her classmates and commanded, *Look at me. See* me.

Gwen knew what Cole Ransom was seeing: a beautiful woman with whom physical intimacy definitely appealed. Gwen had been the recipient of many such looks over the years—though none as searching as his, as wanting.

And none she'd ever wanted more.

He'd never know, and you'd never forget.

And the remembrance would kill her.

Gweneth St. James replied to Cole's query as she'd replied to all such inquiries by men before. "I'm waiting for someone."

"Paige?"

"I beg your pardon?"

"Are you waiting for Paige?"

"You—you know who I am?" she stammered.

"Gwen St. James. We met Saturday. I'm Cole Ransom. Remember?"

"Yes."

"Then why wouldn't I remember you?"

Gwen didn't answer. She had no answer. But she saw her hand gesturing for him to sit.

"Was the rest of your walk uneventful?"

No. We talked about you. "Very."

"No more dropping of keys?"

"You don't believe I dropped them?"

"Not for a second."

"I've always considered myself a pretty good liar."

"Sorry to disillusion you."

"Well, I'm thinking about quitting anyway."

"Just thinking about it?"

"I have a history of making hasty decisions." Hasty, easy, and sometimes monumental—without any soul-searching whatsoever. Was that the reason for her color-less soul? A consequence of having been masked for all these years? Gwen didn't know. But all future decisions would be made with great care. And might not be easy in the least. "I'm thinking about giving that up as well."

"The hasty decision-making?"

"Yes."

"Ah." Cole took a swallow of his coffee, but his eyes never left her face. "You're not working tonight."

"How do you know?"

"You're the Gwen who did the makeup for Louise Johansson, aren't you?"

"You knew Louise?" *Oh, Louise, what do you think of this man?*

"No. We never met. But Louise was much loved. There was a lot of talk over the weekend about how happy she was when she left—thanks to a makeup artist named Gwen who does makeup for FOX's evening and late-night news. You."

"Me. But Louise's happiness was thanks to Paige, not me. My contribution was only skin-deep."

"Only skin-deep," Cole echoed softly. "Is there such a thing?"

He was talking to her, about her, as if he cared. And as if he *saw*, and still wanted to touch.

Gwen looked away, outside, at a foreboding sky on the verge of rain. Then back. To him. "You think the real reason Paige felt faint was because of her kidneys."

"You know about her kidneys."

"Of course. Paige is my friend." Gwen made the pronouncement the way Paige had made the identical pronouncement—about her—on Saturday afternoon, with fondness and pride. And reverence, Gwen had decided as she reflected on Paige's tone, as if Paige knew what a rare treasure friendship was. And wishfulness, as if it was a treasure she hoped she'd found at last—with Gwen.

Okay, Gwen had conceded. Maybe it was her own wishfulness she heard; she'd realized, on reflection, that Gwen-the-imposter's many friendships had been...superficial. Yes, she truly cared about her friends. And, yes, they truly cared about her. But they didn't know her. She hadn't trusted them to know her. Not the astonishing way she'd trusted *her friend* Paige. "Although, admittedly, Paige isn't always forthcoming about herself. But I've done some reading on my own, and I'm beginning to understand. I think. I know you can't reveal specifics about Paige, but I do have a few general questions...."

"Ask."

"Okay. Great. Well, I know when you felt under her coat sleeve it was to check her hemodialysis access site. But I'm not sure why."

"I was feeling for the thrill."

"The *thrill?*"

Cole Ransom smiled. "The turbulent blood flow caused by the creation of a fistula between an artery and a vein. If the resultant shunt is too great, it could explain her low blood pressure."

"And a too-great shunt could be surgically corrected?"

"That's right. It could."

"But there wasn't a thrill?"

"There was, but no more than I'd expect."

"You created the fistula, didn't you?"

"Guilty."

And, based on her research, Gwen felt certain it was

a Brescia-Cimino fistula. Cole wouldn't have given Paige—or any of his patients—anything less. The so-called "native" fistula, created by the sewing together of the patient's own artery and vein, lasted longer than the more easily inserted prosthetic graft.

Gwen had concluded, on the night of the port-wine moon, that Paige was on hemodialysis. Her conclusion was now confirmed. And the fact that Paige had the kind of vascular access that was used only for long-term dialysis meant she had end-stage renal disease.

Long-term dialysis also meant that Paige had failed at medical—and dietary—management of her disease. She'd become acidotic, perhaps, or her serum potassium had been too high, or maybe she was simply so malnourished that dialysis had been the only logical next step.

But not an entirely successful one. Paige was still malnourished. Gwen even knew why. Protein intake, so rigorously restricted in patients before dialysis, was encouraged once dialysis began. Protein was washed away during dialysis, and, if it wasn't adequately replenished, muscle mass was lost.

Which was why Paige exercised even when she was fatigued, to keep her muscles toned and strong.

But Paige was thin, and her bones were fragile, and by her own admission she hadn't gotten the hang of keeping her blood pressure high enough to avoid fainting, but not so high as to flood her lungs.

Dr. Paige Forrester, who masterfully balanced chemotherapy with quality of life for her patients, was failing miserably in finding balance for herself.

"What are you thinking?" Cole asked.

"That Paige isn't doing well on dialysis."

"Has she told you that?"

"No. But it seems pretty clear. So what about transplantation?"

"What about it?"

"Is she a good candidate?"

A flash of silver sparked in his dark gray eyes. "Why do I get the feeling Paige hasn't spent much time discussing her renal failure with you?"

"Because you know how not forthcoming she can be."

"But there's more, isn't there? You've decided it would be easier to seduce information from me than from Paige." The silver glittered. "If so, Gwen, you're succeeding. I'm hopelessly seduced. The answer is yes. Paige is an excellent candidate for renal transplantation."

Hopelessly seduced. "When?"

"Today. Yesterday. Eight months ago."

"So she's waiting for a donor." A wait, Gwen had read by port-wine moonglow, that averaged three to four years. Unless there was a living-donor volunteer.

"Is she waiting, Gwen?"

"*Isn't* she, Cole?"

Primum non nocere. First, do no harm. It was every physician's solemn pledge. As was doctor-patient confidentiality. Cole chose to permit the first tenet to trump the second. The more Gwen knew about Paige's illness, he reasoned, the more she could help her. "To the best of my knowledge, Paige hasn't authorized her nephrologist to add her name to the national transplant registry."

"Why not?"

"Now *that's* a question to be pursued by a friend."

She intended to pursue it, Gwen would've told him, had they still been alone.

But they weren't.

A pretty blonde, wearing a scrub-dress and lab coat embroidered *Surgical ICU,* stood beside the table, quite close to Cole.

She also wore a wedding ring. And a smile.

"Cole?"

"Jen."

"I'm sorry to interrupt. I thought you'd gone home. Why *haven't* you?"

"I knew you'd need me. What's going on?"

"Mr.——our patient in bed four spiked to 38.8."

"When?"

"Fifteen minutes ago. Everything's under control. Well, the on-call vascular team's in the O.R., but they asked us to get the usual labs and put in a *stat* infectious diseases consult. Since you're still here, and you just *know* ID's going to want to examine the abdominal incision, I thought I'd let you know what's up."

"I examined and redressed the wound less than an hour ago. It's not the source of the fever."

"I know. I read your progress note. But—"

"I'll be right up, Jen. Two minutes. No one touches that dressing until I arrive."

"You got it, Cole. I'll guard it with my life."

Jen's final comment was embroidered with a little flirtation, the sort in which the imposter Gwen had been known to engage, as safe behind her mask and the fiction of David as Jen was behind her wedding ring.

And did the sexy bachelor smile at Jen as she walked away? No. His solemn gaze focused intently on Gwen. "I have to go."

"Thank you for answering my questions."

"You're welcome, but you owe me, Gwen. Next time," Cole said, "you answer mine."

13

Then why wouldn't I remember you?

After Cole left, Gwen began to imagine her replies. *I have this birthmark, you see. Maybe you didn't notice it.*

And his. *I noticed, Gwen. But you think it would matter to me? What kind of man do you think I am?*

"Gwen?"

"Paige!"

"Hi. Sorry I'm late."

"It's fine. I was just…"

"Daydreaming."

Fantasizing.

Gwen stood and gave Paige a gentle hug.

When they sat, Gwen took stock of the woman who needed a renal transplant today, yesterday, eight months ago. Paige's eyes were dark-circled. A chronic halo. But

Paige looked stronger than she had on Saturday. Rosy, not ashen. Even if she'd taken the stairs, as undoubtedly she had, she was in no jeopardy of an impending faint. "You look better."

"I *am* better. Thank you."

"So?"

"So?" Paige repeated quizzically.

"What happened," Gwen asked her friend, "with Jack?"

"Oh!"

"You don't have to tell me."

"No, I *want* to. It's just that…I'm not used to…" *Having a friend.* "It was good, Gwen. Seeing him was good."

"He remembered you. *Of course!*" Gwen asserted, even as that unanswered question, from Cole, echoed in her brain: *Then why wouldn't I remember you?* "Didn't he?"

"Yes." Her rosy cheeks became rosier. "He did."

"And he was dazzled."

"Well," Paige said, smiling, "I don't know about that."

"But you *are* going to see him again."

"I think so. Yes," Paige said, sparkling now. "I am. But enough about me! Is this just one night off, Gwen, or are you on vacation?"

"Vacation. Much to the delight of a woman named Maria. She's been doing freelance work for the station's afternoon talk show and is overjoyed to have some full-time pay. It's good to know that if I decide I need more than two weeks, I'll be making someone who's nice—and very talented—extremely happy."

"More than two weeks for what?"

"To think. Make decisions." *Search my colorless soul.* "And keep my Friday-afternoon appointment at the Laser Surgery Clinic. It's an initial consultation to see what the physicians there think."

"They'll think what you've assumed—that you'd have a wonderful result. I did a little reading about port-wine stains over the weekend. I'm sure I didn't discover anything you don't already know. The information available online is about as detailed as anything in the medical texts, and a lot more current. I did learn things *I* didn't know, however. Beginning with the reason for the birthmark itself."

Gwen paraphrased one of the definitions she'd found. "Chronic pooling of blood in tiny veins—*venules*—due to a diminished or absent nerve supply to the vessel walls."

"I'd never known that," Paige said. "I also hadn't realized how uncomfortable laser therapy—for port-wine stains specifically—can be."

"The dreaded repetitive snapping of rubber bands on the skin?"

"Yes." The laser beams had to be directed specifically at the pooled blood in each and every dilated venule. Depending on the age of an infant or child, and the extent of the area to be treated, anesthesia was often required. Even in adults, when the birthmark was as extensive as Gwen's, anesthesia was sometimes chosen.

"The discomfort during the treatment doesn't worry me. It's the blistering and scabbing afterward that I'd need to decide how to deal with. I probably couldn't use makeup for seven to ten days following each session, and since I'd likely be zapped—and snapped—every couple of months for at least a year, that's a lot of time off work. True, Maria would be thrilled. But it might just be easier to quit my job at the station altogether."

"Or go to work without makeup."

"Or go to work without makeup," Gwen affirmed.

"Do you really think your co-workers—your *friends*—would care?"

"They would. In a good way. With sympathy and understanding. But they'd also feel betrayed. They trusted me with their secrets, and I never trusted them with mine. That's not really friendship, is it? And, even worse, I lied. I need to think carefully about the best thing to do."

Gwen took a sip of her latte and noticed Paige's mug on the table. Her drink was unsipped but not untouched. Paige's hands were curled around the porcelain. For warmth, perhaps. As thin as she was, Paige Forrester probably always felt cold.

Just as she was always thirsty. And no wonder. Based on what Gwen had read, Paige's daily liquid quota was three cups—plus whatever cc's of urine she happened to have. And, Gwen had learned, for hemodialysis patients fluids were defined as anything that was liquid at room temperature.

Ice cream.

Jell-O.

And, of course, lattes.

Long before Gwen's call to schedule their cafeteria rendezvous, Paige had undoubtedly carefully measured and poured today's fluid allotment. True, she could take a sip or two now and deduct a sip or two later. But the physician who'd failed medical management of her renal failure and wasn't doing well on dialysis was unlikely to upset the precarious balance she'd achieved.

With a transplant, however... *Now that's something a friend should pursue.*

"I did some online research, too. About kidneys on the fritz. I've decided you're on dialysis and that it's not going well."

"You're right, Gwen. On both counts. But the situation's about to get *much* better." Paige's hands tightened around the mug, as if embracing a promise, and her dark blue eyes brightened with hope. "My nephrologist and I have agreed on a whole new approach."

"That's wonderful, Paige! You mean—oh, don't look now, but there are two girls standing by the latte bar who seem to be extremely interested in you."

"In me? I'd better look." Paige did, then smiled and beckoned.

The girls approached.

"Dina. Beth. Hi."

"Hi, Paige!"

"Hi...Paige."

"This is my friend Gwen. Would you like to join us?"

"Sure!" Dina plopped into a chair.

Beth settled more gently.

"We were on our way to your mother's house," Dina explained, "but decided to stop by the hospital and check it out."

"And?"

"It's beautiful," Beth said.

"And huge," Dina embellished. Then, as if cutting to the chase, she focused on Gwen. "Did you go to Stanford?"

"No."

"But do you know Beth's dad?"

"The builder who's renovating Paige's mother's home? No to that also."

"Gwen's a makeup artist," Paige said.

Dina, on the verge of deflating, instantly perked up. "Really?"

"Really. I've been doing TV work for the past seven years, and before that I did makeup for a portrait photographer."

"Have you made up anyone famous?"

"I suppose that depends on your definition. I've certainly done makeup for people who *regard* themselves as famous."

"But do you do it for regular people, too?"

"For friends, and friends of friends. I enjoy that the most."

"What do you think about *my* makeup?"

"Well," Gwen murmured as if just noticing it, as if it wasn't way overdone. "You obviously have a knack. But is there a reason you're wearing it?"

"A reason?"

"Something you're trying to cover up?"

"No. Why?"

"Because I think it's best not to wear makeup until you're quite a bit older."

"That's what my mom says."

"She's probably worried about your looking too grown-up too soon. My reasons are more…mystical."

"Mystical?"

"I'm an advocate of letting your unconcealed skin soak in the ambience of wherever you happen to be. That makes it healthier, I think, more vibrant, with more colors of its own. The greater your treasure trove of colors, the more you can do with makeup later on. The more colors you can wear."

"So you don't think each person has just one right color of makeup she should wear?"

"I've never thought so, no. But that goes against a mountain of conventional wisdom. I bet there'll be all sorts of interesting colors you could wear."

"I could take off this makeup and you could see."

"I'd be happy to, Dina."

"Great!"

With that, Dina was off. Beth waited for Paige's directions to the nearest ladies' room, then followed.

"You certainly have a knack," Paige said as Beth and Dina disappeared. "You really know how to talk to eleven-year-old girls."

"I'm not so sure about that. I'd say Dina did the talking. I do think there's an agenda, though. I think they've come specifically to talk to you."

"I can't imagine why," Paige replied as her beeper sounded. *Especially since they're on their way to my mother's and can talk so effortlessly to her.*

14

"What do you think?"

Gwen looked up at a smiling, pretty, makeup-free Dina. "*Fabulous.* You have so many great colors. About a million years from now and just for fun, you can tinker with eyeshadow and lipstick."

"Just for fun?"

"You bet. Makeup should be an accessory to match your mood. That's why I don't adhere to the notion of one face, one palette. Many moods, I say, and many colors."

"Cool! Thank you. Where's Paige?"

"A family member of one of her patients needed to see her." Paige had left with apologies after saying two things. She'd love to "do" another latte. A more leisurely one. Then, with quiet worry, she'd asked Gwen not to men-

tion her dysfunctional kidneys to her mother—if and
when Gwen dropped by the mansion. "Was there something you wanted to discuss with Paige?" she asked the
girls.

"Yes. But we didn't think we'd run into her today. We
were just planning to figure out where her office is and
make an appointment for Beth to see her."

"Are you okay, Beth?"

"Beth's fine!" Dina replied. "But she'll be even better
if Paige knows her mother from Stanford."

"Why's that?"

"Because *Beth* doesn't know her. Her parents got di-
vorced right after Beth was born."

"Oh," Gwen murmured. "I see. I have no idea, Beth,
whether or not Paige knows your mother. But I'm absolutely certain she'll want to talk to you about it. Why
don't we go to her office and set up an appointment
right now? We can leave her a note, if you like, explaining why."

The appointment, for 3:30 the following afternoon,
was made, after which Gwen composed the note. It was
short; the girls were standing close by. But the salient
facts were communicated, including Beth's—but not
Dina's—uncertainty about seeing Paige at all. Gwen
didn't state the obvious: how tricky, how delicate, such
a conversation with Jack's daughter might be.

Paige would know.

And she would handle it with grace.

After handing the note to Alice, who'd give it to Paige as soon as she returned, Gwen escorted the girls to the main lobby. Beth was far more animated now, the die having been cast, and she reminded Gwen of Paige, of her hopefulness when she'd said that she and her nephrologist had a new plan.

Gwen should come with them, the girls insisted as they neared the place where Beth and Dina would veer right to the mansion and Gwen would go left to Belvedere Court. Mrs. Forrester wouldn't mind. She was— *Oh, my gosh!*—so *amazing!*

Gwen was a little tempted, especially since the girls' portrait of Paige's mother was so different from the image Gwen had gleaned from Paige: a cherished blossom, delicate and beloved, and needing every ounce of the protection her daughter so willingly gave.

But the puzzle of Mrs. Forrester—Gwen didn't know her first name—could be solved another day. Right now, her thoughts were on Mrs. Forrester's daughter.

Gwen wanted to reread one of the many kidney-related articles she'd downloaded over the weekend, one article in particular—a review of the results of transplanting kidneys from living donors who were immunologically compatible but unrelated. Strangers, for example, and spouses.

And friends.

And if the results were as positive as she'd remembered? And it was something she could do.... The decision, Gwen realized, had already been made. A quick decision, but not a hasty one.

And so easy, Gwen thought as she let herself into the apartment building foyer, so easy. So right. All the soul-searching in the world wouldn't change her mind.

Gwen expected to find a cardboard box propped against the wall beneath her mailbox. That was where the oversize packages from the cosmetic companies were set. There *was* a delivery for her, the one for which she'd signed, a large envelope—and thick.

The return address label read:

Sister Mary Catherine
Sacred Heart Villa
Buffalo, New York

Sister Mary Catherine. The mother Gwen had hoped, perhaps most of all, to reassure.

Today was the day she'd find out.

Gwen opened the envelope flap during the elevator ride to her floor. Once inside her apartment, she started to extract the contents.

Then stopped.

And wiped away the camouflage cream.

She wanted to be Angel as she read, the girl who'd roamed the world with her skin unconcealed, soaking up the vibrant colors of Carmel-by-the-Sea.

And, she recalled, she'd signed her letter to Sister Mary Catherine as Angel—which was the way the nun's reply began.

My dearest Angel,
What joy to hear from you! And what a lovely letter you wrote. There's nothing for you to apologize for. We understood why you never answered our letters. (We *believed* we did, I should say. We didn't allow ourselves to imagine the extent of your isolation—which I'm quite sure you've minimized greatly in your letter, to protect me.) We debated traveling to San Francisco and bringing you back to Santa Fe. But you weren't destined to spend your life in a convent. We knew that. And we knew you'd find your way—as, beloved Angel, you have.

I was in Africa when your letter arrived, which explains part of the delay in my reply. The rest is explained by the information within. I decided to wait until I received it before writing to you. The enclosed documents were gathered by a police detective I'd known in Carmel, and trusted absolutely. He's retired these days, but he welcomed the chance to do a little investigating once again. I told him everything I knew about how you came to be with us (yes, dear one, I *did* have additional information that I'd never shared) and he followed the trail from there.

He found your mother…and more. His report is clear, and the documents are self-explanatory. You could skip to them now. *But* I hope you'll first finish reading what I have to say. It's a selfish wish— I want to explain myself!—and, selfishly, it's my fervent wish that you'll be able to forgive me once I do.

So (if you're still reading): What I told you in the convent was true, as far as it went.

You *did* arrive at St. James at 10:00 p.m. on October twenty-ninth.

And the woman who brought you to us *was* a tourist from Iowa.

And she *had* found your mother walking in the storm.

And your mother *did* ask her to give you to us.

But your mother gave the Good Samaritan other information, as well. Your father was violent, she said. He'd hit her and she felt certain he would hurt you, too. She was going to tell him you'd died. It was the only way, she believed, for you to be safe. So, she said, we mustn't notify the police.

We mustn't take you to a hospital, either, for the same reason. The health care professionals would be obliged to let the proper authorities know. You didn't need to go to a hospital, anyway, for you'd already been. You were healthy and had been since your birth thirty-four hours earlier. Yes, your real birth date is the twenty-eighth. It seemed more...kind to tell you you'd just been born.

I never met your mother. Just before she and the tourist rang the convent bell, she gave you to the other woman—and fled. But I believed the story she'd told. I had no reason to doubt it. I did, however, have responsibilities to you. I needed to determine, if possible, that the woman claiming to be your mother really was your mother and as such had the right to give you away. Once satisfied that you were a legitimate foundling, you see, I'd have no qualms about filling out the requisite paperwork for the state.

Fortunately, I'd worked often enough with the Carmel police and medical establishment—primarily in cases of domestic violence—that I was able to make inquiries with the utmost discretion. I wanted to do nothing, of course, to alert your (allegedly) violent father to the fact that you were alive, after all.

For that reason, I waited almost a month before making calls to newborn nurseries of local hospitals. It didn't take long to find the one where you'd been—and fortunately, the memory of the nurse who'd cared for you was precise and clear.

You'd been born on October 28th, at the site of a car crash near Monterey, and were immediately transported to the small community hospital in

Carmel. The thought, I gather, was that your mother would follow. Her condition deteriorated, however, and she was rushed to a hospital in Monterey. Her deterioration was related to obstetric complications, not traumatic ones. She'd witnessed the crash, but had been traveling in a different car.

Your father and paternal grandparents *were* involved in the trauma. Your grandparents died at the scene and your critically injured father was taken to the same Monterey hospital as your mother.

According to the nurse who cared for you in Carmel, your mother came for you the following evening (the 29th). Whether she'd been discharged or was simply out on a pass, the nurse didn't know (the detective's report concludes the latter). The nurse who released *you* to *her* did say she looked quite ill. Despite her precarious health, however, she'd made the trip from Monterey to Carmel expressly to get you—and did, the nurse told me, at about 9:30 p.m. Fifteen minutes later, the Iowa tourist spotted her wandering in the rain and, at your mother's request, drove her—and you—to the convent.

To us.

The nurse told me your mother's name. It meant nothing to me, beyond the fact that it enabled me to call the hospital in Monterey to inquire about your father.

(He was a good man, as you'll discover when you read the enclosed. A *wonderful* man. Your mother's allegations of abuse and violence were entirely false—just a ploy to ensure that no one made inquires to the police about you).

Your father died, I'm afraid, five days after the crash.

It didn't occur to me to inquire about other patients with the *same* last name who were hospitalized at the same time. Nor did I attempt to find your mother. She knew where you were. She'd come for you when she could...if she could.

I've wondered, over the years, about finding you and telling you her name. Obviously, I've always decided *no*. She didn't deserve the joy of knowing you. She'd abandoned you, never returned for you, lied about your father—and who knew what else?

She didn't deserve to know our Angel. Besides, I thought, she wasn't a mother *worth* knowing.

The odd thing is that for the past year or so, I've been rethinking my decision. Indeed, as remarkable as this may seem, during my flight home from Africa I'd resolved to get in touch with my police-detective friend to see what, at this late date, he could find (and if whatever he uncovered was something I believed you needed to know).

Imagine my surprise when I returned to find a

letter from you that proposed, in essence, a similar pursuit!

We'd both begun thinking about your mother. Our reasons, however, weren't the same. Yours was the generous wish to reassure her about the decision she'd made on that rainy night. And mine was the sudden worry, the heart-pounding fear, that she had no idea where you were. She looked terrible, the nurse had said, and her husband was dying, and what if she was so distraught, in such a daze, she had no clear memory of what happened next?

What if she believed she'd left you to die in the storm? Or, having a vague recollection of the tourist, that she'd given you to a total stranger to raise as her own?

Let me reassure you, before *your* heart begins to pound with worry, that my fear was quite unfounded. The detective uncovered nothing to suggest the above scenario (and, as I've subsequently remembered, both the nurse who cared for you and the tourist who gave you to me noted that, as ill as she appeared, she was completely lucid).

The detective also found nothing for which she needs, or deserves, to be reassured. (Quite the opposite.)

But there's something else he discovered.

Something you *must* know, and should have known long ago. (And would've known had I not been so convinced that finding your mother would do you no good.)

But I was wrong, as you'll discover. I do hope, in time, you'll be able find it in your heart to forgive me (but I will understand if you don't).

The first document you'll see, dear Angel, is the birth certificate of your twin....

15

Her twin: Paige Elizabeth Forrester.

Her parents: Claire and Alan Forrester.

And the unwanted daughter's long-held vision about the location of her birth? In the lee of a sand dune or beneath a canopy of pines? Maybe there *had* been sand dunes and cypresses at the site of the crash. Maybe that tiny bit of Gwen's imagined history was true.

And as for the revelation itself, that Gweneth Angelica St. James was Alan Forrester's firstborn daughter—and heiress…

An attorney named Stuart Dawson, described by Sister Mary Catherine's investigator as a "renowned San Francisco litigator and close Forrester family friend," would undoubtedly insist on confirmation by DNA. There was a fortune to consider, after all. Any lawyer worth his salt would require more than documents and hearsay before turning over half of Paige's inheritance to her supposed twin—even if Claire Forrester confessed all.

Gwen St. James, ever the imposter, could be an imposter still: an opportunist who'd discovered the existence of the forsaken Forrester, had a similar birthmark and decided to cash in.

She'd have needed help in making the discovery. A paramedic father. A nurse mother. Or the reverse. Some adult who'd reminisced throughout her childhood about that late October day when Alan Forrester's widow—yes, of *the* Forresters of San Francisco—had discarded a baby girl with a birthmark that was remarkably similar to hers.

The attorney would demand proof—especially given the utter absence of physical resemblance between Gwen and her twin, Gwen and her mother, and Gwen and the two generations of Forresters who'd perished on the day of her birth and five days later.

The photographic documentation was enclosed. The first image, a newspaper clipping dated January twenty-eighth thirty-one years ago, pictured the new Dr. and Mrs. Alan Forrester. Next came three images, parents and son, that had appeared, along with a full-page memorial in the *Chronicle,* in November of that same year. The final photograph, colorful and recent, had been published in the June issue of *Town and Country.* The event, hostessed in her "splendid" Pacific Heights home, the historic Forrester mansion, by "San Francisco benefactress" Claire Forrester, had been the annual "lavish" fundraiser for Pacific Heights Medical Center's neonatal ICU. The intensive care unit for precarious newborns was, the accompanying column noted, Mrs. Forrester's favorite cause.

The society columnist also noted that she sponsored at least two other moneymaking hospital galas every year. Claire's physician daughter was pictured, as was attorney Stuart Dawson, as was Mariel Lancaster, "close friend" and co-hostess of the event.

A note from Sister Mary Catherine's investigator was stapled to the *Town and Country* clipping, an explanation of Claire's passion for the neonatal ICU.

Unlike Gwen, who'd been born healthy and robust, the small and fragile Paige had spent the first six weeks of her life in intensive care; she'd been saved there. It wasn't uncommon, the investigator had discovered, for such discordance in size and health to occur in multiple births. The discrepancies were usual in the case of quin-tuplets, sextuplets, septuplets, but were well-described in twin births, as well.

It had to do with placental blood supply, and the nu-trients each twin received, and...the investigator was a little vague on the physiology, but he'd been assured by the obstetricians he'd consulted that it was eminently possible and made medical sense.

But the disparity in their health as infants was yet an-other reason the handsome, tuxedoed attorney in the

Town and Country photograph would demand an inspection of Gwen St. James's DNA.

But the abandoned twin herself already knew.

Claire was her mother.

Paige was her twin.

Gwen embraced those truths as if she'd known them all her life, and for several too-brief moments, the elation she felt was shimmering and pure.

She had a sister—a sister!—whom she was already planning to help in a most sisterly way...*and who'd been planning, in turn, just how and when to best betray her.*

The *why* of the betrayal was obvious. Paige needed one of Gwen's healthy kidneys to carry on the work of Paige's damaged ones. And the execution of the betrayal that was unfolding even now? Meticulously plotted. Elaborately conceived.

Gwen would expect nothing less from her brilliant twin.

She *was* right, wasn't she? She *was* being betrayed by Paige? It wasn't just that Gwen was sensitized to betrayal, had every reason to be. No, it wasn't. It stretched credulity just a bit too far, to the point of snapping entirely, to accept as fact that she and Paige just *happened* to meet.

It had to be conspiracy, not coincidence, with careful preparation every step of the way—including research to determine which of Gwen's traits would be easiest to exploit.

The truth of Gwen's character must have been a happy discovery, indeed: a woman who was everyone's friend.

A woman who was always willing to listen and to help. A woman who could be manipulated with ease.

Of course Gwen St. James would offer to do Louise's makeup. And of course she'd notice—and worry about—the troubled woman who approached the hospital at the same time as she. And when the dying Louise cradled her blemished cheek, *as if she knew,* Gwen's already swirling emotions would be primed. She would talk.

Confide.

Confess.

Gwen's emotions swirled now. But she managed to rise above her despair just long enough to dismiss Louise as a true conspirator. The great-grandmother's role would've been unwitting, and eager. Once told that Gwen had a secret she really needed to reveal, Louise would happily cup Gwen's face and speak the carefully scripted words—as a result of which Gwen would share her secret. Or so Paige had hoped.

Louise wasn't complicit in the treachery. Was *not.*

Nor was Robyn. Both Johansson women were pawns—ideally situated, from Paige's standpoint. In the right place at the right time.

But if there'd been no Louise and no granddaughter who worked with Gwen, the makeup artist could still have been easily, and logically, approached. The scenario was a simple one to construct. One of the 8-North nurses would call the station, at Paige's request, and explain that Dr. Forrester, a cancer specialist, had a patient who'd been hoping to go home to die—until she saw her ghastly reflection in her hospital-room mirror.

The idea of makeup arose, the nurse would say, and Paige had mentioned that she'd recently attended a hospital benefit and seen a Madolyn Mitchell she almost didn't recognize. Her selfapplied makeup was...different from what San Francisco television viewers were accustomed to seeing. Paige didn't say that Madolyn's technique left much to be desired; Paige Forrester would *never* say such a thing. But the nurse would explain that Paige had come away with a profound appreciation for makeup as art...and for the talented makeup artist at FOX.

Dr. Forrester wanted the best for her patients, the nurse would tell Gwen. That was why the oncologist was wondering if Gwen would consider applying the makeup that would enable the dying patient to go home. Money was no object. Dr. Forrester would happily pay Gwen's fee and arrange for a limo to transport her to and from the medical center, and...Paige would convince that grateful patient to speak the same words Louise had spoken—so that, on cue, Paige could deliver her own practiced line.

May I join you? she'd asked, with—feigned—uncertainty when she returned to Louise's room. And, on cue, Gwen had begun to reveal to Paige what she'd never shared with another living soul. And when she'd paused to inquire if this was something Paige really wanted to hear, Paige had offered an impassioned reply. *I really do.*

So impassioned, in fact, that it felt as if Gwen was doing the gracious—but friendless?—cancer specialist a favor by trusting her.

The sisters bonded. And when it was time for Paige to leave and Gwen saw her "dread," Gwen, being Gwen, accompanied her and witnessed the *almost* faint. Which prompted Paige's fond, proud, introduction of Gwen St. James as her "friend." Not only that, it had prompted her to do some confiding of her own.

Gwen's renal failure research was nice but not necessary. Paige *and her co-conspirator* had already decided to deliver, over lattes, the only medical data Gwen had to know: Paige needed a transplant today, yesterday, eight months ago.

Paige's co-conspirator... Cole.

Gwen's initial assessment—*he cares so much about Paige*—had been correct. Cole was in love with Paige, and Paige was in love with Cole, and even Gwen's diagnosis of her sister's faint wasn't that far off the mark. Paige wasn't pregnant with Cole's baby. Yet. But she *would* be. There was abundant clinical experience, Gwen had learned, with successful pregnancies following renal transplants—especially when the kidney came from an HLA-matched sib. Over time, with such a match, the immunosuppression could be dramatically reduced, or even discontinued altogether.

It was nice, but not necessary, that Gwen had initiated today's latte get-together. Had she not, Paige would have set it up for tomorrow. Today also worked for Paige, though. And for Cole. He'd merely stayed at work a little later than he otherwise might have after his weekend on call—something the man who loved Paige was happy to do.

And as for Cole's recognizing Gwen, *remembering* her... He hadn't, wouldn't have, without helpful hints from Paige. Gwen would be at a window table, as per Paige's voice mail, and Cole could easily identify her by her copper hair.

So Cole made sure that Gwen learned what she needed to know. And the magician's sleight of hand was particularly cruel, letting Gwen believe she was seducing the information from him...as if she could seduce anyone.

So there it was. The grand plot to lure Paige's generous new friend into giving her a kidney. Gwen would offer to be tested, and voilà, there'd be a perfect match.

Voilà...Gwen had forgotten about April, *Avril,* a name uncannily similar to Angel, *n'est ce pas?* Another astonishing bond between the strangers who'd so rapidly become friends—and quite likely a spur-of-the-moment fabrication.

Paige's self-proclaimed attempt to reinvent herself at Stanford was an invention in itself. Obviously. There was no reason for such a makeover. The April coincidence had been an impromptu decision—and opportunity. Yet another chance to make sure Gwen felt such a connection to Paige, such a closeness, that she'd happily donate a kidney to her friend.

Gwen would make the donation. Happily.

Paige would be saved.

And Claire Forrester, the delicate blossom, wouldn't have to face the daughter she'd abandoned—to see *that* face ever again.

And once Paige Forrester got what she needed? What only her sister could provide? She'd withdraw from Gwen, so graciously that Gwen would be unaware their surprising "friendship" was shutting down. Paige had patients to care for, emergencies to which she must respond. *Adieu, Angel. Au revoir.*

It was a workable scheme from start to finish. A triumph of determination and deceit.

Paige Elizabeth Forrester would get her new kidney.

She was lucky, that unblemished twin, that it was her kidneys that had failed. Nature provided friends—and twins—with spares.

Lucky. And scheming. Committed to getting what she wanted, when she wanted it, no matter what treachery was involved.

But what if, oh what *if,* the untarnished daughter had needed not a kidney but a heart?

16

"Gwen." Cole's surprised but gentle greeting came as he opened his apartment door seven hours after he'd seen her last. She was such a different Gwen than the woman in the hospital cafeteria. Her hair, that glorious mane of every color of autumn, was a chaotic tangle, and her bright blue eyes were shadowed. Stark. And her port-wine stain, concealed then, was fully revealed. "What's wrong?"

"Nothing!"

"Okay," he said softly. "Come in."

She didn't, yet. "You seem surprised to see me. Didn't Paige tell you I live here, too?"

"No, I haven't seen Paige or spoken with her since Saturday."

Of course you have! Cole Ransom was a better actor,

even, than that gifted actress, Paige. The duo's carefully crafted script undoubtedly called for Cole to pretend, should the situation arise, that he had no idea Gwen lived at Belvedere Court. His surprise at seeing her was so convincing, though, that if she hadn't known better, she'd have believed it to be real.

But Gwen did know better. Cole was a terrific actor. A great pretender. And Gwen also knew what had given him license to pretend. His love for Paige.

"Well," she said. "I do. My apartment's two floors down."

"That's a very nice coincidence, Gwen. Please come in."

His feet were bare, his attire well-worn denim, his black hair shower-damp. At home...and no longer on the prowl.

"Are you alone?" *Or is Paige—*

"Alone, drinking bourbon." *Thinking about you.* Cole didn't speak the most important truth aloud. He feared it might send her fleeing before she even crossed the threshold. "Join me, Gwen."

The invitation—*join me*—sounded like *be part of me, Gwen. Be part of my life.*

Of course it did. Cole Ransom wanted her kidney for the woman he loved. So, in a way, Gwen would—or at least her kidney would—become part of his life.

And an important one at that.

Remember why you're here, she admonished herself.

Why she was here. Logically, and it had seemed very

logical for a while, she was planning to confront one—
or perhaps both—of the conspirators in the treachery
against her. She'd do so with dignity, of course, just as
she—Angel—should have faced her San Francisco classmates and proclaimed herself *not* a ghoul.

Dignified confrontation had seemed the only option.
For a while. But the more Gwen had envisioned the
scene, the worse she'd felt. She'd known anger. Betrayal.
And how destructive they could be.

Gwen didn't want such corrosive emotions in her life.
Not if she had a choice in the matter.

And, in this matter, she did.

So she wasn't here to confront the betrayal. Or the be-
trayer. Quite the opposite. She was going to proceed as
if there'd never been a letter from Sister Mary Catherine. She was going to donate her kidney—assuming there
was a match—to her new "friend."

Cole and Paige would believe they'd succeeded in
duping her. *So what?* Giving a kidney to her twin sister
was what Gwen wanted to do. And it was the kind of sister, of *person,* she wanted to be.

Do unto others as you would have them do unto you.

With that remembrance, one of many that had swirled
in her brain this evening, Gwen stepped into Cole's
apartment.

The floor-plan was the same as hers, the similar furnishings identically arranged. It wasn't that makeup artist
and escape artist—*con artist*—were of one mind when

it came to selecting furniture and placing it just so. Both had simply chosen to rent furnished apartments. And neither had bothered to make even the slightest change.

Both lived their lives elsewhere. Gwen at the television station, surrounded by nice, nonduplicitous people; and Cole at the hospital, working his magic in the operating room.

After work, however, only Gwen—typically—returned to her Belvedere Court apartment. Cole continued to live his life elsewhere. At Paige's condo, she assumed. Or perhaps, on occasion and with the woman he loved, in a grand suite in the Forrester family home.

Gwen caught sight of the living-room clock. It hung on the same wall as the clock in her apartment.

Same wall, same clock…but wrong time, surely.

"It's not ten-fifteen."

"Yes, it is. Give or take a minute or two."

"I had no idea it was so late."

"It's not that late," Cole reassured her. But…where had she been? he wondered. *Some private hell.* Cole knew such journeys. Intimately. And that they were measured in timeless—endless—anguish. "Would you like something to drink? I have bourbon. Water. Ice."

Gwen didn't usually drink. Though this was far from a usual night.

But she needed her wits about her, and she was already far more scattered than she'd thought. She'd lost time, in the emotional chaos of the evening. Large chunks of it.

She had to be very careful not to lose her resolve. She needed to be particularly circumspect about over-reading the concern in the smoke-gray eyes.

Cole didn't care about her. Not really.

But he cared very much about her kidney.

Make thine enemy thy friend. Or, she amended, *pretend to.*

"I'm fine, Cole. Thank you. I don't need anything to drink."

"Okay." Good. It wasn't his style to ply women with liquor. Didn't need to. Never would. And, if she'd said yes, he'd have prepared a dilute mixture with an abundance of ice. But even a little bourbon might have been too much. "Gwen, please sit." *And talk to me.*

Gwen sat, and surprised him again.

"How's your patient in bed four?"

The fever had been due to phlebitis at an intravenous site, and entirely unrelated to the aortic aneurysm repair he'd done.

"He'll be all right."

"Good. You're probably wondering why I'm here."

"I'm a little curious, Gwen. But mostly," Cole said softly, "I'm glad you are."

Liar! No, Gwen gave herself a stern reminder. Again. This was precisely what Cole was supposed to do. What she'd known he'd do. Pretend to be bewitched *by her.* Seduced *by her.* Because, of course, this kind of attention from the gorgeous surgeon would make someone *like her* do anything to please him. Such as donating a kidney to a friend.

Gwen had believed she was prepared for this. She wasn't. Cole's pretense hurt. Too much.

She made herself recall the convent teaching that had, at least earlier this evening, almost made her smile.

It was certainly apt.

Turn the other cheek.

Cole couldn't guess what thought had lured the faint smile, wild but lovely, to her lips and put the slightest sparkle in her cloudy blue eyes. But he was grateful for it.

"So tell me."

"Okay. Well. I wanted to follow up on what we talked about this afternoon. Paige's need for a transplant and her reluctance to add her name to the registry. She and I didn't have a chance to discuss either of those issues, but I have a feeling it's not necessary. That she's no longer reluctant."

"A feeling?"

"More than a feeling. Paige told me that she and her nephrologist have come up with a new plan."

"Longer dialysis runs."

"What?"

"That's the new plan. Longer runs. Eight hours instead of four."

Was this revelation—probably untrue—considered an essential piece of the grand scheme to seduce her out of a kidney? It seemed an unnecessary contrivance. But not, she supposed, if despite their efforts she remained wary about donating. The longer dialysis runs might make her believe the need for transplantation was quite urgent, and underscore just how poorly Paige was doing on dialysis. Not that longer dialysis runs necessarily meant either of those things, at least not according to Gwen's reading.

But she played along.

"Will the longer runs help?"

"Hopefully."

"But Paige would still be better off with a transplant."

"Much better."

"From what I've read, and assuming an HLA-match, a kidney donated by an unrelated living donor can be almost as good as one donated by a relative."

"Maybe *as* good," Cole replied. "The data's still evolving. Either way, an HLA-matched kidney from a living donor can give excellent long-term results."

"I was thinking about having myself tested as a potential donor for Paige."

Gwen paused. Watched. And saw—what looked like—pride in her, wonder at her generosity, and not even a hint of the satisfaction Cole must have felt at his remarkably effortless triumph. Gwen didn't see any indication, none, of the thoughts that surely danced within. *We did it, Paige. Your damaged twin fell for it hook, line and sinker.* Nor did Gwen sense any restlessness in Cole, wishing she'd leave so he could give his beloved Paige a call. He was a patient fisherman. Gwen was on the line...but not yet in the boat.

Well, she would be soon. Would jump right in. This was

beginning to hurt far too much, and she felt herself want-ing—too much—to believe she was wrong about Paige and Cole. They weren't lovers. Or conspirators. Maybe there *was* no conspiracy, after all—just coincidence.…

"More than thinking about it, actually. I'd like to."

"That's very generous of you, Gwen."

"Paige is my friend."

"Still, it's—"

"What I want to do." *What you want me to do.* So why was he acting as if she should give the decision a little more thought? Because *acting* was what this was all about. "And what I'm going to do."

"Okay." His voice was soft, and that look of pride still glimmered there.

"I wouldn't want Paige to know, though, unless there happens to be a good match."

"Makes sense."

"The problem is, if Paige hasn't even started to ex-plore transplantation as an option, there won't be her HLA results to compare with mine."

"But there are."

Of course there are. "Oh?"

"Paige's nephrologist did the tissue-typing as a matter of routine."

"That's who I should see, then? Her nephrologist. And swear him to secrecy."

"Secrecy comes with the territory, Gwen. The fewer secret-keepers, however, the better. There's nothing

Paige's nephrologist can do that I can't, from ordering the HLA studies to comparing the results."

"You can get a copy of Paige's HLA profile?"

"Sure."

"And you don't mind?"

"Not at all. I have surgery until about one tomorrow. Could we meet in my office at two? If not—"

"Two's fine." Gwen stood. "I'll see you then."

"We're leaving?"

"We?"

"When you're ready to go home, I'll walk you to your apartment."

"That's not necessary."

"I never said it was. It's also not necessary for you to leave."

"I thought you might like to—" *call Paige, give her the news* "—go to bed."

Only if you do. Only when you do. "It's not an emergency," he said. Or was it? "Stay. Talk to me. Answer my questions from this afternoon."

Then why wouldn't I remember you?

Only skin-deep...is there such a thing?

Gwen hadn't forgotten the questions. Nor, Cole's expression told her, had he.

What she *had* forgotten was her blemished cheek. Angel's cheek. Wiped bare before she'd read Sister Mary Catherine's letter...and naked still.

She was fully exposed before him. Again.

And nothing in his intense gray eyes had reminded her. No shadow of disgust, no grimace of pity.

Gwen even wondered, *imagined,* a silvery glitter of desire.

The mirage shimmered even now as she answered the first of his two questions.

"Because of this." Her faintly trembling hand touched her cheek. "Most people would've seen this, remembered this, and nothing more."

"And?"

"There was a time when I believed that things like birthmarks were only skin-deep."

"But not anymore."

"No. Not anymore."

"I'm sorry you've been so hurt."

"I'm okay!"

"I know that, too."

She was hallucinating now. Seeing all sorts of wondrous things that couldn't possibly be there. Desire and tenderness. Caring and longing. She shook her head; she had to get back on track. She asked him a question she was quite certain he didn't expect, a question that would elicit a reply he'd failed to rehearse.

"What did you think when you saw my birthmark?" *It was even worse, wasn't it, than you and Paige had imagined it would be?*

"That it was entirely below your eye. How good that was."

Good for her, Gwen knew. For her future. A port-wine stain involving the eye or forehead raised the specter of Sturge-Weber Syndrome, in which both glaucoma and seizures could occur.

"I'm lucky," she murmured.

"And what else?"

"What do you mean?"

"I'm wondering what happened during the seven hours between the time I saw you in the cafeteria and when you came here tonight."

Don't tell him. You're turning the other cheek, remember? You're not ever going to let them—the lovers, the conspirators— know that you know who you are and what they've done.

"What do you want?" she asked. It was a soft plea of disbelief.

You. Cole wanted her as he'd never wanted any woman before. In every way. All ways. He wanted to talk to her and touch her, to laugh with her and listen to her, to watch her from afar, as one would marvel at a sunset, and to hold her close.

Cole wanted all that. Stunningly. Ferociously.

And Cole Ransom wanted something more.

"I want you to trust me."

Gwen looked away. Down. At the floor.

She saw familiar carpet, and familiar hands.

Surgeon's hands. Lover's hands.

And felt their touch.

Cole lifted her chin. Then, because her face was mostly

veiled, he carefully parted the copper tangles. His fingers caressed her blemished cheek as he did so, and her perfect cheek. Equally. Naturally. As if there wasn't the slightest difference between the two.

"It's okay," he said, when he could see her eyes…and she could see his. "I don't blame you for not trusting me. As a matter of fact, it's probably smart not to."

He was telling her he couldn't be trusted. *Confessing.* To what? Something that filled his voice with darkness and put fury in his eyes.

"But I do trust you, Cole," Gwen heard herself say. Astonishing words, confident ones, that could only have come from her heart. And they were defiant, too. Those words. That heart. And ever more certain as wonder replaced fury in his eyes. "I *do*. It's just that—"

"It's already been a long day's journey into night?"

"Yes. I guess. Is that all right?"

"You don't have to tell me anything, Gwen. Ever."

"I *want* to, though. I just need a little time to think things through."

Things—like whether it was possible that she hadn't been betrayed, after all, by either Paige or Cole.

17

Yes, Gwen told herself an hour after Cole had escorted her from his apartment to hers....There was a way to believe, *and she did,* that she hadn't been betrayed by Paige.

Or Cole.

And the only conspiracy—yes, there was one—belonged to fate.

Paige Elizabeth Forrester and Gweneth Angelica St. James were destined to meet. And, upon reflection, it wasn't really that far-fetched to envision it happening precisely as it had.

One of Gwen's co-workers at FOX would have a relative with cancer. Inevitably. So many people did. And because the family would want the best for their loved one, they'd go to Paige.

And when that loved one, worried that her great-grandchildren might be frightened of the physical ravages even Paige couldn't prevent, makeup artist Gwen would volunteer her expertise.

The twins would meet. If not this year, then the next, or the next.

But it was so lucky it had been this year that Louise needed her.

For it was this year that her sister—her sister!—needed her, too. Just in time, at the right time, destiny had conspired to reunite the Forrester twins.

It was an easy reunion to orchestrate, little more than a two-block walk. Both lived in San Francisco, after all—thanks to the one human conspirator in the scheme.

Gwen herself. She was a major conspirator, in fact, and had been conspiring for quite some time. Since age thirteen. She'd known then, some part of her had known, that she mustn't leave California with the nuns. And she'd known, at fifteen, to conceal her birthmark from the world. She'd become friend and confidant to everyone she met that way—including the woman whose grandmother with cancer would lead her right to Paige.

But even if thirteen-year-old Angel had ignored the finger of destiny that pointed her to northern California and the City by the Bay—even if she'd become Sister Angelica instead of makeup artist Gwen—destiny would not have been foiled. From the very beginning, a fail-safe was in place. Sister Mary Catherine. The nun who'd loved the blemished infant, and who alone knew the whole truth of that rain-drenched night, was always destined to be jolted by one heart-stopping worry—that the mother who'd abandoned her baby girl had forgotten where she'd left her.

Sister Mary Catherine would've found Gweneth, or Angel, wherever she was. Santa Fe, Rome or Timbuktu. And the forsaken twin would have gone to San Francisco, moved there, to meet her sister.

Gwen would've been the schemer then, contriving a pretext through which she and Paige would meet. As doctor/patient, perhaps. Physician/nun. Or precisely as they had, as makeup artist and oncologist. Gwen, the camouflage expert, would offer her services. Life might be a little easier for Paige's patients, mightn't it, if cutaneous tumors could be concealed? Kaposi's sarcoma came to mind.

The sisters would meet, as they'd met on Saturday, and the result would be the same. Joy. Homecoming. And Gwen's fast but confident decision to offer Paige one of her kidneys.

Because of Sister Mary Catherine, Gwen would know the true relationship. And would she tell her sister? Her sister!

Yes! Yes! Yes!

No, she was informed by an astonishing sense of calm. Paige must never know. Because of Claire.

Sister Mary Catherine's investigator had found nothing to suggest amnesia in Claire Forrester. The new mother had simply chosen to keep the perfect twin and discard the damaged one.

And, for thirty-one years, Claire had hidden the truth from the daughter she loved—and who so obviously loved her.

What would happen if Claire's three-decade deceit was revealed to Paige?

The cherished daughter would know the pain of betrayal, just as the unwanted daughter had.

It *wasn't* going to happen. Gwen would never hurt her sister that way.

She'd be Paige's friend. And kidney donor.

Nothing more...and, for Gwen, more than enough.

And if her conspiracy-of-destiny scenario was dead wrong? If she was being played for a fool, befriended for her kidney?

Then so be it.

But unless and until she was otherwise compelled, Gwen would believe in Paige, trust in Paige.

And unless and until otherwise compelled, Gwen would believe in, trust in, the man who'd told her, so persuasively, that he'd been hopelessly seduced.

It was raining in her dream, and dark and cold. And she was desperate...until she saw his shadow. The rain became warm then, just as she did, heated with joy.

She'd find what she was searching for, he promised. They'd find it together.

In a while.

For now, for a while, the search could wait.

But he could not.

She'd been a virgin when they'd wed. Shy. Wary. Fearful, perhaps, that once he discovered everything there was to discover, he might no longer want her.

And so, in the first and only year of their marriage, their lovemaking was traditional. And wonderful. And destined to become more wonderful—and more intimate—over the years of love that lay ahead.

But Alan had died, and so had those years. Now he'd returned to her, and now he wanted her so much.

She ran to him in the shadows, floated into his arms. She was so bold as they loved. And now she was laughing. Laughing! And so was he. That was new, too. But after all these years, they knew each other so well, felt so comfortable with each other, that the intimacy was easy.

When the laughter stopped, he whispered, his voice hoarse with desire, *I love you, Claire. I love you.*

And I love you, Stuart. I love—

Claire awakened with a start. Aching. Wanting.

And vividly remembering her dream.

She'd had erotic dreams before. Many. Of course. Over the years. But her lover had been Alan, *Alan,* not his—and her—dearest friend. Hadn't he?

Claire didn't know. She'd never awakened with such clear memories of a dream. And now that she had? She ached.

She wanted.

Her bedside clock glowed. 4:22. Stuart would be asleep. And alone? Claire didn't know that, either. Didn't want to know. She'd finally said as much to the friends— and friends of friends—who'd dated him, fallen in love with him, and who, when their feelings weren't returned in kind, had come to *his dear friend Claire* for comfort and advice.

Claire had no idea who Stuart was dating. *If* he was dating. But she could call him. Share the joke. *It's me, Stuart. Claire. You'll never guess what I just dreamed.*

And when she told him, he'd laugh. They'd laugh together, as they often did, because they knew each other so well after all these years.

Would Stuart laugh about her dream?

Could she?

No. Nor could Claire permit herself to yield to the harmless wish to curl back into bed, into dreams, *that* dream—or to the fearsome wish to call him with a very different message.

It's me, Stuart. She wouldn't need to say her name. *Could you come over? Now?*

Claire got up, stood up, and swayed as the pain seized her. It was in her stomach, as it had been for months, and it was gnawing. *Something* was gnawing. Perhaps the same demon that tormented her with memories that wouldn't quite come clear had now added to its mischief the remembrance of erotic dreams.

Tonight the demon gnawed, chewed away. But at other times it burned. Or sometimes churned.

The worst, though, the greatest pain, was when it made her queasy. She was reminded of her pregnancy then, that soaring happiness, that boundless joy.

And their wonder, hers and Alan's, their hopes and their dreams for their baby girl.

Claire Forrester made no predawn phone calls. But five blocks away, her abandoned daughter did. It was morning in Buffalo, and Sister Mary Catherine had always been an early riser.

She'd become quite a modern nun, she'd noted in her long P.S. to the letter she'd sent. She could be reached, around the clock, by e-mail, voice messaging or fax.

The early-rising Sister was already out and about by seven, Eastern time, when Gwen called.

Gwen left a message of thanks, reassurance, and the repeated insistence that there was nothing to forgive. Sister Mary Catherine couldn't possibly have imagined Gwen had a twin. And it might not have been the right time, before now, for Gwen to learn about her sister. It might even have been the wrong time.

But now was the *perfect* time, Gwen said, more than once, in the message she left. Absolutely perfect, as she'd explain in greater detail when she and Sister Mary Catherine talked...which she couldn't wait to do.

After the call to Buffalo, and for the next few hours,

the makeup artist doodled. Then sketched. The eventual result was her rendition of an HLA pedigree, but not just any pedigree—the four possible patterns of inheritance from Claire and Alan Forrester to their girls.

Gwen knew from her reading that each parent had two Human Leucocyte Antigen—HLA—haplotypes. One of which, one from each parent, was given to a child.

So:

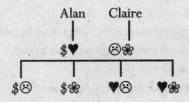

The choice of a dollar sign for the first of Alan's two haplotypes was obvious. He was the Forrester scion. And as for the second haplotype symbol, the heart? Gwen decided to believe that her father would have loved her, wanted her, kept her.

There was a frowning face for the mother who'd gazed in revulsion at her firstborn daughter during those first all-important fifteen seconds. But for Claire's second haplotype, Gwen chose a flower. She was, at least in Paige's view, a cherished blossom.

There was a one in four chance, a twenty-five percent hope, that Paige and Gwen would be a perfect match. Say a flower and a heart.

Then there were the less-than-perfect possibilities, the

fifty-perfect chance of sharing only one haplotype—and the twenty-five percent chance of sharing neither.

Neither. It was possible, Gwen had discovered, for DNA-confirmed sisters, as she and Paige surely were, to be entirely incompatible when it came to HLA. In fact, the chance that Paige would be ♥♣ and Gwen would be $☹ was the same as the chance of their being a perfect match.

Twenty-five percent.

One in four.

That wasn't going to happen, Gwen told herself as she traced and retraced the flowers and the hearts.

The match would be perfect.

Destiny wouldn't have it any other way.

18

Division of Vascular Surgery
Pacific Heights Medical Center
Tuesday, November 5

"Gweneth Angelica St. James." Cole read the hospital
card Gwen had given him, the one she'd gotten in Clinic
Registration the afternoon before. "Beautiful name."

A beautiful name, Gwen thought, that wasn't really
hers. Not today. Not anymore. Her birth date, the October twenty-ninth embossed on the card, was also wrong.

Merely off by a day, however.

Unlike her name, which was off by a lifetime.

She was Baby Girl Forrester.

Blemished Girl Forrester.

The other twin.

"Gwen?"

"Yes? Oh. Long story." She looked at him, believed in him. Trusted him. "Which, sometime, I'd like to share."

"Is tomorrow too soon? We could spend the day together."

"You're not working?"

"No. Not tomorrow. Or Thursday."

"Because you worked all weekend."

"Because, Gwen, I was hoping to spend some time with you. Tomorrow?"

"Yes. Tomorrow."

"Good. I'll call you tonight."

"Okay." Gwen knew he only had fifteen minutes now. He'd told her as much, with apologies, when she arrived. But Cole was a man who could simultaneously assemble blood-drawing equipment, fill out lab slips and, as he'd just done, sense her quiet sadness—and talk. So she said, "I wonder why Paige has resisted being considered for transplant."

"I don't know."

"But why do you think?"

"Probably for the same reason she's refused to cut back at work. Her partners have urged her to take less call and manage fewer patients. But she won't."

"She wants to be a worthy standard-bearer for renal dialysis patients everywhere."

"I think so. I've also wondered if she feels she needs to do dialysis well, to perfect it, before moving on to transplantation."

Gwen nodded. She'd wondered about that, too. Then there was that other possibility, that Paige had been compelled to wait, not knowing why, just as, without knowing why—until now—Gwen had made decisions that led her to Paige.

"Do you know your blood type?" Cole asked.

"O. Universal donor."

"Good. And your health?"

"Also good, as far as I'm aware."

"I could draw blood for the donor-screening panel, if you like. With your permission."

"My permission?"

"The panel includes tests for HIV, hepatitis, syphilis, any one of which could be transmitted with the transplant. But running those tests without express permission to do so is occasionally viewed by patients, not to mention their attorneys, as an unacceptable invasion of privacy."

"Their attorneys?"

"The legal argument is that it's assault and battery to take any blood sample, no matter how routine, without the patient's consent."

"Assault and battery? Isn't that a little extreme?"

"Assault, in the eyes of the law, is the threat to do bodily injury. As I recall, the tourniquet qualifies as an instrument of assault, as does the swabbing of alcohol at the venipuncture site. Battery is the attack itself, the piercing of skin and invasion of the bloodstream."

"You have my permission to draw whatever you like. Whatever Paige needs."

"Okay." Cole added several more tubes to the colorful array he'd already assembled, then reached for the tourniquet.

And there was no assault. No battery. No unwanted touch.

Just gentle expertise.

Gwen watched as her blood flowed into the syringe and was cradled in his palm. "How soon will you get the results?"

"Seven to ten days." Cole didn't look up. "You really think you're going to be a match."

"What? Oh. I hope I am. I *want* to be."

Cole's gaze remained on her arm, the needle, the syringe. But his voice, his words, were far more than skindeep. They reached all the way to her heart.

"I know," he said. *I know*.

Every Tuesday after school, Beth and Dina went their separate ways. Beth had piano lessons. Dina took dance. The third friend, Larry, swam on Tuesdays. Swam every day, in fact.

The girls reunited for dinner. Every Tuesday. One week at Dina's, the next at Beth's. The visiting girl spent the night. They went to bed early on those Tuesdays. Beth had orchestra in the morning, before-school rehearsals beginning at 6:30. Dina respected her friend's need for rest.

Today was a "Dina's house" Tuesday. Beth wouldn't be

coming from her piano lesson, however, but from her appointment with Paige. She'd canceled her lesson, of course. Yesterday, after the appointment was made.

Neither Dina nor Larry had canceled their after-school plans. Both offered to, though, with increasing insistence throughout the day.

But Beth was firm. She could go by herself. She was *okay* by herself.

She felt...comfortable with Paige.

And girl and doctor did all right.

They did just fine.

And because of who they were, both serious, both gracious, they'd each thought about the small talk that might precede the reason for their meeting. And, not surprisingly, both had arrived at the same topic: Beth's Monday afternoon at Claire's.

"Did you have a nice time?" Paige asked.

"Really nice." Beth held out the necklace she was wearing, had worn on purpose for Paige to see. "Your mother gave me these. They're love beads. You know, from Haight-Ashbury? I like them a lot."

Paige touched the symbol of that fabled time in San Francisco. She knew only a little about the era of Hells Angels and flower children, of making love not war. She knew even less about the street artist's life before Alan. The love beads before love, before loss. Before Paige.

Before Claire Forrester became such a wonderful mother to so many other daughters.

"I'm glad you like them, Beth. I'm sure she's glad, too."

That was it. The end of small talk.

Beth was wondering about her mother.

"Dina and I thought she might be the girl my dad was dating," she began. "The one you knew."

"No, Beth. I'm sorry. That girl was someone else. Not your mother." *Just me.*

"Oh." Beth's bright green eyes, Jack's eyes, clouded with disappointment. "So you don't know her?"

"Maybe I do. She might have been in my freshman dorm, or one of my classes." Assuming she'd even attended Stanford. Jack had met her at a wedding, he'd said, and hadn't seen her since. Based on that, Paige had concluded she'd gone to school somewhere else. Stanford was large enough, of course, that the wedding-night lovers need not have encountered each other again. And, for someone like Paige, who'd studied, devoured her pills, then studied some more, Stanford had been so small that even if Beth's mother had been a classmate, Paige wouldn't have known her. Still, long shot though it was... "Can you tell me her name?"

Beth shook her head. "I don't know it. It should be on my birth certificate, Dina says, but I don't know where that is."

And Beth hadn't searched for it, Paige realized. Beth wouldn't rifle through her father's things, even with encouragement—and persistence—from Dina.

"What does your dad say about your mother?"

"That she left when I was a baby because it didn't work out for the three of us to be a family."

"When did he tell you that?"

"We talked about it one time. When I was little."

"I'll bet he also said he was the lucky one, because he got to be with you."

"That's *exactly* what he said."

"Your dad loves you very much, Beth. More than anything in the world. And," Paige added gently, "you love your dad so much you don't want to hurt his feelings by asking about your mother. You don't want him to think you've been missing her all this time."

"I *haven't* been!"

"I know. And your dad knows." *I'm the one who's been missing my mother...all this time.* "But you're getting older now. It makes sense that you'd begin to wonder about her."

"It does?"

"Absolutely. Perfect sense. So much so that I'll bet your dad won't be the least bit surprised when you ask him about her."

"I'm not even sure what questions to ask."

"That doesn't matter, Beth. You could say you've been wondering about her and go from there." That wasn't Beth's approach any more than it was Paige's at Beth's age—or now. Beyond the carefully thought-out questions was the attempt to consider possible answers before the questions were even asked. But the universe of potential answers about a never-known mother was simply too vast. "You know what? I really wish, when I was your age, I'd told my mother there were things I was wondering about—and asked her if we could find the answers together."

"But your mom's so *easy* to talk to!"

"She is, isn't she?" *My mom. My mom?* "Just like your dad."

"Are there still some things you're wondering about? Because you could talk to her now!"

Paige knew the unasked questions. She'd never forgotten them. *Why can't we be close? What's missing between us?* And the answer, a question, too: *It's because of me, isn't it? Me.* "I could talk to her, couldn't I? Maybe I should, Beth." *Maybe I will.*

"And maybe I should talk to my dad."

"More than maybe. He'll want you to, and I *know* he'll understand. Don't you?"

Beth nodded and her green eyes glowed. "I know. And I will. But...I have to think about it a little longer. About the *kinds* of questions I want to ask."

19

Jack Logan's cell-phone number, retrieved four months earlier from his ad in the Yellow Pages, was right where Paige had put it—in the top left-hand drawer of her desk.

After about a two-second debate, she dialed.

And about eight seconds later, he answered.

"Logan."

"It's Paige, Jack." The reception was good. His voice was clear, as were the construction noises in the background. "Is this a bad time to call?"

"Not at all. How are you?"

"Good. Thanks."

When Jack spoke again, the background noises had disappeared. "But something's wrong."

"No. In fact, something's good. I think." Jack would

be relieved, she'd decided, to learn it wasn't fascination with ecstasy that was troubling Beth. Or that despite her slenderness, she'd become obsessed with her weight. Or that she was suffering from the kind of teenage angst that could so tragically lead to death. Very relieved, regardless of his own emotions concerning his ex-wife. "I'll have a better idea how good after I discuss it with you."

"That sounds interesting. When does our discussion get to take place?"

There was ample time to forewarn him. Beth would be mulling things over, she imagined, for a few more days. But the sooner Jack knew, the sooner his relief—and the sooner he could help Beth begin to talk.

"Tonight? After Beth's in bed?"

"It doesn't need to be that late, depending on your schedule. Beth's spending the night at Dina's."

"Oh. Well, then I can call you anytime after seven-thirty. Whenever's best for you."

"And I can pick you up anytime. Whenever's best for you. We'll go to the restaurant of your choice."

"I can't, Jack."

"You can talk—anytime—by phone, but not at all face-to-face?"

"Tonight's a dialysis night for me."

"You're on—"

"Yes."

"No one's listening, Paige. It's just us. Is it uncomfortable?"

"Dialysis? No. It's a little confining, but worth every second."

"How long is each dialysis?"

"I've been doing four hours three times a week. Beginning tonight, though, we're going to try increasing each run to eight hours. That's why I can call you anytime."

"You're not planning to sleep?"

"I'm planning to try—maybe. I'm not sure I'll be able to."

"Because you're in an open area with other people?"

"No. The HDU—Hemodialysis Unit—is in the main hospital, on 5-West, a typical ward with private rooms. Sleep is possible. But, as marvelous as dialysis is, there's something a little unsettling about having so much of your blood volume being laundered through a machine."

"What can go wrong?"

"Nothing! At least not for more than a second or two. We're carefully monitored, lots of alarms, and the backup generators have backups of their own. But you know me, Jack. I'm compulsive. And a worrier. So I watch."

You know me, Jack. Yes, he did. Vulnerable Paige. Who didn't begin to know herself. "Something just occurred to me, Paige."

"What?"

"That if all the rooms are private, visitors must be allowed."

***

I know, Cole had said, a quiet assertion, and an honest one.

And hours later it still felt devastating to Gwen.

Last night, Gwen had asked him what he wanted. And Cole's answer, that she trust him, was undoubtedly true. The more Gwen trusted Cole, believed in Cole, the more likely he'd be able get what *he* wanted most: a new kidney for Paige.

Gwen had been right all along. Cole cared, so much, about Paige.

But Cole and Paige *weren't* lovers, any more than they were conspirators in a treacherous plot. Neither knew that Gwen was Paige's twin, and Paige had no idea about Cole's passion for her.

The torch Cole secretly carried for Paige was glowing. Burning with the surgeon's determination to save her life.

Cole's decision to involve Gwen in that goal was an impromptu one. When they'd met—by chance—on Saturday, he'd seen that Gwen felt as protective of Paige as he did, and might be an ally in his campaign to convince Paige to get a transplant.

That's something to be pursued by a friend.

In fairness, that was undoubtedly all Cole had ever imagined Gwen would do. Talk. Pursue. Convince.

And when Paige's friend proposed donating the kidney herself, Cole had been grateful. And interested, and caring. Gwen was, after all, the woman who just might save Paige's life.

Cole hadn't betrayed her.

Gwen had betrayed herself.

With impossible fantasies of him.

Jack arrived at the Hemodialysis Unit at seven forty-five, the time specified by Paige. She should be settled in her private room by then, hooked up to the machine.

And she was.

Dressed in an oversize white shirt, loose-fitting jeans and heavy woolen socks, she sat on the bed, atop the covers, propped up by pillows.

The two large-bore needles in her dialysis fistula were concealed, as was the fistula itself, cocooned in snowy gauze. Should a disconnect occur in either the arterial line carrying blood to be filtered of its poisons, or the venous line returning the detoxified blood to her, the gauze would become wet and red.

And alarms would sound.

For now, there was only the soft whirring of the dialysis machine—the mechanics of which interested the engineering major from Stanford. Impressed him.

"Remarkable," he said.

"Yes," Paige agreed. "It really is. How it works, what it does, and how available it is to whoever needs it. That wasn't always the case. As recently as thirty years ago, committees reviewed applications from dialysis-hopefuls and decided who to accept—and who to reject."

"Who lived and who died?"

"Yes. I don't know how they did it. How they were *able* to."

"Were these physician committees?"

"No, although I imagine some physicians were involved. As I understand it, though, most committee members were just citizens from the community. The equivalent, I suppose, of a jury of one's peers. They reached the impossible verdict, the death—or life—sentence was imposed, and there wasn't any appeal. Very difficult all around."

"I'll say," Jack said, scanning the machine once again, and the plastic tubing filled with her blood, his expression darkening as he did.

"It *is* rather an out-of-body experience, isn't it? You could go home, Jack, and I could call you."

"I'm not leaving, Paige. There isn't any part of me that wants to. I was thinking about your not wanting your mother to know. Agoraphobia or not, it would be hard for her, for any parent, to be here. Watching. She'd want to do something. Trade places with you if nothing else. But she could do more than that, couldn't she?"

"Yes. She could."

"And she would, in a heartbeat. She'd give you both of her kidneys if you needed them. You know she would. And isn't she likely to be a pretty good match?"

"Yes."

"So?"

"So...I used to wonder, *obsess,* about whether she and I were really mother and daughter."

"Do you doubt it?"

"Not anymore. I'm definitely Alan Forrester's daughter—and therefore also hers."

"So?"

"I can't shake the feeling that I'd reject her kidney, no matter how good the match. It's irrational, I know. But we're so different, in every way."

"What if you did reject her kidney?"

"It would feel like rejecting *her.* Which I don't want to do."

"I'm very sure she wouldn't consider that a reason not to donate. Especially since it's far more likely that your immune system wouldn't reject her kidney at all. Isn't that right?"

"Medically, yes. Statistically. But not if you factor in my apprehension. If a patient truly fears a surgical procedure, to the point of being certain it will fail, most physicians are very reluctant to proceed, no matter how irrational that worry might seem."

"Self-fulfilling prophecy?"

"It happens." Paige drew a breath. "But, Jack, I *am* thinking about talking to her about this." *And maybe, while we're at it, she and I can talk about the mother-daughter relationship that's never quite worked.* In the meantime, there was that other mother-daughter relationship to explore. "Beth came to see me today."

"She did? Why?"

"She's curious about her mother and wondered if she was the girl I said I knew. The one you'd been dating at Stanford."

Oh, my Bethie. She'd been worrying all these months, and he hadn't pushed her to tell him what was wrong. But he should have. Should have.

"Helen didn't even go to Stanford," Jack said. "She was a senior at Ohio State. What did you tell Beth?"

"That she wasn't the girl you were dating, but maybe I knew her anyway, if Beth could tell me her name."

"Could she?"

"No." Paige didn't mention the birth certificate.

After a moment, and to the whir of the machine that filtered toxins from blood, Jack Logan, too, opened his veins....

20

"I told you how we met, at a wedding that summer. I was an usher. She was a bridesmaid. And during the ceremony, she also played the harp."

"The harp. That's so…"

"Heavenly? That's the right word for the way Helen played—and the way she looked as she played."

"Optical illusion?"

"It didn't seem to be. She had an ethereal quality. Even her name. Helen Grace. When we met, she'd just sent an audition tape to the Carillon Conservatory in Great Falls, Montana. It's a small school, privately endowed, world-renowned for the success of its graduates. Helen wasn't optimistic about her chances. She was self-taught on several instruments and had been playing the harp less than three years."

"But she was a gifted musician."

Jack nodded. "Like Beth. In the morning following our night together, I drove Helen to the airport, wished her luck getting into Carillon, predicted she would, and until she called that Monday in November, I never expected to hear from her again."

"Did she want to get married? Was that why she called?"

"I'm not sure why she called or what she expected me to say. She'd just found out that morning and, I guess, needed to tell someone. Me. I don't think she'd given any thought to the future yet. She was stunned, but willing, when I suggested marriage. And very much relieved."

"Because it meant she could pursue her musical career?"

"It did mean that, but I think her relief was something else. Maybe she knew she couldn't be a mother to Beth, and was grateful I'd be there. She'd gotten into Carillon. They were eager to have her, and wanted her to begin in early January. I encouraged her. There was no reason we couldn't live in Great Falls. I moved there—briefly— when she did. My plan was to find a home for us, a job for me, and, during the months before the baby came, learn a bit more about the woman I'd married than the scant—and worrisome—facts I knew."

"Worrisome?"

"She came from a large family. She was the oldest of five children. None of whom—or her parents—attended our wedding. Or called. Or wrote. Ever."

"Did she tell you why she and her family were estranged?"

"No. She merely confirmed the obvious—that they were. I didn't learn much about Helen during those months before Beth was born. She had a room at the conservatory, where she preferred to stay. The rehearsal rooms were always open and she liked playing in the middle of the night. So I returned to San Francisco, lived with my folks and worked with various contractors I knew. I made enough money before Beth was born to be able to stay home with her for the first year. I flew back to Great Falls two days before Helen's due date."

"You and Helen must have spoken over the phone during that time."

"Some. Not much. When I'd call to ask how she was, I'd hear about her passion for her music, and how thrilled she was to be at Carillon, and even how grateful she was that I'd encouraged her to go. Unless I specifically asked about her pregnancy, she didn't mention it—and even when I asked, she always seemed a bit startled, as if she'd forgotten it...or built a fire wall between her baby and the rest of her life. I'm quite sure she never talked to Beth during her pregnancy."

"But Beth heard music. Helen's harp."

"And, I imagine, the instruments other conservatory students played. Helen delivered two days after her due date. It was a long, difficult labor. The doctors wanted her to remain hospitalized for several days, but she insisted on leaving after only one. I drove her to the conservatory. She wanted to play her harp. Then I returned to the hospital to be with Beth. Two days later, I took my baby girl home."

"And Helen?"

"She lived at the conservatory, just as before. Helen was where she wanted to be, and so was I. I felt sorry for Helen, missing the daily miracles, but on the rare occasions she was home, she was so uncomfortable with Beth it was a relief when she left."

"Do you know why Helen was uncomfortable?"

"No. She acknowledged it, but refused to talk about it—beyond saying that she'd never been good with babies."

"But *you* weren't uncomfortable with Beth."

"Not for a second. I worried about SIDS, because of Jason. SIDS," the vigilant father repeated softly, "and everything else. But caring for Bethie was easy. Joyful. Even though it wasn't always so easy or joyful for her. She slept fitfully in the beginning, short spurts, and she'd wake up crying. I didn't mind. For me. And I could usually calm her by holding her. Singing to her. It was her response to the singing that made me figure out why she cried."

"She missed the music."

"Yes. She'd become accustomed to, maybe even addicted to, the sound of Helen's harp. And she was suffering a withdrawal of sorts from her nightly dose of music. I asked Helen to make us a tape, and from then on, Beth slept peacefully throughout the night. Helen moved home, temporarily, toward the end of summer. She had no choice. The dormitory where she lived was being painted. Beth's fussiness had ended weeks before. I told Helen as much, and Beth showed her. When I put Beth in Helen's arms, she smiled at Helen, and patted and cooed. But it didn't matter. Helen immediately became anxious and it wasn't long before she insisted on handing Beth back to me. And over the next few days, she never touched Beth at all. Midway through Helen's two-week eviction from her dormitory, Beth became a little sniffly. Her first real cold. We didn't have a humidifier, and I thought we should. Normally I would've taken Beth with me. But Helen was there, and I left only after Beth and I had spent some time in a steamy bathroom and she'd gone to sleep. I promised Helen I'd be back in less than an hour. I thought I'd pick up some groceries while I was out. In the end, I decided against the groceries and was home in under thirty minutes. Helen had seemed so anxious about my leaving. She'd even offered to go instead. I thought it would be good for her to be alone with Beth. Of course I didn't expect Beth to awaken."

"But she did."

"Yes." Jack's voice was quiet. Dangerous. "She did. I heard screaming even before I opened the door. Helen's screaming. At Beth. Who was crying in a way I'd never heard before. I ran to Beth's room, afraid of what I'd find—Helen hovered over the crib, screaming. Hitting."

"But she wasn't?"

"No. She was cowering in the farthest corner of the room, her back pressed against the wall. Her eyes were wild. And her screams were actually frantic pleas to Beth, imploring her to be quiet. I told Helen to get out of the room and stayed with Beth until she was calm again, sleeping. Then I went to find Helen. She looked, *was,* terrified. Of me. I kept my distance and our conversation was brief. I didn't ask why she'd done what she'd done. I didn't care. No answer would have swayed me. I didn't want her anywhere near my daughter ever again. It wasn't a particularly understanding approach on my part."

"But completely understandable."

"And fine with Helen."

"She gave you sole custody of Beth."

"Happily."

"Have you heard from her?"

"No. Not from her, or *of* her. I've made a point of not looking for Helen Grace CDs, or special concerts on PBS. I'm not certain either one is something she'd do—let's face it, I don't know her—but I'm not interested in finding out. Haven't been." Jack drew a breath. Sighed. "But now...I suppose I should've known Beth would eventually be curious. We talked about it once, when she was six. I'd read the books and even discussed the situation with a child psychologist. I planned to tell Beth that

Helen was a good person and a gifted musician. And, should the question arise, that the reason the marriage didn't work had nothing to do with her. Beth. But the question didn't arise. Beth, at age six, didn't really care."

"But she remembers what you told her, Jack. That it didn't work for the three of you to be a family and that you're the lucky one to have gotten to spend your life with her."

"She remembers that?"

"Vividly. And she also made it very clear that she hasn't been missing Helen all this time. Doesn't, for that matter, miss her now. She's just curious. She's going to talk to you as soon as she figures out what questions to ask."

"I'd better start thinking about the answers. They're a lot trickier now than they would've been when she was six. Thank you for telling me, Paige. It's good news." Jack smiled. "It *is*."

"She loves you, Jack."

"I know she does. How are you feeling?"

"I look tired, don't I? Dare I say *drained?*" Paige cast a wry glance at her extra-corporeal blood. "That's typical of my dialysis runs. I lose energy, and then I regain it—once the run is complete and I've had a little sleep."

"I bet you could sleep now. I could watch the machine."

"While I sleep?"

"Why not?"

"I don't know if I could sleep if you were here."

"We could see. Or, if you promise to *try* to sleep, I

could leave you in the care of the many monitors and alarms."

"That's probably what you should do."

"I will then. But one of these days, Doctor, I'm going to feed you. And kiss you." *And watch you sleep.*

Paige's sleepy blue eyes widened. "Kiss me?"

"Didn't I mention that was something else I was hoping to do twelve years ago?"

"No. You didn't."

"Well, it was. Is."

"Oh."

Arguably, at that moment, Paige Forrester was as captive an audience—and recipient of kisses—as she could possibly be. But the woman tethered to the dialysis machine had never felt freer.

And as for the words to which she'd tethered herself, words like *brittle* and *driven* and *rigid* and *tense,* they, too, were breaking free.

"Oh?" Jack echoed.

Then, as he kissed her and Paige kissed him back, both whispered, on a smile of wonder, *"Oh."*

21

Gwen was online, at MapQuest.com, when her phone rang at 9:48 p.m.

She knew who it would be. He'd said he'd call. She wished he had done so hours ago, three to be exact, just moments after she'd bade Sister Mary Catherine a glorious good-night. Gwen had felt so calm then, wrapped in a cocoon of love that spanned decades and continents.

So she'd had a little skirmish with a fantasy of her own making. So what? Romantic fantasies were de rigueur in the world of men and women where Gwen St. James, imposter, had never truly dwelled. *You can't make some-one care about you, no matter how much you want him to.* How many times, based on no personal experience whatsoever, had she said that to one of her friends?

Gwen had been saying it to herself as the evening wore on. *You can't. He doesn't. Not his fault. Get over it.*

She answered her phone with a breezy hello.

Cole's echoing hello was more subdued, but smiling. "Your routine labs are all entirely normal."

"So I'm good to go, donor-wise, assuming Paige can be convinced and the cross-match is negative."

"I wondered if you knew about the cross-match." It was a potential last-minute glitch, a test run shortly before the transplantation itself. A recipient, especially one with a history of blood transfusions, previous transplants or pregnancy, could have developed antibodies against antigens in the donor kidney. In which case, the transplant from that donor might be postponed, or even canceled. "I should've known you would."

"Has Paige had many transfusions?"

"No. She's been receiving erythropoietin instead."

"Good."

"Have you thought about what you'd like to do tomorrow?"

Oh yes. Fantasy upon fantasy. "Nothing."

"Meaning?"

"You don't need to do this, Cole."

"Do what?"

"Be nice to me." *Pretend to care...so much.*

"What are you talking about?"

"You had yourself tested, didn't you? That's the reason you have Paige's HLA results. You wanted to give her one of your kidneys."

"Just like you. Is that so terrible?"

"No. Of course not. That's what people who love each other do."

"I'm not in love with Paige. And unless you know otherwise, which I seriously doubt, Paige has no such feelings for me."

"But you care about her. *So much*."

"You're right. I do. Paige reminds me of someone I once knew."

"And loved."

"I did love Eileen. In the way I would've loved a sister, if I'd had one. A sister, Gwen, not a lover."

The distinction, and his desires, were eloquently clear.

Paige was the sister.

And Gwen was the lover, his lover, if she wanted to be. If she dared.

"Could we go to Carmel?"

"Sure." Cole's voice was soft with pleasure. "We can go wherever you like."

"There are some places in Carmel—and Monterey—I'd like to see. Two hospitals and a bed-and-breakfast that used to be a convent." *And the spot on the highway where a car took flight.* The spot might be just as treacherous tomorrow. The rain that had just begun to fall on San Francisco was the front edge, the forecasters said, of the first winter storm. Just as treacherous. And not treacherous

at all. She'd warn Cole of the danger. Would tell him...
everything. "I have maps."

"Okay. We'll see those places."

And spend the night at one of them?

Gwen heard his unasked question—or maybe it was
hers. "Cole?"

"Gwen?"

"Nothing."

"Everything?"

"Yes."

"We're going to have a nice time, Gwen. Just being
together will be nice."

"This is Stuart Dawson," the recording began. "If you'd
like to leave a message, please do so after the tone."

Claire did. "It's Claire, Stuart. You're probably still at
Mariel's dinner party, meeting her latest love. She's amazing, isn't she? So resilient. And fearless. I hope you like
her new man. I must confess I had a feeling you'd still be
out, but there's something I want to say to you, need to
say to you tonight. *Now.* I don't know why I feel such urgency. But I do. So. Here goes.

"I've been thinking about us. You and me. How much
you mean to me, how grateful I am. You've always been
there for me. *Always.* Since Alan's death...and before. Remember the times when Alan had to spend all night in
the hospital and I called you? Just to talk?

"And it was you I called—remember?—the first time

I felt Paige move. Alan was in surgery and I was so excited. You rushed right over and felt her, too. I would've called you anyway. Alan and I would have. But it was just the two of us that day. The three of us. You and Paige and me. Even before Alan's death, she probably heard your voice as much as his. Maybe more. And after he died, you became the father she needed so desperately. She didn't have a mother to speak of.... Oh! I paused, didn't I? Awaiting your rebuttal. Which, in turn, I would've had to rebut. But this voice messaging is better. So. Where was I? Paige needed a father. And you were there. And you were wonderful. Paige loves you so much."

Claire had been clutching the phone tightly, as if it were the last lifeline in a raging storm. She couldn't let go. *Was afraid to.*

"This is such a strange time. Emotional. Yesterday I found a box of my belongings, my life, before I met Alan—and you—on that Halloween in Ghirardelli Square. My street-artist days were there, as was my single memento of Sarah's Orchard—our family Christmas card, a photo of all nine of us, taken a month before I left.

"I was a daughter, Stuart, and a sister, who left at seventeen and was never heard from again. I *loved* my parents, my sisters, my brothers, my twin. I just didn't fit in. Alan wanted to invite them to our wedding—but I couldn't do it. Trying to fit in with the Forresters was overwhelming enough.

"Once I was pregnant, though, and becoming closer to Rosalind, Alan and I decided we'd have a true family Christmas. The MacKenzies, the Forresters and you, of course, and Mariel. We were going to discuss it with the four of you in Carmel, and maybe even phone my family from there. I have no memory, after the deaths, of deciding *not* to get in touch with my family. But that's what happened.

"They deserve an update on the daughter who disappeared. They deserved it years ago. I'm a hole in their hearts, just as they are in mine.

"I'm going to reach out to my missing family, Stuart. Soon. But first I'm going to reach out to Paige—my own missing daughter. I *have* to. Maybe if I start at the very beginning and share with her my joy at learning she was inside me, we can discover the place where we got so terribly lost...and get past it. I've wondered if that's what I've been searching for in my blurry memory of running in the rain. The place where I lost my Paige.

"I'm rambling, aren't I? In another moment, I'll be describing a dream I had about you and me. I'm not as fearless as Mariel. Not fearless at all. But...I *am* going to tell you—your machine—about my dream. You can always pretend your voice messaging system mysteriously crashed, and that the message from me was erased. Feel free to pretend that happened, Stuart! Or just stop listening right—"

The pain hit with a vengeance, a sharp-clawed fist that

gripped her stomach, then twisted and twisted, its talons piercing deep.

"—on second thought," she managed, barely. Then summoning energy, forcing cheer, she said, "I'm going to bed! The dream was a dream, silly and foolish, but the reason I called was important and real. To thank you, Stuart, with all my heart and forever, for everything."

"So, Stuart, what did you think of him?" Mariel's question came shortly before midnight and just moments after the last of her other dinner guests had departed her Nob Hill estate.

"What I think, Mariel, is that he's married."

"And?"

"That he's fifteen years younger than you."

"Perceptive as always, Stuart! And incisive legal eagle that you are, you've homed right in on two of his most appealing aspects—the other two being that he's wickedly sexy and enraptured by me. Oh, Stuart, don't look at me like that! Is it so difficult to imagine he'd be interested in me?"

"Not difficult at all. It's why you're interested in him that's baffling."

"He's sexy, young, in love with me—and, best of all, *married*."

"You don't need to go after another woman's husband."

"For the record, he's pursuing me. And I don't want him to leave her. I don't want to be married to him, or any man, ever again."

"You're better than this, Mariel. You can *do* better than this. It's beneath you."

"Do you hear yourself, Stuart? It's demeaning for me to be involved with another woman's husband, but it's just fine for you to be in love with another man's wife? Because Claire *is* Alan's wife. Now and always."

22

Jack sensed the presence behind him in the kitchen of his Pacific Heights fixer-upper. He turned toward his father——the officially retired housepainter who, until it was time to apply the colorful gift-wrapping to the entire home, had taken up carpentry. And plumbing. And any other construction hat his son would permit him to wear. Which, in general, included anything that didn't involve climbing ladders or scaling rooftops.

"Hey, Dad."

"Jack. Fancy meeting you here in the middle of the night."

"Did I wake you?"

"With your pacing, you mean?" Pete Logan smiled. "I was awake, happened to hear you. What's up?"

"Beth's wondering about Helen."

"What did you tell her?"

"Nothing yet. She doesn't know—yet—that I know. She told Paige Forrester, thinking Helen and Paige might have known each other at Stanford, and Paige told me. Beth's planning to talk to me. Eventually. I'm just trying to decide how long I can wait."

"I figure until six-fifteen tomorrow morning when you pick Beth up at Dina's."

"That's what I think, too."

Pete nodded, paused, then said, "Paige Forrester."

"What about her?"

"That's the question."

And the answer. And another reason for Jack's restless pacing late into the night. Their kiss had been brief. Chaste. Life-changing...

It was as if he'd been missing her for twelve years. And now she was found. And, miraculous technology notwithstanding, Paige was in precarious health.

"She's terrific, Dad."

Pete Logan smiled. "I figured that, too."

It was actually almost six-seventeen by the time Jack broached the issue of what was worrying Beth. He collected her first, at Dina's door, then dashed with her through the pouring rain to his car, then made sure she'd safely buckled up.

"I saw Paige last night."

"She told you, didn't she?"

"Yes, honey, she did. She knew I'd been concerned that something was worrying you, and she also said you were planning to tell me yourself."

"I thought she might tell you. I was hoping she would. But...are you mad, Daddy?"

"That you want to know about your mother? No, sweetheart, not at all. I'm a little mad at myself, though, for not realizing you'd want to."

"Dina says it's a girl thing."

"Which is why Paige gets it."

"And Gwen."

"Gwen?"

"Paige's friend. Gram would probably get it, too."

Eve Logan *might* get it. But given her feelings about Helen, she'd be ferocious in discouraging any discussion of her ex-daughter-in-law.

"Probably," Jack agreed. "But you know what? Even *I* get it now. I was thinking we could take the day off and go somewhere, just the two of us, and talk. Or," he continued without a pause, "we can talk later. Anytime. Lots of times. I know you're busy rehearsing for the Thanksgiving pageant."

"We really are."

"So maybe you should go to school?"

"I...yes. If that's okay."

"It's more than okay, Beth. Besides, it's not such a terrible idea for me to go to work, too."

She laughed, and they traveled in silence for a rain-drenched block. In another block they'd reach the school.

"Could you tell me her name?" Beth asked.

"It's Helen. Her name is Helen."

"Helen," Beth echoed softly, wonderingly.

Jack had believed he "got" it. But he hadn't. Not really. He was hearing it now, in his daughter's voice, and feeling it in quivers of fear deep within. But there was no going back. And for the daughter he loved, Jack moved forward.

"We met at a wedding. She's a musician, sweetheart. Like you. She was playing the harp."

"The *harp?*"

Jack didn't see her eyes widen. His own eyes were where they needed to be. On the road. Keeping her safe. But Jack knew her eyes were wide and bright. "The harp."

"Do you know where she is?"

"No." *Oh, Bethie, no.* "But I'll find out." Jack pulled to a stop in front of the academy. "I'll tell you what I've found, and we'll take it from there. All right?"

"Yes. Daddy? I love you."

"Oh, sweetie, I love you, too."

Jack watched Beth scamper toward the redbrick building. It was a short scoot, beneath an awning, at the end of which stood Charlie, the school's security guard.

Charlie waved when Beth reached him, as did Beth, and, after Jack waved in reply, she went inside.

Before driving to the Forresters' mansion, Jack placed a call to his own home.

Pete answered on the first ring, and in moments both parents were on the line.

"She's okay," Jack said. "Relieved. A little overwhelmed. She wants to go to school. To talk to Dina, I'd guess. I told her Helen's name, where we met and that she played the harp."

"You're not going to tell her about Helen screaming at her."

"No, Mom. I'm not. It's not the past she's interested in. It's the present. Maybe the future."

"Meaning she might want to meet Helen?" Eve asked sharply.

"Because if so, Jack, your mom and I don't want Helen anywhere near our girl."

"I know, Dad. Neither do I. We'll cross that bridge if and when we come to it." *Which we will.* And then the mother who would've preferred to run an errand rather than spend an hour under the same roof as her sleeping infant would have a chance to really hurt that little girl. *I don't want to see her, Jack. Why would I? We agreed, years ago, that she was all yours.* Jack wouldn't let Helen hurt her, of course. Would not. Somehow. "For now, let's just take it one question at a time...."

The mansion was aglow when Jack turned into the circular drive. Claire must be awake, brewing coffee and baking muffins for his crew. He didn't think she was expecting anyone this early.

He made the long-distance call from his car. The conservatory offices in Great Falls would be open at seven-forty. At least, twelve years ago, they'd been open by seven.

And still were.

"Carillon Conservatory, Dolores speaking. What may I do for you?"

The voice was like the bells for which the conservatory was named. A beautiful voice, and an unfamiliar one.

"I'm an old friend of one of your graduates. I was hoping to get in touch with her and thought you might be able to point me in the right direction."

"I expect I can," Dolores chimed. "We keep close track of our graduates and their brilliant careers. It will depend, of course, on the information she's authorized us to reveal. What's her name?"

"She was Helen Logan her first year. But she might have gone back to using her maiden name. Helen Grace?"

"Yes. That's the name she uses. Helen Grace."

Uses. Present tense. Jack hadn't known, until that moment, if Helen was even alive. But she was. She could—or could attempt to—do harm. "Do you know where she is?"

"Indeed I do. Where she is, and where she's *not*." Jack wasn't a musician. But even he could detect a sour note. "Helen *should* be performing on the great stages of the world."

"But she isn't."

"No. Not anymore. She had such *promise*."

"What happened? If you feel you can tell me…"

"I honestly don't know what happened. But I *do* feel I can share some of the facts. It's not a violation of her privacy. The entire debacle was very public—the *talk,* for quite a while, of the classical music world. And, of course, there were all those patrons who paid good money to hear her perform, only she'd fail to show. She wasn't *forced* to quit, though, despite her erratic behavior and the embarrassment she caused. Her talent was so remarkable that she was given another chance. And another. Genius is quirky. Temperamental. Concessions are made for a gift as rare as hers."

"Was she temperamental?"

"Helen? Heavens, no. I thought you knew her."

"I just wondered if she'd changed."

"No. She's still the quiet creature she's always been. And she could return to the concert circuit in a heartbeat if she wanted to."

"What's she doing instead?"

"Giving piano lessons. To beginners. *Children.* And not particularly gifted ones, I gather. Just whoever's parent happens to call."

"Piano, not harp?"

"That's right. When she quit the tour, she quit the harp. It's such a shame. Maybe an old friend could remind her of her talent and convince her to start playing again. At least convince her that if she's determined to teach, she should do it here. She's been offered a position. Many times. In my opinion, she owes the trustees that. They took a chance on her and she let them down. She could've been our most celebrated graduate."

"Can you tell me where she is?"

"San Francisco."

Jack's blood turned to ice.

"Since when?"

"Oh, I suppose it's been eighteen months. Maybe two years."

"Do you know where she lives?"

"I'm pulling it up on the computer. It's slow this morning. Not quite awake. Ah. Here we go. I just need to confirm that Helen hasn't asked that we withhold more specific information. No. She hasn't. I didn't think so. I can give you phone number, address, both."

"Both, please."

"All right. Her phone number is area code (415) 346..." Dolores provided a phone number with a Pacific Heights prefix.

And an address, including apartment number, within four blocks of Marine View Academy.

Jack probably thanked Dolores. He probably didn't just sever the connection with neither a murmur of gratitude nor a word of goodbye. But he really didn't remember.

The man whose brain was hard-wired for pattern recognition was already assembling the pieces into a terrifying whole.

Helen was in San Francisco.

She lived along a route Beth took when she walked to and from school.

And she was teaching the musical instrument Beth loved to play.

And why did Helen live where she lived? Why was she teaching what she taught? Because of Beth, of course. Because in the disturbed mind of Helen Grace, Beth was responsible for her failed career. *And would pay.*

That was the most ominous scenario. The presumption of danger for Beth. Which was what the vigilant father had to presume, and act on accordingly. Very soon, he would confront Helen face-to-face.

First, however, he needed to know that Beth was safe. She would be, within the school, unless Helen was there, as well. Jack's ex-wife wasn't one of Beth's teachers. Jack knew them all. But she could be teaching other classes, other grades, or be a nonteaching member of the staff.

Jack's call to Marine View Academy was answered by the principal's assistant, a woman Jack trusted to inform the principal of the situation when she arrived at eight. The assistant provided reassuring information. There were no Helens on staff, teaching or otherwise, nor anyone who matched the description Jack gave. Security hadn't reported anyone loitering on the grounds, and would have, and there hadn't been any phone calls—or other inquiries—about Beth, or Dina, or Larry. And there'd been no attempts to take Beth out of school early, as only Jack, his parents and Dina's mother were authorized to do.

Beth was safe at school. Jack would meet with the principal at two. By then he would have confronted Helen, and they'd take it from there.

It was a brief conversation, but a calming one. He'd feel even calmer after he'd said good morning to Claire. She'd undoubtedly seen his car and would worry if he suddenly sped away.

Another car pulled into the drive just as Jack reached the front door. He recognized the driver and waited. Claire must have been expecting the family attorney.

"Hello, Stuart."

"Jack."

The men shook hands, opened the door and entered a mansion fragrant with coffee and muffins...that were burning. Or had burned.

"Claire?"

Stuart's alarm was obvious in his voice and in the urgency with which he led the way to the kitchen.

The muffins *were* burning. The oven was smoking. And, most alarmingly, there was no Claire.

Jack grabbed an oven mitt, then the smoldering muffins. By the time he'd set them on the stove and turned around, Stuart was gone.

Running. Calling to Claire.

Jack ran, too.

But it was Stuart who reached Claire's bedroom first, found her first...and saw the woman he loved lying in a pool of blood.

23

The Emergency Room staff wasn't accustomed to checking if Cole Ransom was on call. He almost always was.

Nor would it have occurred to anyone to ask the page operator if the surgeon happened to be taking the day off. He never had.

The phone call to his apartment would've been made even if all the facts had been known—that he wasn't on call and had signed out for the next two days. And it would've been made, as in fact it was, without apology.

There wasn't time for such niceties. For anything but the words that greeted him when he answered the phone.

"We need you."

"Talk to me," Cole commanded four minutes later when he entered Trauma Room Three.

The wall of nurses and doctors parted at the sound of his voice, permitting him to see, to touch, while he listened to the salient facts.

Cole saw a lot. A woman translucent from blood loss and with a distended belly. She had an ulcer, or maybe cancer, from which there'd been not only a massive hemorrhage but a perforation as well. That was why her abdomen was distended. The through-and-through erosion of her stomach wall permitted air, blood, acid and bacteria unfettered access to her peritoneum.

Cole also saw what he expected to see in a state-of-the-art trauma center. In the short period of time the critically ill patient had been in the Emergency Room, all appropriate interventions had been implemented and the requisite lab work had been sent. It didn't happen by accident. Every member of the trauma team that had cared for her had a preassigned task, from scissoring away her garments to drawing the arterial blood gas to starting an intravenous line—by cut-down if necessary—to inserting a urinary catheter to endotracheal intubation to emergency type and cross.

When done by a well-trained team, the stabilization process was swift, comprehensive and virtually silent. No one needed to call out a reminder to check the blood count or to make sure all the labs were requested *stat*. Words, spoken calmly, primarily communicated relevant findings on physical exam: vital signs, gunshot wounds, racoon-eye bruising, open fractures, cerebral spinal fluid leaking through the nose.

There was little modesty for the patient in those moments of life and death. There couldn't be. Survival itself depended on the trauma experts' ability to see—and assess—everything.

Cole was seeing, assessing, as one of his trauma colleagues spoke.

"She was found, unconscious and shocky, in a pool of blood. She hadn't been down for long. She'd recently been in the kitchen of her home."

"History of belly pain?"

"None, according to the family friend who brought her in. He's in the waiting room."

"Other history?"

"Agoraphobia. No known allergies."

Cole didn't ask about her hematocrit. Her shock and her pallor told him it was perilously low—but being fortified. The first unit of blood had already been transfused. The second was hanging, ready to be infused.

Cole asked for a laboratory value not so easily determined by physical exam—but which, based on what he could see, he believed would be elevated.

"Amylase?"

"Sky-high."

Meaning the ulcer had burrowed into the pancreas, causing inflammation and injury—which, in turn, would cause more. The spill of pancreatic enzymes, digestive enzymes, into the abdominal cavity would begin the digestive process there—in essence, a cannibalization of the host.

Cole noticed her hands. Ringless. But the indentation on the wedding-ring finger suggested that a ring was usually worn, and had recently been removed—likely for safekeeping—by the E.R. staff.

"Is there a husband?"

Cole's query prompted a few seconds of stunned silence.

"Paige is her only family," the E.R. chief finally replied.

"Paige?"

"This is Claire Forrester, Cole. Weren't you told when you were called?"

The information *had* been provided. But Cole had already hung up his phone and was on his way. If he was needed, he was needed. The patient's name, and even the diagnosis, simply weren't relevant.

They never had been—until now, when the patient was the dying mother of the woman who reminded him so much of Eileen.

Cole Ransom knew the story of Claire and Alan Forrester. *Everyone* at Pacific Heights Medical Center knew. Cole's office was even located within the Alan Forrester Pavilion—the funding for which had been raised by Claire.

"Where is Paige?"

"We don't know. We've tried pager, home phone, cell phone, office, Alice—"

"The HDU?"

"She *was* there," the triage nurse said. "Her eight-hour run ended at three-thirty this morning, and after that she went home. She's probably in the shower. Forgot her pager and can't hear the phone. The other man who brought Mrs. Forrester in is on his way to her apartment now."

"The hospital administrator's already on board," the chief added, "if you feel you need to start operating before Paige can be found to give consent."

Cole didn't give a damn about a duly signed consent to operate, any more than the E.R. staff had required a signature before rushing Claire Forrester into the trauma room and initiating every possible intervention in the hope of keeping her alive long enough to make it to surgery. When time mattered, when life mattered, the approach was care for the patient first and deal with the attorneys later.

But Cole wanted Paige to have at least a few minutes' warning that her mother was going to die.

"Call this number." Cole recited the phone number he'd dialed once and knew by heart. "Tell Gwen what's happening and that we can't find Paige."

"You got it."

"Give the O.R. a ten-minute heads-up," Cole said. "And have whoever's on for trauma meet me there. Right now I'd like to put in a second central line."

* * *

Gwen reached the Emergency Room's waiting area just as Cole was approaching a man she recognized from the *Town and Country* photograph Sister Mary Catherine had sent.

Tuxedoed then, Stuart Dawson was wearing a suit now, and blood.

So much blood.

Her mother's blood. Everywhere: his clothes, his hands, the handsome face savaged by fear.

He loves her, Gwen realized. *And he knows, and it's killing him, that she's going to die.*

No! Cole won't let her—

Gwen's defiant thought was severed by Cole himself.

Yes, the surgeon looked calm and controlled. But Gwen saw a heart-stopping darkness in his storm-gray eyes. As if Cole doubted there was anything he could do. He would experience an even greater darkness, a darker shadow, if he could not. She was sure of it.

Cole saw her then, and—for her—he vanquished the darkness.

"I don't know where Paige is," Gwen told him.

"Don't worry. We'll find her."

"She'd want you to operate." *I want you to operate. I trust you. Believe in you.* "I know she would."

"I'm going to operate, Gwen. There's really no choice." Cole's calm gaze focused on the Forrester family attorney and friend. "There are a couple of things I'd like to know. If *you* know. I understand Mrs. Forrester is agoraphobic. Is she on any meds?"

"For the agoraphobia? No," Stuart replied. "Or for anything else. Claire doesn't take any medication at all."

"So her health is good?"

"Excellent. She's always been in perfect health." Stuart fought against a surge of emotion and forced himself to concentrate. "No. Wait. That's wrong. Claire had a placental abruption when Paige was born, and there was a reaction to the anesthetic received."

"What kind of reaction?"

"She was groggy for a number of days, and intermittently confused. The doctors attributed it to an unusually prolonged amount of time for her system to clear the drug."

"Do you know what anesthetic she was given?"

"No, I'm sorry. I don't. I could try to find out."

"That's all right."

Cole's voice was reassuring. And he found a comforting smile for Stuart Dawson. It was a valiant effort, but he couldn't quite pull it off. Stuart had carried Claire's virtually lifeless body, after all, and held her close to him while Jack drove.

There wasn't time to track down an anesthetic given at another hospital thirty-one years ago.

There wasn't any time at all.

The short journey to Paige's condominium would be brightly lit, even in the middle of the night. And safe, around the clock. It was a journey the oncologist—and dialysis patient—had made hundreds, perhaps thousands, of times.

And which Jack Logan was making now. He knew where she lived. He'd dropped her off after the swim meet, and walked her to the building's always-locked front door.

Always locked. But opening now, and repeatedly, as Paige's neighbors left for work.

At any other time, Jack would've been quite unhappy about the ease with which he slipped inside. Now he was simply grateful.

He fully expected to find Paige in her twelfth-floor condo. She'd be out of her shower by now, and getting dressed. Any moment there'd be a shadow in the peephole, in response to her doorbell's melodious ring, and a moment later, she'd open the door.

But moments passed. No shadow. No Paige. And the morning paper, curled in a water-repellant plastic sheath, hung on her doorknob. Beneath that, also in plastic, were the minutes of the most recent meeting of the condominium association—which had been delivered this morning. Or last night?

24

Cole did not, as he prepared to operate, think about the death in Texas twenty-two years before.

His focus was on Claire.

But that West Texas day and its brutal murder were always with him. The memory was carved deep, as Eileen had been carved with a jagged-edge knife, the kind of brutal wounding that left scars so hideous—and so bloodless—there wasn't the slightest diminution over time.

Cole's scars were invisible to the naked eye. But he knew the gaps they created in his heart and in his soul, the spaces where blood wouldn't flow and nerves had been severed.

The places, now spaces, where love should have flowed.

Such blood-warmed places had existed in the sixteen-year-old he'd been. His life until then had been a grand adventure, a nomadic odyssey with the rodeo cowboy and cowgirl parents who'd been teens themselves when their son was born.

They were kids in love, who loved their baby, and who took him happily from town to town and rodeo to rodeo. Cole trotted along beside them, an eager puppy, then rode beside them, becoming a cowboy, too. He was going to be a good one, like his father, a rare breed rugged enough and talented enough to make his living solely from money earned in competition.

Cole Ransom. Rodeo cowboy—and cowboy scholar. Cole loved to learn. Loved school. His parents were bemused by the son who preferred school to playing hooky, but could hardly disapprove. Nor would they. For years, perhaps from the start, Cole had been more of a pal to them, a favorite buddy, than a child.

Cole's education was erratic, as wandering as his life, a situation he vowed to change as soon as he found a school he wanted to attend in a town where he wanted to live, and where he could remain behind when his parents moved on.

The town was West Fork, Texas.

The school was West Fork High.

And the reason was Eileen Lake.

She was *Miss* Lake to her students, Cole included— for a while. She was thirty-six, and taught biology. And he was sixteen. And infatuated with Miss Lake?

No. Although the bright, handsome sixteen-year-old cowboy had been known to have sex with adult women who didn't have a clue about his true age. Cole had been known to have sex, in fact, with whomever he wanted, whenever he wanted.

But there was nothing even remotely sexual in Cole's feelings for Eileen Lake. She was his friend, his bossy big sister.

His inspiration.

Eileen's passion for science awakened the answer to who, *what,* the cowboy scholar was meant to be. A physician. A surgeon. Cole knew he belonged in the operating room even then.

Eileen agreed. Encouraged him. She herself had considered a medical career. But her true calling, she believed, was to be a teacher of doctors, not a doctor herself.

A teacher and a mother. Her truer calling.

Eileen wanted a family. The man with whom she lived, Brad Tilton, kept promising her that one day she would. They'd get married, Brad told her, as soon as he got the job promotion he so richly deserved. They'd buy a real home, too, not the "pitiful excuse for a house"—Brad's words about her cottage—that he'd moved into, at her invitation, two years before.

Then they'd have kids.

Eileen became pregnant six months after Cole enrolled in West Fork High. It was Cole, her friend, with whom she first shared the news.

And it was to Cole that Eileen Lake lied the follow-ing day. She'd fallen, she told him when he noticed the bruises on her neck. She'd gotten the whirlies, she was pregnant after all, and had stumbled down the stairs. Dumb, huh?

Cole believed that lie, and the next one and the next.

At sixteen, the cowboy for whom everything was easy and everything was good, didn't know about lying.

Or violence.

Or men who hit women.

Nor did Cole know, at sixteen, that some women pro-tected their abusers.

By the time Cole recognized Eileen's lies for what they were, Brad's violence had escalated to the point where, in retrospect, the outcome was inevitable.

If he'd recognized the lies sooner, Eileen and her baby would have survived. That was what Cole Ransom be-lieved, and always would. And it was the reason he'd been on the lookout for lies ever since. Why he feared them, feared missing them, until it was far too late—as it had been for Eileen.

Eileen wanted to get away from Brad. His fury was growing, and his accusations were becoming more bizarre. Eileen had *planned* the pregnancy, he shouted. Expressly to sabotage *his* career plans. And, he raged, the baby probably wasn't even his.

But Eileen was afraid to free herself from Brad—which, Cole told her, he didn't understand. In fact, speaking from the arrogance of inexperience, Cole convinced her it was the hormonal roller coaster of her pregnancy that was making her fearful. Irrational. *Rationally,* he insisted, she had nothing to fear.

And speaking from the arrogance of a charmed life untouched by tragedy, Cole defined Brad as a bully, hence a coward, hence not a threat.

Trust me, Cole had said easily, persuasively.

At sixteen Cole Ransom didn't know about bullies who murdered women they claimed to love. Or that the greatest danger for the woman was when she dared to end the relationship.

Eileen didn't know it, either. But she felt it. Feared it. Still, she told Brad to leave her home. She had to. For her baby. For herself.

Brad complied with a shrug.

You see? Everything's fine. With those words, Cole lured a smile from her. Brad was gone from her life. But if the cowardly bully ever returned, Cole would protect her. He'd sleep on her living-room couch, as he had for the ten nights since Brad had left.

Ten nights was long enough, Eileen told him. Too long, according to the high-school principal. Too long. Too wrong.

Four nights later, Brad Tilton broke into Eileen's pitiful excuse for a house and slaughtered her. Slowly. With the jagged-edge knife.

It wasn't a private slaughter. Eileen managed to call

9-1-1. So there was a standoff, and a dialogue between Brad and the police, a negotiation in which Brad offered to let Eileen go in exchange for the chance to meet man-to-man with the sixteen-year-old cowboy trash who'd gotten her pregnant.

The hostage negotiator said no. And was listened to. He'd been flown in from Dallas and was a pro. If they allowed Cole into the house, there'd be two potential victims instead of one.

Cole didn't care. Anything to protect Eileen, to save Eileen. Who *trusted* him.

Trusted *him*.

Cole made it to the front door before he was tackled by the West Fork police. He was restrained after that, handcuffed to a patrol car. The single self-inflicted gunshot sounded fifty-two hours into the siege, and the SWAT team, also from Dallas, confirmed they saw Brad Tilton lying dead. At that point, the officer who was watching Cole, and had played football in high school with Brad, uncuffed the teen cowboy. He truly believed Cole had seduced Eileen and was ultimately responsible for the carnage inside. The officer wanted him to see it.

So Cole saw Eileen's blood, her baby's blood, splattered on floors, walls, ceilings. The white satin comforter on the four-poster bed. The massive hemorrhage, like crimson moonbeams, was out of his reach. Beyond his control.

25

Gweneth Angelica St. James, the forsaken Forrester, and Stuart Dawson, the Forrester family attorney, stood together in the Emergency Room waiting area—which, except for them, was empty.

This was the quiet time in emergency rooms everywhere, the morning lull between seven and eight. Patients too sick to wait till daylight had come in hours before. And those determined to hang on until their own physicians could be seen were en route to those doctors' offices now.

Gwen and Stuart stood together, in silence, each lost in painful *what ifs*.

What if he'd gone to Claire last night? Within minutes of listening to the message she'd left? He'd wanted to, was tempted to. But she'd said she was tired. Going to bed.

So Stuart had fought the temptation. *You mean so much to me, too, my Claire. And the way your voice softened—did you hear it?—when you said you wanted to talk about us. You and me. Tell me your dream, Claire, and I'll tell you mine.*

And he'd fought, too, an icy shiver of fear. The feeling, haunting but real, that Claire was saying goodbye.

A different set of *what ifs* tormented Gwen.

What if the anesthetic, which left Claire Forrester groggy and confused, had encouraged her to give her blemished daughter away—by mistake—then blocked her ability to retrace her steps? And what if it was the anguish of that irrevocable deed that had caused an ulcer to bore its way to an exsanguinating bleed?

Yes, Gwen had read the new thinking, the scientific data, about ulcers. In fact, she'd come across something in *Time,* or was it *Newsweek,* quite recently. In most cases a bacterium, *Helicobacter pylori,* was implicated. And if not, or sometimes in addition, non-steroidal anti-inflammatory medications, like aspirin, naproxen, ibuprofen, played a role. As did aggravating factors such as family history, tobacco and caffeine.

The old notion of *stress* causing ulcers hadn't been thrown out entirely. There remained "strong anecdotal evidence" that stress and ulcers were intricately entwined.

So what if her mother—oh, her mother—had been drinking coffee, worrying about the daughter she'd lost, and taking an occasional anti-inflammatory pill for a touch of arthritis, not bad, just there—and *that* was why the ulcer had burned and bled?

And if only Gwen had dropped by the mansion, as Paige had encouraged her to, or accompanied Beth and Dina to spend Monday afternoon with the *oh my gosh, so amazing* Mrs. Forrester...

Claire might have recognized her firstborn daughter *somehow,* despite the family resemblance that wasn't there and the makeup mask that was. Somehow...because Claire was the mother and Gwen was her lost baby girl.

Claire would have recognized her, if, if, if, and the ulcer would've started to heal. The mother and her twin daughters, reunited at last, would be having decaf lattes in the cafeteria even now—Claire's agoraphobia vanquished, too—discussing the renal transplantation that would happen just as soon as the *perfect* HLA-match was confirmed.

"Mr. Dawson? Ms. St. James?"

The Emergency Room nurse waited for at least one of them to focus. Both did, eventually, but the attorney answered first.

"Yes?"

"Dr. Ransom wanted me to give you these." The nurse gestured to the clothes—tailored suit, button-collared shirt, spotless blue tie—she was carrying. They hung, in plastic, on hangers imprinted with a dry cleaner's logo, and with the invoice still attached. "These are his. He thought they'd fit. He keeps a supply of freshly laundered street clothes in his office."

Cole's secretary, who'd brought the garments to the E.R., had explained to the nurse the reason for the supply. The surgeon, and frequent expert witness, could go from O.R. to deposition without the inconvenience of going home.

"There's a call room in the E.R. where you can change, if you like. And there's a shower, too."

It took Stuart a few aching, *what if* moments to comprehend his need for Cole Ransom's clothes. And a few more to overcome his immediate resistance to shedding the items that bore Claire's blood.

But it was necessary, for Paige, that he do so.

"Thank you." Stuart took the clothes. "Is there any word?"

"Mrs. Forrester is in the operating room and the surgery has begun."

"And Paige?"

"Mr. Logan called to say she wasn't at her apartment. When we told him we hadn't found her either, he said he had an idea where she might be. He's going there now. As soon as he finds her, they'll go to her office, rather than come down here. Cole thought Paige's office might be a good place for everyone to wait. It's on 8-North, quite close to the surgical ICU, which is where Mrs. Forrester will be once she gets out of surgery."

Once she gets out of surgery.

If she gets out of surgery.

What if.

"I'd be happy to show you to Paige's office. Her secretary, Alice, is there, so the office is open, and there's coffee...."

"I know where her office is," Stuart said. "But thank you."

"I know, too," Gwen added. "Thank you. I think I'll just head on up."

Jack hoped he knew, prayed he knew, where Paige was. He knew with certainty that she hadn't been home. According to Paige's across-the-hall neighbor, the condominium association minutes had been delivered between eight and ten last night.

His hope, his prayer, was that despite what the dialysis tech had said, Paige hadn't left the Hemodialysis Unit, after all...hadn't made the middle-of-the-night journey across the brightly lit street...hadn't encountered danger where she'd always felt safe—either outside her condominium building or from an intruder, like Jack, who'd so effortlessly gotten in.

Jack also hoped, prayed, that Paige would be asleep in the HDU, merely sleeping, in the bed that wasn't hers and beyond the hour when she usually awakened.

It was possible, Jack told himself as he sprinted up the stairwell to 5-West. Her room was remote from the nursing station, at the far end of the ward. And since it was believed that Paige had gone home at 3:00 a.m., the room would remain undisturbed until housekeeping arrived to clean it.

Paige would be sleeping, merely sleeping. She would *not* have begun her journey home, down the same stairs Jack was ascending now, and woozy from her first eight-hour dialysis run, tripped on a step, fallen, hit her head.

Nor would Paige's dialysis fistula have leaked after her removal from the machine. And the leak that didn't happen would not have become an exsanguinating gush.

The daughter would not be found in a pool of blood less than an hour after the mother had been.

Or ever.

Paige wasn't on the stairs that Jack was ascending three steps at a time. No one was. Not on the first flight, the third flight, or the fifth.

Breathless, he arrived at the room where he'd kissed her good-night.

The door was closed.

He opened it swiftly, and quietly.

And swiftly, quietly, he walked to the bed where she lay.

Sleeping. Merely sleeping.

No pool of blood haloed her sable head, as it had encircled and stained her mother's blondness. Paige's breathing, unlike Claire's, was deep and slow.

And far from ashen, Paige was flushed pink with the warmth of her dreams.

No smile had curved the blood-caked lips of Claire Forrester, and her expression had been anguished—as if, in her final moments of consciousness, she'd understood what was happening and whispered, implored, *No, please. No!*

Claire's daughter, in sleep, was smiling.

Jack reached to wake her. But stopped before touching. Why rouse her from happy dreams to a wide-awake nightmare?

Her consent to operate wasn't needed. The surgery was already underway. Her awareness of what had happened, was happening, wouldn't affect the outcome—which would be, Jack feared, a nightmare in itself.

He'd seen how much blood Claire had lost.

And he'd seen Claire.

Jack wanted to touch Paige. But he withdrew his questing hands, then withdrew from the room to make some calls.

Gwen rushed to Paige's office as Jack Logan had rushed to the HDU. She wanted to be where she belonged, with her sister, the moment Paige was found.

Where she belonged. It was a legitimacy that only she knew about.

As far as Paige was concerned, Gwen St. James was the makeup artist with whom there'd been some sharing of confidences on Saturday afternoon, and a brief conversation on Monday, and from whom there'd been a note explaining the purpose of Beth Logan's meeting with Paige.

That was it.

If asked, Paige would undoubtedly say that their interactions had been pleasant. And she might even voice amazement at how immediately comfortable she'd felt with Gwen. And that she'd like to see more of Gwen. Paige Forrester might even confess that although Saturday afternoon's description of Gwen as her friend was chosen to convince Cole she was in good hands, it felt nice. Right. Something she believed she and Gwen *could* be.

But in another setting, Paige would likely have introduced Gwen as what she was, the camouflage specialist who'd created a mask for Louise Johansson so that she might die at home.

All of which meant that Paige would wonder, with reason, what Gwen was doing in her office so early in the morning, on this days of all days. Indeed, she might wonder what Gwen was doing in the medical center at all.

But Paige wouldn't ask. She was too polite. Besides, on a conscious level, she'd be consumed with worry about the mother she loved.

But there might be subconscious wonderings, disturbing ones.

Was Gwen St. James, nice though she seemed, a vulture of sorts? Did the makeup artist sense an impending death and circle in watchful silence until her talents— her talons?—could be put to their best use?

Perhaps Gwen had heard that Claire Forrester would soon be needing a colorful enhancement to her ashen face…so that Alan would recognize his beloved, and want her, when they were reunited at last.

At best, Gwen's presence would be a surprise to Paige. At worst, a torment.

And it wasn't as if Paige needed her. Jack was there for her. And Paige's Jack, *Avril's* Jack, was enough.

But Stuart would be there, too. For Paige. As would Alice. As would the concerned gathering of nurses, doctors, social workers, X-ray techs, and so on. Gwen saw them as she rounded the final corner toward Paige's office.

Gwen was the outsider and would be viewed as such, a voyeur who would've stopped at the edge of a seaside cliff to gape at a grandfather impaled by a drive shaft, a grandmother with half a face, a father who was dying—and a mother hemorrhaging from a placental tear that had also torn her twins' in utero embrace.

Gwen alone knew that she and Paige had hugged in their mother's womb. And touched, and smiled, and comforted, and soothed.

Before reaching her sister's office, she turned and fled.

26

Jack had told her, just last night, that he would happily keep vigil while she slept. And he'd vowed, when she demurred, that someday Paige would trust him to watch her as she dreamed.

And now, having returned to her room after making the calls, he was watching her sleep, and marveling at how much better she looked than when he'd left her last night.

More comfortable, too.

No longer lying palms up, veins opened, taking great care not to dislodge the needles in her forearm, she was lying on her side, gently curled, secure and snuggling in her blanket cocoon.

Had Jack been able to choose the kind of sleep he wished one day to witness, it would've been what he was seeing now.

A heavenly peace.

Paige was oblivious to the sadness that would greet her when she awakened. Jack dreaded the cell-phone vibration he was expecting. He'd seen Claire, after all, and feared the worst.

And, judging by her expression when he and Stuart found her, so did Claire.

The very worst.

The call would come, and Cole Ransom would inform Jack when he answered that if Paige wanted to see her mother one last time, now would be the ideal moment. Claire's color was much improved in death, a consequence of the transfusions she'd received. And she looked serene, Cole would tell him.

Sleeping in heavenly peace.

Eternal peace.

But it would be an illusion, Jack thought. Claire hadn't been ready to die. She'd been fighting it, pleading with it not to claim her, even as she'd been vomiting stomachful upon stomachful of blood.

Pleading. Fighting. As if there was something unfinished she had to do.

Or say.

To Paige…who might have things to say to her mother, too. Or might want to be with her, touching her, when Claire died.

If so, or even if not, Jack had no right to withhold the truth from Paige, to delay the revelation a second more.

He touched her cheek. Whispered her name.

"Jack," Paige murmured, sleepy and unalarmed. It made perfect sense that Jack would be here. He'd been with her throughout the night in her dreams. "Hi."

"Hi."

"What time is it?"

"About eight-fifteen."

Paige frowned, propped up on one elbow. "In the morning?"

"In the morning."

Paige glanced around the room, a search for bearings. And remembrance. "I fell asleep after you left, and didn't wake up until the run was through. I was going to leave then, I started to, but I heard the wind and the rain, and I decided to stay right here." In this bed, where he'd kissed her, with such wonder. Paige didn't see wonder now. "Jack? Why are you—oh, it's Beth, isn't it? You talked to her and she's upset that I told you. I'm sorry!"

"Beth is fine. We did talk, and she's glad you told me. I'm here because of your mother, Paige. She's in surgery."

"What?" Paige sat up. Too quickly. Her blood, still sleeping, still dreaming, lagged a few racing beats behind. But it caught up before she fell back again. She compelled it to. "Why?"

"They think she has an ulcer."

"An ulcer without pain?" She shook her head. *Denial.*

Dr. Forrester knew the stages of death and dying—the normal human response to news of a catastrophic disease. Denial was the first. And here she was, denying. *It can't be an ulcer. She's never had any pain. And she's always been so healthy. She's the picture of health.* Denial. And an overreaction. Jack had said nothing about death, dying, catastrophe. "Why do they think it's an ulcer?"

"She had some bleeding."

"But...no one operates on bleeding ulcers anymore. It's not necessary. They just do endoscopy. Who decided to take her to the O.R.?"

"Cole Ransom."

"Oh," Paige whispered. Death. Dying. Catastrophe. *No.* "She perforated."

"That's what they think."

"When?"

"Stuart and I found her about ninety minutes ago. It'd just happened. She'd put muffins in the oven." *And the blood on the bedroom carpet was warm.*

From the viewpoint of everyone in the Emergency Room, and—as word spread—within the medical center at large, Cole Ransom was the right surgeon to operate on Claire. Beyond the simple fact that he was the best, and that she was bleeding and he was the vascular surgery chief, was his expertise in trauma.

A peptic ulcer that perforated and bled *was* traumatic, and could even, as Claire Forrester's devastating perforation did, mimic a gunshot wound to the abdomen—like the self-inflicted gunshot wound that had ended Brad Tilton's life.

Eileen Lake's abuser hadn't intended to kill himself. Brad was far too cowardly to do so, and was without a scintilla of either remorse or shame. Instead of firing a bullet into his heart or his brain, he'd aimed for his upper belly. And Brad Tilton had hit his mark.

Stomach. Pancreas.

Fatal.

Sixteen-year-old Cole Ransom hadn't seen Brad Tilton's internal injuries. Only the West Texas coroner had. Cole didn't know, although it was true, that the tissue trauma to his patient, Claire Forrester, was even worse.

Cole knew only who he was. What he was.

Not a magician.

Not a warrior.

And most assuredly not a god.

He was a man, that was all, as well trained as he could possibly be. And he gave, to every patient, all that was in his power to give.

Sometimes, it wasn't enough.

"We're losing her, Cole." The statement, from the anesthesiologist, was spoken with neither censure nor alarm. It was merely the not-so-surprising truth. "Her pressure's cratered again."

Claire's blood pressure shouldn't have plummeted. The bleeding had stopped. Cole had stopped it. And her intravascular volume had been restored by transfusions of blood.

So the renewed shock was something else. Septic. Anaphylactic. Cardiogenic. Neurogenic. Except there was no evidence of any of those.

So, perhaps, Claire Forrester had simply surrendered, her body had, collapsing from what must have been months and months of pain—the ulcer was huge—that she'd fought, apparently successfully, to conceal. But the battle had been too long, too hard, too costly.

She had nothing left.

"Don't do it." The command, Cole's, was fierce. And stunning to the operating-room team. He seemed to be speaking to the patient herself. "Don't. Quit. Yet."

27

Gwen the outsider ran outside—into a rainfall more drenching, more punishing, than the rain that had pelted her during her frantic dash from Belvedere Court to the Emergency Room.

A rainfall now, perhaps, like the torrential downpour through which her mother had run on that storm-ravaged night—when, as ill as she'd been, she'd gone to Carmel to get her firstborn child. So that she could give her daughter away?

No. *No.* So that the Forresters—father, mother, twins—would be together, under one roof, in the hospital in Monterey. That had been her plan. A reunion of family.

Claire probably didn't know about the birthmark. She hadn't really seen her just-born daughter, not clearly, between that baby's birth and her own clinical deterioration. Claire had known only that one of her baby girls had been born at the crash site, and was in the newborn nursery in Carmel.

She must have taken a cab. She would've been too ill to drive, and she'd been on foot when the tourist from Iowa offered her a ride to St. James Convent.

Claire had likely learned about the convent from the cabbie who drove her from Monterey. Maybe he'd said how good the nuns were, how excellent the convent school—and maybe, seeing how distressed she looked, he'd even mentioned that its chapel was a calming place to pray.

And Claire had remembered the convent when, having retrieved her blemished daughter, she'd become confused again, uncertain what to do. And somehow, in her confusion, she'd given her daughter away.

But Claire had wanted her family together.

That had been her intent; Claire's firstborn daughter was sure of it.

Had it not been for Claire's confusion, both baby girls would have lived with the new widow in the Forrester family home—where Gwen was now. The mansion. She'd been running here all along, in the rain, guided by a heart that felt no confusion at all.

Gwen had forgotten about the renovation. The circular drive was a parking lot of SUVs and trucks. Also, she noticed, a dark green Lexus and a bright blue Jag.

In the foyer, Gwen discovered the Jaguar's stylish owner. Mariel Lancaster. The fourth of the foursome pictured in *Town and Country*. Co-hostess of Claire's gala for the neonatal ICU, and one of Claire's closest friends.

High heels clicking on the marble floor, Mariel was shedding her coat, her umbrella, making herself at home, and hadn't—yet—noticed Gwen.

"Claire?" she called gaily. "Where are you?"

"She's not here." The reply came from the far end of the foyer. From one of the workmen on Jack's crew.

"Of course she is! We're plotting the Christmas fund raiser for the Pediatrics wing. Oh, I get it, Stuart put you up to this, didn't he? Whoever you are. Because he's still angry with me."

"I'm Kyle. Jack Logan's foreman."

"Terrific. And nice try. But since Stuart's car is parked right outside—"

"There was an emergency," Gwen said from the doorway. "She's at the med center."

"What kind of emergency? Oh, no, *Paige?*"

"No," Gwen replied. "Not Paige." *Claire. Paige's mother. My mother. Mommy!*

"Mrs. Forrester," Kyle said. "She's in surgery."

"For what?"

"An ulcer."

"An ulcer? Claire? No way."

"I'm sorry, ma'am. That's all I know. That's all Jack said when he called."

Mariel turned to Gwen. "Is this really true?"

"Yes."

"And you are?"

"Paige's friend. Gwen."

"Where's Stuart?"

"At the medical center, in Paige's office, waiting."

"Uncle Stuart." Paige punctuated her greeting with a warm embrace. When had she become a hugger?

Stuart, a little surprised, hugged back. And he said, as he had for decades, "Hey, kiddo." Then added, "She's still in surgery."

Paige nodded. Alice, whose desk she and Jack had passed en route to her office, had said as much. "You were at the mansion at six forty-five? You and Jack?"

"Yes," Stuart said. "I was. We were."

And it was lucky. So lucky. Claire had needed both men, one to cradle her close to his heart, the other to make the three-block drive.

"Did she call you?" Paige asked. And she worried that Claire had tried to call her, too, a frantic early-morning plea to her physician daughter. *Help me, Paige. Please. Something's terribly wrong.*

"No, Paige, she didn't call. Not this morning. But she left a message last night that made me decide to drop by early today. It had nothing to do with her health. And this morning, before we arrived, she'd obviously been up making coffee and muffins. The bleeding must have come without warning. I don't think she made any calls."

"Without warning," Paige echoed. "But she must've had pain. Did she ever mention it to you?"

"No," Stuart said. "Never. But there were times when she suddenly stopped speaking. I wonder, now, if it was because of the pain. She always said she'd just lost her train of thought. And that she was fine."

Like her daughter.

Fine, fine, fine.

Lies. Lies. Lies.

"Were you ever going to let me know?" Mariel asked when she walked into Paige's office. Her question, an accusation, was directed at Stuart. And the reason Mariel's first question wasn't about Claire was that she'd gotten multiple updates between the hospital's main entrance and the eighth floor. Tearful updates. And determinedly hopeful ones. The entire hospital knew, and cared, about the woman—Paige's mother—who hostessed parties *just for them,* the hospital staff. Parties, not galas. Thankyous, not fund-raisers. "Stuart?"

"Yes, Mariel. Of course."

"Oh, Stuart, I'm sorry! I should never have said what I said last night."

"It doesn't matter." Besides, what she'd said was true. Claire was Alan's wife, past, present, future. At least that was what Stuart had believed, told himself he must believe, until he'd heard the message that awaited his return from Mariel's. And then... *If only, if only, he'd gone to her.* "I'm just going to walk down to the atrium and back."

"I'm going with you, Stuart," Mariel said. "Just to walk. I won't say a word."

"Will you tell me how it went with Beth?" Paige asked Jack when Mariel and Stuart were gone. "Please? It would help."

"Okay. It went well. She *was* glad, really, that you'd told me."

"Did she have questions yet?"

"She wanted to know Helen's name. And I volunteered how we met and that Helen played the harp."

"Do you wish you hadn't?"

"No. I've discovered something I need to know, and I might not have if I hadn't piqued Beth's curiosity to the point that she asked me if I know where Helen lives."

"Oh, Jack. Are you saying Helen lives in San Francisco?"

"In an apartment building overlooking the route Beth and Dina take when they walk to school."

"What are you going to do?"

"Talk to her."

"And the police."

"I'm not afraid of Helen, Paige. But Beth..."

"She wouldn't talk to strangers."

"Helen wouldn't feel like a stranger to Beth. Not if she was playing the piano—or the harp. She isn't Beth's piano teacher. At least she isn't the one I pay. But for all I know, she and Beth see each other all the time."

"You'd know."

"I didn't know Beth had been wondering about Helen."

"You knew she was wondering about *something*."

"I also had no idea she'd canceled her Tuesday-afternoon piano lesson and scheduled an appointment with you. I wonder what else I don't know."

Paige wasn't about to let this man, this wonderful father, believe he wasn't a vigilant shepherd after all.

"She's a responsible girl, Jack. Just like her father. That's why she informed her piano teacher beforehand that she wasn't going to show. And as for scheduling an appointment with me, it's not like she was arranging a rendezvous with a stranger."

"No," he said softly. "It was like she was meeting with the woman who could have been her mother. Should have been. And might still want to be?"

"Jack..."

"I fell in love with you, Paige. You. Paige. Twelve years ago. I've never fallen out. In fact, I'm still falling."

"I fell in love with you, too. I *am* in love with you. I never stopped. Don't want to stop."

"Then don't."

"But..." There were so many *buts*. And yet, as she looked at him, and saw his love and his hope, suddenly there were none. They'd love each other, protect each other, and, and, together, they'd banish the bad things. Her smile for him was radiant and pure. "Then I won't. I love you, Jack. You...and Beth."

"And we love you."

Jack held her then, and she held him, and they swayed together, a slow dance to music they alone could hear.

"Jack?"

"Paige?" It was a muffled kiss, his lips whispering into her hair.

They'd banish the bad things that could be banished, and the ones that could not? Together they'd see them through. "Helen. You need to talk to her, Jack. Today. *Now.*"

"I need to be here, Paige. Now. With you. And Beth's safe. I've spoken to the school. At some point I'll call my parents and tell them what I've learned. They'll keep the two o'clock meeting I've scheduled with the principal and take Beth and Dina home after school. Even that may be an overreaction. Helen's been in San Francisco for at least eighteen months."

It wasn't an overreaction, Paige knew...and felt certain Jack did, too. If not for his concern about *her,* Jack would be at Helen's apartment now. "If you'd found out this morning that Beth was taking ecstasy, you wouldn't have decided to discuss it with her some other time— even if you'd also discovered that she'd been taking it for eighteen months. Would you?"

"You know I wouldn't. But I can, and will, wait to see Helen until your mother's safely out of surgery."

"No, Jack. Please go now. I'm okay. *We're* okay. I just want to be certain our girl's okay, too."

"You're sure?"

"I'm positive."

"I'll be back soon."

"Drive carefully," said the daughter who'd lost her father on a rainy day like this.

Jack smiled solemnly. "I will, Paige. I always do."

Paige believed him and believed that he'd return safely. And would her mother return safely from the very edge of eternity?

Or would she die without ever knowing all the things Paige had planned someday soon—too late—to say?

I love you, Mother. And admire you. And regret—so much—that we were never close...and that I never told you how I feel.

Paige was so proud of Claire. She'd always been proud of her. When she was twenty-one, she'd tried to imagine her mother's twenty-first year, the perfect love, the impossible loss, the courage it must have taken to survive. But Claire *had* survived, smiling above the pain, loving beyond the loss, making the happiest life she could for her baby girl.

And as for the agoraphobia Claire had overcome, when she had to, for Paige... Far from ashamed of it, Paige had longed for it—the wonder of finding a place so safe she never wanted to leave.

But I've found a place like that now. With Jack.
Paige wanted her mother to know.
Don't die, Mother. Please don't die.

28

Gwen followed the trail of blood from the marble foyer to the pastel haven where, in a different lifetime, the twins and their parents would have lived. And Gwen kept following the crimson drops until she reached the moonglow-and-gardenia bedroom where her parents had loved…and where, this morning, Claire had bled.

And bled.

And bled.

And when she'd lost so much blood that her blood pressure had plummeted, Claire had collapsed. She'd fallen into the pool of her blood.

Gwen saw the imprint of her mother's face, the place on the bloody carpet where Claire had lain. Mother and daughter had almost been twins this morning, their cheeks identically stained.

Gwen sat on the carpet and touched the imprint as if touching her mother's face. The blood was cold—oh, too cold—but wet. Still wet.

And, as she touched, Gwen envisioned the life that might have been. There she was, cantering into her mother's room at dawn. *Good morning, Mommy!* And there was Claire, rising from beneath the rose-petal comforter to greet her. *Good morning, sweetheart! Come give me a hug!*

And Gwen imagined entering this bedroom in the dark of night. *I had a bad dream, Mommy. May I sleep with you?* The rose-petal covers opened in welcome then, and a loving voice assured her frightened daughter, *Of course you may.* But Gwen didn't crawl in. Yet. *I'd better get Paige, too. I don't want her to wake up and be alone.*

Gwen saw the happiness that might have been. *Felt* it. This was her home. Where she belonged. This was where, but for a tragedy on a cliffside highway—followed by confusion induced by anesthesia and grief—she and her twin and her mother would have lived.

The ringing phone intruded into Gwen's reverie, and then became part of it. On the fourth ring, the answering machine on Claire's dressing table picked up—and Baby Girl Forrester heard her mother's voice.

"Hello, hello! I'm here, somewhere, most likely on the phone. You know me and call-waiting! But leave a message, please, and I'll call you back!"

It was a beautiful voice, lilting and soft. It sounded

hopeful, Gwen thought. And so welcoming. As if every caller might be Claire's long-lost daughter, found at last.

She thought about her mother's *You know me and call-waiting!* That meant, surely, that Claire Forrester's friends knew what Gwen St. James's friends knew: She didn't *have* call-waiting. Never would. Gwen couldn't imagine, and obviously neither could Claire, severing a conversation with one friend in favor of beginning one with another.

The friend who was calling Claire now was named Joanne. Her message began promptly after the beep. "The grandkids will be in town next week and the girls are already wondering when they'll get to see Aunt Claire. I realize you're under construction, but...call me. And if it's simply too much of a nuisance, just tell me. Be honest! Talk to you soon."

When Joanne's message ended, Gwen rose from the bloodied carpet and walked to the dressing table where the answering machine—and its hidden treasure, Claire's voice—had become silent.

A rapidly blinking green light signaled there were more messages, treasures in themselves, for the messages from Claire's friends gave insight into Claire.

The other three messages had been left that morning, by callers blissfully unaware of the real reason Claire wasn't answering her phone.

The first was left at 7:15, when Dr. Cole Ransom was inserting a second central line into Claire's chest.

"Hey, Mrs. F! It's Ron-the-grocer. I'm looking at an

order on my computer screen. It says it's from you, posted at 9:08 last night, but I just wanted to double-check the quantities ordered. Either my computer program is engaged in wishful thinking or you've started baking for an army. Give me a call, and I'll send the correct amounts over pronto."

At 7:30, when the E.R. nurse was offering the blood-drenched Stuart Dawson a clean change of clothes, an elegant British-accented voice said, "Hello, Claire? It's Juliana Whitaker. Thank you so much for your gracious offer to host next spring's Pearl Moon fashion show at your splendid home. I accept! Garrett and I will be in San Francisco next week, and I'll talk to you then. Thank you, *thank you.*"

At 7:40, when Gwen was fleeing from the medical center, the first sound recorded after the beep was the gasping end of a sob. "It's Nell. Your friendly basket case. You were right, Claire. He *is* still seeing her. You tried to tell me. To *prepare* me. And you did. Really! I'm far better than I sound. But when you have a moment, could you call me?"

After listening to the messages, Gwen replayed Claire's greeting. And replayed it. And replayed it. And heard its echoes of hope and welcome long after she began to wander to other places in the bedroom.

It was a slow exploration, and a reverent one. And a survey, only, of what Claire had left in plain sight.

Which included her wedding band. The golden circle—simple and traditional—lay on the nightstand beside a telephone. The gold was engraved—simply, traditionally—with her parents' initials and their January twenty-eighth wedding date thirty-one years ago.

Her parents. Alan and Claire.

Neither of whom Gwen resembled in any way. Although she wanted to. Desperately. Here, in this place that felt like home, and where she felt like a daughter, she wanted *proof* that she was…and permission to feel as she did.

A mother-daughter aversion to call-waiting wouldn't suffice. And no matter how many times she listened to the lilting voice on the answering machine, Gwen couldn't detect the slightest resemblance to her own.

Spotting a computer in an alcove, Gwen went to it— with the hope, perhaps, of discovering a screen-saver identical to hers.

In fact, the Blue Mountain Arts screen-saver wasn't one she'd ever seen. But she loved it. Instantly. Would have chosen it, too.

A lamb hopped, floated, across a meadow of flowers beneath a sky of fleecy clouds. Then, when its cavorting journey was through, more images of spring appeared. Spring and Easter, for polka-dot eggs tumbled gaily onto the screen, followed by bunnies. Then the lamb's dance began anew.

You are my mother. You have to be.

But the blissful screen-saver wasn't proof. Neither

were the tidy stacks of articles on the desktop nearby—although, like Gwen's own tidy stacks of computer-desk articles, the subject matter was medical.

Indeed, many of the articles had been downloaded from the same Web sites visited by Gwen. WebMD. PublicMed. The topics Claire had researched were not, however, the ones Gwen had: renal failure, hemodialysis, transplantation or HLA. Claire *would* have sought that knowledge, however, would have scoured the Internet night and day, if she'd known Paige's kidneys had failed.

But Claire hadn't known, so she'd searched instead for information about herself—the demons that haunted her, and made her bleed: postpartum psychosis, repressed memories, agoraphobia, panic attacks, peptic ulcer disease.

It was a search for answers. Clearly.

A tormenting search, perhaps, for her misplaced child.

Yet, there were no articles on port-wine stains. No articles on birthmarks at all. And no treatises on the wonders of laser surgery.

The artist-mother *would* have remembered her first-born daughter's blemish. Even if she'd forgotten where she'd left that baby girl. And she'd have cared so much about the fate of the baby with the unfortunate blemish that instead of simple stacks of paper she'd have stored the data within the computer itself.

Or so Gwen told herself.

There might be links on her computer desktop. To

laser-surgery sites, and more: to the Web sites one visited in search of missing and misplaced loved ones. Sites where a mother could post everything she could recall about the night she'd given away her precious baby girl—in the hope that someone, perhaps the lost and searching girl herself, would help her bring her daughter home.

Might there be such desktop links? There *would* be, Gwen's racing heart promised as her trembling fingers hovered over the computer's mouse. And she'd have her proof.

Gwen touched the mouse. The frolicking lamb froze midleap, then disappeared.

And, an instant later, Gwen St. James saw her mother's computer desktop—and the wallpaper Claire had chosen to adorn it.

29

Jack pressed the intercom button labeled *Helen Grace, Apartment 522*. Then, in the event that she was inclined to view the image of her visitor on a closed-circuit TV, he looked directly into the camera positioned above the apartment building's main door.

Helen might be in hiding. But Jack was not. He wanted her to know that she'd been found, and that he wasn't going anywhere until they'd talked.

Maybe his expression communicated just that.

The door buzzed and Jack was in.

Helen's apartment was near the elevator. Its door was open wide.

And there she was. Helen Grace. The stranger with whom Jack had created a baby. Because of this woman, because of Beth, because he believed it was right, Jack had said goodbye to the girl in the drama library who'd captured his heart.

In Jack's memory, the stranger he'd married—the woman who'd screamed at his baby girl—was a monster. His memory had made her a monster.

But the Helen who stood before him was the Helen he'd met at the wedding. Delicate. Ethereal. And looking older, now, than her thirty-four years. Her eyes looked old. Weary.

But not wary, Jack realized. And, he realized, she *had* been wary before. Wary…and afraid.

Not anymore.

This new Helen, still a stranger, was a little defiant, and very determined.

"Hello, Jack."

"Helen."

"Come in."

He did. It was a studio apartment. The otherworldly musician's worldly possessions all in one room. There weren't many possessions, but there was a sense of crowding nonetheless. The forsaken harp, cloaked in canvas, commanded the space.

There wasn't a piano in the piano teacher's small apartment. Helen gave her lessons, Jack supposed, in her students' homes.

"So," she said. "You noticed me, after all."

"Noticed you where?"

"At Saturday's swim meet. Even with my very short

and much darker hair, wearing a baseball cap and glasses and sitting in the middle of a row of swimmers' parents."

"You were at the swim meet." Jack's words were measured. His tone was harsh. "Why?"

"Why do you think?"

"You don't want to know what I think."

"I'm *not* stalking her, Jack! And," Helen added quietly, "I'm not stalking you."

"You just *happened* to be at the swim meet?"

"I just happened to *decide* to be there."

"Just like you happened to decide to move to San Francisco and live within blocks of our home and Beth's school."

"I *want* to live here."

"Because of Beth."

"Yes, because of Beth! *Of course*. Seeing Beth, being able to see her, is the reason I'm here. That's not a secret. My being here isn't a secret. I'm sure you had no trouble finding me once you chose to look."

"I hadn't imagined I'd ever need to look."

"To be on the lookout, you mean. You think I should've consulted with you first."

"It would have been nice."

"For you, Jack."

"And for Beth."

"I would *never* do anything to hurt Beth. You don't believe that, do you? Can't believe it—given what I did."

"I have a hard time believing you'd want to see her at all."

"Can I tell you, Jack? Will you listen? And try to hear?"

"I'll try."

"Will you sit, please?"

The small apartment had two chairs. And the sofa bed where Helen slept.

Jack sat in one of the chairs.

But Helen remained standing. She needed to be taller than he was, as tall as she could possibly be, as she explained to the father of her daughter why she'd always felt so small.

"As you might recall, I was the oldest of five children. We had very little money. My parents worked nights. They made more money that way. But even then, there was never enough. What my parents didn't spend on drugs, they spent *while* on drugs. It was my responsibility to watch the younger children when they were stoned, and I was also supposed to keep the little ones quiet, virtually silent, during the daylight hours when my parents slept. But...I wasn't any good at it. Wasn't any good *with them*. I couldn't find ways to keep them happy, or even distracted, and when they cried, I couldn't comfort them. As a result, we were punished, all of us, even the babies."

"Punished," Jack repeated softly. But he churned with fury. "Hit?"

"Hit. Beaten." *Screamed at, sworn at, starved.* "It was my fault. I was to blame. And if I'd been the only one who was punished... But I wasn't, and the others were so young. They didn't understand, and their confusion made them cry all the more, and I couldn't make them stop."

"No matter how much you pleaded with them."

"Yes. How do you know?"

"You were pleading with Beth that day, begging her to be quiet."

"That day." Helen drew a breath, as if the gulp of air might make her taller. More buoyant. But no amount of air could lighten the leaden memories. Nothing could. Her delicate frame seemed crushed beneath the weight. "She started crying about twenty minutes after you left. I went to her right away, and touched her, and tried to speak to her in the calming way you did. But my touch was wrong, *awkward,* and she sensed my fear, I think, heard fear not comfort in my voice. It made her afraid, too. Anxious and confused. Her crying became more shrill, and filled with panic, just as my brothers' and sisters' crying did. They loathe me, by the way. For failing to prevent the abuse. And they've all gone on to repeat the cycle of violence with their own children."

"But you didn't."

"Didn't I? I screamed at her, Jack. I can't forgive myself for that, nor do I expect you to. Or her. I'm telling you about my childhood so you'll understand the reason I did what I did. But what happened to me as a girl is not, and never could be, an *excuse.*"

The reason I did what I did. Helen spoke of her wrongdoing as the most vile of crimes. But what, Jack reflected, had the damaged young mother actually done? She'd tried to comfort her crying daughter. Her soothing touch had caused distress, at which point she'd retreated to the farthest corner of the room, cowered there and screamed at her own demons, not her baby girl.

"I should've given you another chance."

"I didn't want another chance, Jack. And even if I had, you shouldn't—and I think wouldn't—have given me one. You had to protect our daughter. And it would've been impossible, then, for me to assure you that I'd never hurt Beth the way my parents hurt me. That was my greatest fear, of course. That I'd lash out as they had. I didn't *want* to. I'd promised myself I never would. But the sound of Beth's crying, of any baby's crying, triggered such chaos inside me, I felt out of control. I *wouldn't* have hurt her. I can say that with absolute certainty now."

"What would you have done?"

"Hurt myself."

Jack looked at the forsaken harp and realized that as long as the harp remained silent, the apartment would, too. Helen had no radio. No television. No state-of-the-art stereo system and DVD.

Just silence. And the shrouded harp. And a book, a romance novel, beside the sofa.

"Which you have anyway," he murmured.

"No, Jack, I've saved myself."

"By quitting the concert tour?"

"Yes. And moving to San Francisco. And teaching piano. And...seeing Beth."

"From up here?"

"Since September, yes. Before that, I lived about four miles away."

"And saw her..."

"At piano recitals. She has such a feel for the music. And I've attended pageants at the academy, the ones that are open to the public. And Dina's dance competitions. And Larry's swim meets."

"How do you know about Larry and Dina?"

"I ordered copies of the school yearbooks. Long before I even moved to the city. I just wanted to see pictures of Beth. Then, when I got here and saw her, I also saw her friends."

"And me."

"And you. Except for watching Beth from this window, five floors up, there's never been a time I've seen her that you haven't been there, too."

"But there could've been."

"But there *hasn't*. I decided there *shouldn't* be."

"What I meant, Helen, is that it was possible. You could've met her, spoken to her...harmed her."

"But..."

"You didn't," Jack said. *And never would?* Yes, he decided. She would—still—hurt herself rather than hurt Beth. "What about meeting her? Getting to know her? Have you given that any thought?"

"All the time, and always with the same conclusion. It won't happen, and shouldn't. It would be selfish on my part and totally unfair to her."

"What if she wanted to meet you?"

The eyes, sad and weary, became bright with hope. Then darkened, sadder, wearier, than before. "Meet the mother who screamed at her and walked out on her without a backward glance?"

"She doesn't know you screamed at her, Helen. And as for walking out on her without a backward glance— if I'd told her that, it would've been untrue."

"What *have* you told her?"

"Your first name. How we met. That you're a musician, like she is, and play the harp. And that when it didn't work out for us to be a family, I was the lucky one because she stayed with me."

"So she doesn't hate me."

"No."

"Thank you," Helen whispered.

"What I told her was for her, not for you."

"I know. But thank you, anyway."

"You give piano lessons to children?" he asked.

"To anyone who wants them. Mostly children. As young as four. And I'm fine with them, Jack. I know I'm not going to snap. I've worked through that. I'm calm. Content. It feels right for me to be here." Helen drew a breath. "But it feels very wrong, doesn't it, to you?"

"Less wrong than it felt on the way over. But...not entirely right."

"I'll leave, Jack. If you want me to. I don't want you to worry that I *will* do any of the things I've told you I

won't. Like meeting her. Talking to her. Even being somewhere she is and you're not. I know I can trust myself.
Still, there's no reason in the world that *you* should trust
me. But will you do me a favor before deciding?"

"What favor?"

"Discuss it with the woman you were with at the
swim meet."

"Do you know who she is?"

"No. And I have no plans to find out."

"Why do you want me to discuss it with her?"

"Because it's obvious what she means to you, and what
you mean to her. If she thinks I should leave, I will."

30

"Mrs. Forrester's still in surgery," Alice told Jack when he called. "Which everyone, I gather, thinks is a good sign. Shall I connect you to Paige?"

"Please."

Paige was on the line within seconds. "Hi. How did it go?"

"Surprisingly well," Jack admitted. "Very smart of you, Doctor, to insist that I go."

"I'm inferring you don't need to speak with Stuart about legal options, then?"

"Nope. I don't. In fact, I'm going to cancel this afternoon's meeting with the school principal. So," he said gently. "Your mother's still in surgery."

"And Cole's already begun involving all the relevant

consultants, the specialists who'll be caring for her once she's transferred to the surgical ICU."

"That sounds promising."

"It does, Jack. It *is*."

He heard the emotion in her voice. The soft worry. The quiet prayer. "Are you okay?"

"Wonderful...and weepy."

Jack heard her tears, too. And a decisive—tear-halting—sniffle. Then silence. As if the sniffle hadn't stopped the flow of tears at all. "It's all right to cry, you know."

She gave a watery laugh. "It's going to have to be."

"It is, Paige."

"But..." She sniffed again. Laughed. "I'm determined to get this out. I'm so grateful. To you and Stuart. For finding her and getting her here so quickly. You saved her life, Jack. You saved my mother's life." *And mine.*

"Paige, I..." He faltered. Emotional, too. "I think Cole played a fairly major role in that."

"Only because you and Stuart gave him the chance to." There was a smile in her voice now. The tears were gone—for the moment. Jack tucked his own emotion away. "Cole won't be handling her care in the surgical ICU?"

"The surgical aspects, yes. And I have no doubt the physicians he's consulted will keep him up-to-date on all significant aspects of her medical care. But he won't be calling the shots on the minute-by-minute management she'll need. Cole never does with any of his patients in the ICU. It would be impossible to do it well, and be operating, too."

"So it's good that he's brought in the consultants?"

"Oh, yes. It's the way it should be. Best all around. Where are you?"

"Parked on a side street around the corner from Helen's. That's a key feature of the careful driving I was telling you about. Cell-phone calls made only from parked cars. I'm going to make a couple more calls, then come to you."

"Good."

Jack heard her relief, and he knew she wished he was already there—an emotion she'd been trying valiantly to hide. "Paige?"

"Yes?"

"It's okay to miss me."

Her soft laugh was even more relieved. "Is that right?"

"Absolutely."

"Then I do."

"I do, too. And I love you, Paige."

"Me, too..."

As eager as he was to be with Paige, Jack remained safely parked while he called his work-crew foreman, Kyle. The two had spoken earlier, while Paige was still asleep in the HDU, and Jack had issued very specific instructions at that time.

Kyle was to remove the patch of bloodstained carpet from Claire's bedroom and cover the divot he created with one of the many area rugs found elsewhere in the mansion.

The instructions, when issued, had been urgent. Jack had believed, then, that Claire wouldn't survive. It seemed likely that Paige and others would congregate in mourning at the Forrester family home.

The promising report from Paige made the task a little less urgent. Still, Jack assumed it had long since been done. He expected no less from Kyle and his crew.

But, Kyle informed him, the pool of blood remained fully visible.

"Why haven't you removed it?"

"Because we can't. Gwen won't let us."

"Gwen?"

"Paige's friend."

"And she won't *let* you remove the stain?"

"No. Or even let us come close. It's like she's guarding the bedroom. Nothing's to be disturbed, she says, until Mrs. Forrester's out of surgery. Gwen's amazingly beautiful, by the way," Kyle added. "Too bad she's so strange."

Jack arrived at Paige's office just as Cole was telling Paige, Stuart and Mariel that Claire was out of the operating room and getting settled into the SICU.

"Thank you," Paige said.

Cole shook his head. "Thank your mother, Paige. She's a fighter."

"Yes. She is. And she's going to have to keep fighting, isn't she?"

"For a while, I'm afraid."

"What did you find?"

"An ulcer," Cole said. "It looked benign, but we did a frozen section, anyway. It's an ulcer. Was an ulcer."

"A large ulcer?"

"Fairly large, Paige. She'd probably had it awhile. It penetrated as well as bled. We did a copious lavage of her peritoneal cavity, and she's on broad-spectrum antimicrobials, of course, and I've left in a number of Penrose drains. But I can't guarantee there aren't residual pockets of gastric contamination that will need to be surgically drained. That would be minor surgery, though, compared to today. I also had to resect pancreatic tissue. There were necrotic areas I didn't feel comfortable leaving behind. So far, her pancreatic function seems unfazed. Her serum glucose hasn't budged. But I've asked endocrine to keep an eye on that for the next several days."

"And her lungs?" Paige asked. "One of the 8-North nurses said she'd heard pulmonary paged to the O.R."

"She may have aspirated a little blood." Cole didn't elaborate on how or when blood could have gotten into Claire's lungs. It wasn't something he *would* elaborate on—unless specifically asked—for Stuart, Mariel or Jack. And it wasn't something he needed to elaborate on for Paige. The blood had undoubtedly been aspirated when Claire was vomiting even as she was losing so much blood that she was losing consciousness. Her gag reflex vanished when her consciousness did, leaving her airway unprotected. "The infiltrates haven't increased much with hydration, and her blood gasses are pretty good, so that may not become an issue. No matter what, she'll need to remain intubated overnight."

"May we see her?" Stuart asked.

"Of course. It'll take the nursing staff a little while to get her situated. But after they have...yes. Certainly."

"And speak to her?" Mariel wondered.

Cole hesitated. "Eventually. But as much as you'd like to let her know you're there, and offer reassurance, I'd prefer you wait until there's an indication that she's beginning to awaken on her own. She's sleeping deeply now, with the anesthetic still on board, and she's very calm. The less energy she has to expend, the more strength she'll have for her recovery."

Cole paused again, this time waiting for more questions...and disinclined to volunteer further on the consultants he had—and had not—called. There was one specialist in particular whose expertise was not required: the nephrologist who treated Paige. Unlike her daughter's kidneys, Claire Forrester's were entirely normal in every way. A transplant surgeon's dream.

When no questions were forthcoming, Cole posed one of his own to Paige. "Where's Gwen?"

"Gwen?" she echoed. "I have no idea. There's no reason she'd be here."

"But she was here," Stuart said. "She and I were together in the E.R. waiting area. When the nurse suggested we wait in your office, Gwen said she'd head on up while I changed. When I didn't see her, I assumed she'd found another place to wait."

"But why," Paige asked, "would Gwen have been in the E.R. in the first place?"

"Because of me," Cole replied. "I had the triage nurse call her. We couldn't find you and I thought Gwen might know where you were."

"I can't imagine why."

"My impression was that the two of you are very close."

"Oh. Well...I did give you that impression on Saturday. The truth is, Gwen and I had just met. Gwen knows Louise's granddaughter from the TV station and was nice enough to do the makeup for Louise."

"But you're not friends?"

"I *like* Gwen. A lot. And it's fine that she was here, Cole, and thoughtful of you to call her. It's just that we don't really know each other very well."

"Maybe someone should tell that to Gwen," Mariel said. "She walked into the mansion as if she belonged there."

"I told her she should drop by anytime. Like so many people do."

"But this *morning,* Paige? When Claire was already in the operating room? Which Gwen knew, by the way. She's the one who told *me.*"

"I don't know why she was there today," Paige said. "But—"

"I can think of some reasons," Mariel interjected. "Millions of them. Rosalind's jewels. A wall-safe full of cash. The two Chagalls. The three Degas. The—"

"Gwen St. James is *not* a thief!"

"How do you know that, Paige? You've just said you scarcely know her."

"Yes, but…she's not a thief. *That* I know. I'm sure there's a very logical reason she was there."

"Such as?"

It was Stuart who replied. "Gwen did overhear Cole asking me about Claire's agoraphobia."

"That's it, then," Paige said. "And it's exactly the kind of *kind* thing Gwen would do. Knowing that Mother might feel anxious when she awakens, she decided to bring in some personal items from home. It's something *I* should have thought to do. Gwen's probably in the SICU, giving the nurses those items right now. I think I'll go see." She smiled at Jack. "Maybe we all should. It's time, I think. She should be settled in by now."

"Why don't you and Mariel go on ahead?"

"Jack?"

His dark green eyes glittered immediate reassurance to the suddenly worried Paige. He'd miss her—desperately. But… "There's something I'd like to discuss with Stuart. And, if it's convenient, also with Cole. It's not a big thing. Just a little man-to-man advice."

Once Paige and Mariel were gone, Jack quietly closed Paige's office door.

"Gwen, whoever Gwen actually is, was at the mansion when I checked with my foreman twenty minutes ago."

"Twenty minutes," Stuart echoed as he glanced at his watch. "And Mariel must have seen her there shortly before eight. That's almost four hours ago. She must've left and come back."

"No," Jack said. "She's been there all this time. In Claire's bedroom, apparently. Guarding it, my foreman says, and preventing the crew from removing the blood-stained carpet."

"We need to talk to her." Stuart looked from Jack, who nodded, to Cole. "How well do you know her?"

"Not very." *Just enough to want her in my life for the rest of my life.* "But I'd like to go with you."

"Good."

"I want to check on Claire first."

"We'll wait, Cole. For as long as you need."

The man who'd spent the past two decades on the lookout for lies knew exactly what he needed: to comprehend how he, of all people, could have been so hopelessly misled by Gweneth Angelica St. James.

It wasn't so incomprehensible, of course. Not if he admitted the truth—that he, Cole Ransom, had been hopelessly seduced.

31

Like a castaway on the shore of a bloodred sea, she knelt on the carpet beside the stain she'd forbidden the workmen to remove. With her right hand, she touched the stain, gentle caresses of love. Her other hand, the left, lay clenched and motionless in her lap.

All three men standing in the bedroom doorway could see her hands. But none of them could see her face. It was hidden beneath her wind-tangled hair.

Jack and Stuart wondered—and it saddened them— if the woman huddled before them had gone quite mad. And, had Cole not given a silent signal for them to wait where they were, both would have followed the impulse to approach and to help.

But it was Cole who went to her, who knelt beside her. "Gwen?"

His voice startled her. The room had been silent for so long. Jack's crew had left her alone hours ago. As, hours ago, the phone had ceased to trill.

The news of what had happened to Claire Forrester had spread, a wildfire of sorrow, from one friend to the next.

There'd been just one disbelieving call. Hours ago. *Pick up the phone, Claire! Oh, don't let it be true. Pick up! Please.*

Then silence.

And now this voice. Kind. Gentle.

And caring *so much*.

But this voice, this man, this surgeon wouldn't be here unless, today, even his magic hadn't been enough.

Gwen looked up from port-wine blood to worried gray eyes.

"Oh, no, Cole. *No.* But it's not—"

"She's alive, Gwen."

"—your fault! You did everything... Alive?"

For a stunned moment, Cole could only nod. Despite her own grief, her own fear, she'd swiftly, even urgently, whispered the reassurance to him. Not his fault. He'd done everything he could. She trusted him. Believed in him. "Alive."

"But you're here."

Where I belong. With you. "That's because she's in the ICU, under the care of the best medical specialists I've ever known—all of whom will let me know if there's even the slightest change."

"Did Jack find Paige?"

"Yes. She's with her mother now."

"Oh, good," she whispered. "Cole?"

"Gwen?"

"Thank you."

He smiled at her tear-streaked face. "You're welcome."

So very welcome, Gwen St. James, whoever you are. But Cole knew who she was, knew the only thing that mattered. She was the woman by whom he'd been hopelessly seduced...and with whom he'd fallen hopelessly in love.

And who, for some reason had been sitting beside the pool of blood for hours now, one hand clenched, the other caressing.

Cole moved one of his own hands then, a slow-motion offering of what could be, if she wished, the beginning of their forever. It was a courtly offer, a gentleman wondering, with upturned palm, if the lady in question would care to dance.

She needed only to lift her caressing hand from the bloody sea.

Dance with me. Cole wasn't at all certain she would. She stared at his hand, as if confused by it and believing that—any moment now—the mirage would disappear.

But the surgeon's hand, the lover's hand, remained where it was, steady and strong, even when her trembling hand, painted red at the fingertips, drew near. And then, finally, her hand found its home, her home, in his.

"Hi," he whispered.

"Hi."

"I was thinking we could talk. That was part of the plan, wasn't it, for today?"

"Yes. *Oh*."

"Oh?"

"We were going to leave at seven this morning. *Seven* instead of eight. But you thought I sounded tired, and should try to get a little more sleep. If we'd left at seven, though, if *you'd* left at seven…"

"I'm not the only surgeon on the planet." Cole's remark was casual. Her bright blue eyes were not. They begged, ferociously, to disagree. She was ferocious, his Gwen. And fragile. And exhausted from this morning's still mysterious vigil beside Claire Forrester's blood. "Did you sleep?"

"No. Not really."

"Neither did I. I was too restless to begin our day together."

"I was, too."

"I still am."

"But we can't…you can't…shouldn't you stay close to the hospital?"

"I am close, Gwen. The mansion is close." *We can begin our day together, our life together, right here, right now.* Cole's first choice, for her, would be to find a bed, tuck her in and let her sleep—if she would. Or could. A glance at the bloodstained fingers he held, and the knotted ones he didn't, convinced him she couldn't. He reached for her clenched fist, not to take but to touch, and, at his touch, she opened her fingers and revealed the prize clutched within. She wasn't mad, Cole believed, her odd behavior this morning notwithstanding. Nor was she the jewel-thief Mariel had proclaimed her to be...despite the band of gold that shimmered in her palm. "What's this?"

"My mother's wedding ring."

Not mad, Cole told himself. And if she was? He was beginning his life with her, right here, right now. "Oh?"

"She left it over there. On her nightstand."

"I see. And you found it."

"Yes. And I held it for her, for luck, during her surgery. She'll want it now. Could you take it to her?"

"Sure," Cole said softly. "But Gwen?"

"Yes?"

"Isn't this Claire Forrester's wedding ring?"

Cole expected confusion. Prepared himself for madness. He got clear blue eyes and a beautiful smile. "She's my mother, Cole. That's what I was planning to tell you today. She's my mother, and Paige is my sister. My twin."

"Cole? Gwen?" Stuart asked from the doorway.

"Oh! I didn't realize... You heard?"

"Yes. But I'd like to hear more, Gwen, if you'll tell me."

"I would, too. I'm Jack."

"Beth's father," Gwen said. "She has your eyes."

"Beth's father."

"And Paige's...friend." *The man my twin sister loves.*

Jack's expression made Gwen wonder if he'd read her

silent thought. The gentleness of his voice confirmed it. "And Paige's...friend."

"You don't have to tell us more, Gwen." The high-powered Forrester family attorney sounded distinctly unlawyerlike. As he'd been in the E.R., he was simply the man who cared deeply about Claire. And about Paige. And who seemed, at this moment, to care about her.

"I'd like to tell you. Both of you. Please come in."

They sat, too, on the carpet. And listened without interruption to what Gwen knew about the first thirty-four hours of her life, from her birth at the crash site to the stormy night when the Iowa tourist placed her in Sister Mary Catherine's loving arms.

"I've only recently learned all of this. I met Paige *before* I knew. I have the investigator's report, if you'd like to see it, and the documents he found. And I'm sure you'll want DNA confirmation. That's fine with me. It's the logical thing to do. But," Gwen said, "I *know* what I've told you is true."

I don't give a damn about DNA. Stuart's unlawyerly reaction was prompted by Gwen's wholly unsubstantiated story—which he believed one hundred percent. "How, Gwen? How do you know?"

"I'll show you."

Gwen led the way to the alcove where, on the monitor, the lamb cavorted once again. This time, instead of suspending its blissful dance in midleap, she waited for its final hop off the screen.

Then she touched the mouse.

Claire MacKenzie Forrester's desktop wallpaper was a family-photo Christmas card. *Season's Greetings from Sarah's Orchard.* The Yuletide cheer, in green script, was inscribed on the right-hand margin. And below, in red, *The MacKenzies, Christmas, 1970.*

There were nine of them, MacKenzies all, and all except one—the teenaged Claire—bore a striking resemblance to Gwen St. James.

Claire's sisters especially. Any one of them, all three of them, could have been Gwen's twin.

"The original is there," Gwen murmured. "In the scanner."

No one moved to retrieve it. The on-screen image provided ample proof of Gwen's pedigree. It was, in fact, an elegant—and dazzling—visual demonstration of DNA.

"I don't understand." Stuart's statement, troubled and soft, was underscored by the way he looked at Gwen, as a father might...the kind of father who couldn't imagine abandoning any child, much less his own...and who, when confronted with proof that such an abandonment had occurred, accepted the revelation with disbelieving pain.

"But I *do,*" Claire's abandoned daughter told him. "It's really quite understandable when you think of what it must've been like for her, what she was going through. Loss. Grief. Worry. Fear. Those are difficult emotions at any time, but when they're compounded by anesthetic-induced confusion and her own precarious physical health… Still, despite all that, she made the journey to the hospital in Carmel—to get me and bring me back to Monterey. I'm sure that was what she intended to do. But when she saw my birthmark it was simply too much to deal with, on top of everything else. One sadness too many. She panicked, I suppose, and in that emotional frenzy had no idea what she was doing, and no concept of what it would mean…"

Gwen's impassioned plea for clemency for her mother faltered as the unconvinced Stuart Dawson shook his head. "If you saw the birthmark, you'd understand. Why don't I show it to you?"

"I don't need to see the birthmark, Gwen." *And I will never understand.* "I take it Paige doesn't know any of this?"

"No. She doesn't know. And I'd decided she never would. But that was when I believed I'd been given away with, I don't know, malice aforethought?"

"Meaning Claire knew what she was doing."

"Yes. And remembered where she'd left me, and could have returned for me if she'd wanted to. I didn't think those were truths about her mother that Paige needed to know."

"But you feel differently now."

"Well, yes. If she was disoriented and so distraught that she really had no idea—but you're not buying that, are you? You think Claire Forrester simply didn't want her unsightly daughter and disposed of her accordingly." Hours ago, in the E.R., Stuart Dawson's handsome face had been smeared with her mother's blood. The face was blood-free now, but as ravaged as before. What had tormented him then was the specter that Claire—whom he loved?—might die. And what was torturing him now, what was killing him, was that the woman he loved could have done such a thing to her baby girl. "That *is* what you think."

"I don't know what I think, Gwen." The attorney had the facts before him, including an additional incriminating bit of evidence Gwen didn't know: Claire's own confession of a blurred memory of searching in the rain. The latter would have supported Gwen's hypothesis, Gwen's *hope,* that Claire's irrational act had a plausible explanation.

So why couldn't he embrace that understandable, even forgivable, scenario?

Because, sane or psychotic, abandoning her daughter was not something Stuart's heart would permit him to believe Claire Forrester could *ever* do.

32

"We won't tell Paige then," Gwen said. "Not today, and maybe never."

"That's not very fair," Stuart replied, "to you."

"But it's fine. Really. *I'm* fine."

"*That*," Gwen's uncle Stuart said gently, "I can see."

"And you'll find out, won't you? The truth of what happened that night?" *Whether Claire discarded her bloody-cheeked infant with the ice-cold calculation that you, and Sister Mary Catherine, seem to believe?* "You'll talk to..."

"Your mother."

"My mother." The words didn't sound, didn't feel, as wondrous as before. "Once she's well enough to talk."

"I will, Gwen. I promise. And I'll also speak with Mariel. She was with Claire for those first two days in Monterey."

"And you weren't?"

"No. I didn't arrive until the morning of the thirtieth." *Twelve hours after you'd been given away.* And what was it Claire had told him about her blurred memory? That whatever it was had happened on the first or second night, before he'd made it out of snowbound O'Hare. She knew that, she'd told him, because she was alone in the memory...and she wouldn't have been alone if he'd been there. *Oh, Claire, this truth will hurt you...perhaps destroy you.* This truth. "I'll find out, Gwen."

"Thank—"

Gwen's reply, and then her heart, stopped as Cole's pager began to beep.

"Every consultant is going to let me know everything he or she thinks," Cole explained, with measured calm, as he walked toward the nightstand phone. He dialed the direct number indicated on his pager, a back-line to the nurses' station in the ICU. "Jen. Cole. I was...Okay... Yes, I do want to know...Good. Good...38?...I agree. And she's still asleep?... Great...Oh?...I'll want to take a look at that. I'll be there in fifteen or twenty minutes."

Cole replaced the receiver. "She's fine. Stable."

"But there's something you need to take a look at."

"Something I *want* to take a look at." Cole smiled gently at a worried Gwen. "One of many routine post-op studies I'll want to see throughout the afternoon. She *is* fine. I would tell you if she wasn't."

They left, together, five minutes later. All four of them. Gwen could have remained at the mansion. But it was time, she said quietly, to go to her Belvedere Court home.

And, with smiling apologies to Kyle, she announced that she was relinquishing her post and he should feel free to remove the carpet at any time.

It was a walk, not a dash, toward the medical center.

The rain was gone, swept away by the wind.

And in the calm after the storm, the bay was a sapphire mirror of the sky.

An unseasonably balmy November afternoon.

"You're sure you're all right with this?" Stuart asked Gwen when they reached the place where she and the men would part.

"Positive. I have no business being in the ICU. Gwen St. James doesn't. My presence would only be confusing to Paige."

"But your mother's there, too."

"Yes. And I have to admit I imagined being at her bedside and saying reassuring things her subconscious mind might somehow hear. *But,*" Gwen said, "that was when I believed without question that she needed to be reassured."

"You're more than a little amazing," Stuart said. *You are, so truly, Claire's daughter.*

Gwen shook her head. "No. Oh! I should give you her

wedding ring. Here. I guess she takes it off at night and hadn't yet put it on this morning."

It was a logical guess. But Stuart knew it was a wrong one. Since Alan had placed the wedding band on her finger, Claire had never taken it off.

Until last night...when she'd needed to say things to him. Urgently. She'd been thinking about him, she'd said. Thinking about *them*. And, had it not been for a gasp of silence, a hush of pain, Claire would have told him about her dream.

Stuart pocketed Claire's wedding band, and he and Jack crossed the street.

Cole would be along shortly, after a few more words with Gwen—who'd already been sufficiently adamant about walking the final two blocks alone that Cole didn't raise the issue of escorting her again.

Instead he smiled at her exhausted, sunlit face. "Hi."

"Hi."

"Do you think you can sleep?"

"Now?"

"Now. While your mother's sleeping and I'm keeping an eye on her, and her lab results, throughout the afternoon."

"The consultants will be doing that, won't they?"

"They'd better be. But I'll be there, too, at least until early this evening and after your nap. At which point, if you're interested, I'd like to be with you."

"I'm interested."

"Good." Cole touched her cheek, the light layer of camouflage she wore. "Call me when you're awake."

"I will."

Thanks to the fund-raising efforts of Claire Forrester, Pacific Heights Medical Center's Surgical Intensive Care Unit was not only state-of-the-art but avant-garde. Its most recent remodeling, completed three years ago, included a redesign of the patients' rooms.

Each critically ill patient had, in essence, a two-room suite. A bedroom and a parlor. The latter, a private waiting area for authorized guests, included an oversize sofa, suitable for sleeping, as well as an assortment of chairs.

The antechamber was not a viewing area. The wall between the two rooms was plaster, not glass. That design detail, as all design details, had been specified by Claire. Modesty was preserved for the patient—and loved ones were spared the discomfort of seeing their beloved displayed like a treasure at a museum—or a corpse waiting to be identified in a morgue.

Claire had not, of course, ever seen the remodeled SICU. She'd merely pored over blueprints and sketches in her home.

Now she was here. And she still hadn't seen it.

Paige was in the bedroom with Claire. Mariel had been there, too. But overwhelmed, it seemed, by the sight of her friend so dramatically transformed, she'd whispered that she was going to sit in the parlor for a while.

Dr. Paige Forrester was accustomed to both critically ill patients and ICUs.

But when it was her critically ill *mother* in such a place...Paige had entered the room with trepidation. And for a frantic moment she'd experienced what all patients' families probably did—the urge to scream *Get up! We're getting you out of here! It's time for you to be you again—not this motionless shell. This isn't you. This can't be you! Enough!*

But Paige hadn't screamed. Or fled.

Instead she'd sat, looked, listened. And heard, from the cardiac monitor, the *blip, blip, blip* of her mother's heart. The measured maternal heartbeats, so steady, so calm, comforted Paige. Made her feel safe.

The gentle heaves and sighs of the ventilator were soothing, too. Claire's motionless body didn't fight the machine that was breathing for her. She surrendered, her body surrendered, to its life-sustaining ebb and flow.

It wasn't long before Paige's breathing came into perfect synchrony with Claire's. And maybe her heartbeat did as well. She didn't check. It didn't matter.

What mattered was that she'd never felt closer to Claire—or more certain that the closeness would endure, would flourish, when her mother awakened.

"Paige?"

Paige looked in the direction of the whisper.

"Mariel!" Paige whispered, too, as she moved swiftly to the hyperventilating woman in the doorway. "What's wrong?"

"Nothing." Mariel backed into the parlor. "Well, I can't really fool you, can I? Your mother's not the only one who gets a little panicky from time to time."

"I'm sorry. I didn't know."

"*I'm* sorry, Paige. But...I have to go. I'm sure that Stuart and Jack will be back soon, and Claire's stable, really, isn't she, and—" Mariel drew a shaky breath. "I *have* to go."

"Of course! But can I get you something first?"

"Valium, you mean? A stiff drink? I'll have both, maybe, *definitely,* once I get home. I just don't do very well in hospitals...."

Especially ICUs, Paige imagined. Not since Mariel had spent those five days and nights watching Alan die and Paige barely survive, all the while worrying about her dear friend Claire.

"I'm sorry, Paige!" she said again.

"Don't be."

Cradling one of Mariel's elbows, Paige guided her out of the SICU and into the same elevator foyer where, on Saturday, Paige had needed to sit down before she fell down.

"You shouldn't drive."

"I won't, Paige. I promise. Not if I'm still like this. But I won't be. The minute I get outside I'll be perfectly fine."

"We'll see."

"No, *we* won't! You stay here, Paige. With Claire."
The elevator door opened, and as if it represented escape from a small, windowless box—instead of entry into one—Mariel stepped aboard. "I feel better already!
Call me...."

33

In Paige's brief absence, a radiology tech had arrived to take a portable abdominal film. She was in the parlor, away from the radiation beams, when Jack and Stuart entered the room.

"You're back," Paige said. "Mission accomplished?"

"I'd say so," Jack replied. "She's stable?"

"Very. They're doing a follow-up abdominal X ray right now."

"And," Jack said softly. "How are you?"

"I'm good." She frowned as her attention was drawn from Jack by a Stuart Dawson she'd never seen. He was quite motionless as he stared at the wall beyond which Claire lay. Motionless but...*agitated,* Paige thought. Churning deep within. "Uncle Stuart? The X ray will only take a few minutes, then it's fine for you to go in."

"Oh. Thank you. But...where's Mariel?"

"She just left. It was upsetting for her to be here. I think she was going home."

Stuart nodded. "May I use your office, Paige? I have a few calls to make."

"Of course you can!"

"Okay. I'll be back."

And with that he was gone.

"What happened, Jack? Where were you?"

"We went to the mansion, Paige. To your mother's bedroom."

"Oh. Where you and Stuart found her. No wonder he's upset. The carpet—"

"Hadn't been removed yet." *Your twin sister wouldn't allow it.*

"But that's what you wanted Stuart's advice about. His agreement that it was the right thing to do. And he insisted on going with you." Jack had also wanted to discuss the issue with Cole. Because he knew, as did anyone who read the newspapers, that an unexplained—or unanticipated—death occurring within twenty-four hours of hospital admission was a coroner's case. Particularly when the patient wasn't under a doctor's care. Jack wanted the carpet removed, and Cole was Claire Forrester's treating physician, so his visual documentation of her blood loss before her arrival at the E.R. would, in all likelihood, placate even the most persnickety of coroners. If it came to that...which it wouldn't.

Paige had heard the slow and steady *blip, blip, blips*. And the ever oh-so-soothing heaves and sighs. "So it wasn't about Helen at all."

"No," Jack said. "It was about your mother. And you." And a secret Jack had pledged to keep from the woman he loved. For now.

"Thank you."

"You're welcome. Or, as I'm trying to convince my daughter not to say, 'No problem.'"

"That *is* the younger generation's new reply to 'thank you,'" Paige murmured. Smiled. "Speaking of said daughter, I'd love to hear about your visit with Helen."

"There's no urgency any longer, Paige. I feel comfortable that she's no danger to Beth. I'll tell you all about it later. It doesn't have to be today."

"Except that..."

"What?"

"I've been sitting beside my mother's bed, feeling closer to her than I ever remember having felt. I'm so hopeful that it's a new beginning for us. I *believe* that it is." Paige's eyes glowed. "I guess I'm just feeling optimistic about mothers and daughters today."

"Then, from Helen's standpoint, this is the ideal time for me to tell you. There's an issue she specifically asked me to discuss with you."

"With me?"

"With you. She saw us at the swim meet—yes, she was there..."

* * *

...and not a stalker, Paige concluded when Jack fin-ished recounting his visit with Helen.

"Just a mother," Paige said, "who wants to be near her daughter."

"And who shouldn't be asked to leave?"

"That's your decision, Jack. Just because Helen wanted you to discuss it with me... Why are you look-ing at me like that?"

"Like what? Like I love you? And would have discussed this with you, no matter what Helen wanted?"

"Pretty much like that." Paige gazed into his glittering green eyes. And there was more. That other part of love. The desire. The wanting.

"Good," he said decisively. "Interestingly enough, I, too, think Helen shouldn't be asked to leave. It turns out I'm feeling a bit optimistic about mothers and daughters myself."

Admittedly, Jack wouldn't have chosen *optimistic* to describe his feelings. But—in the spirit of optimism— he was willing to embrace it. *Appreciative* was the word he would've chosen. Appreciation of the resilience and forgiveness of the mother-daughter bond.

The epiphany had come in Claire's bedroom, when he'd witnessed a forsaken daughter clutching the wed-ding ring of the mother she'd never known. And it had been reinforced by the wonder he heard in Paige's voice when she spoke of her hope for greater closeness with Claire, a new beginning.

Jack Logan no longer feared the harm that his daughter's mother might inflict on her. But he churned with fury when he envisioned the sadness that might be looming for the Forrester twins.

"Hello?" Mariel's breathlessness was primarily the consequence of her race from her hastily unlocked door to her ringing telephone. Though she still had every intention of pouring herself a stiff drink.

"It's Stuart."

"Has something happened?"

"No. But I wanted to ask you about those first two days and nights in the hospital in Monterey."

"Oh, Stuart, *why?* It's bad enough seeing Claire lying in the ICU. More than enough déjà vu." Mariel crossed to her living-room liquor cabinet, pinioned the phone between her chin and her shoulder, and reached for a bottle and a glass. "That sound you hear is me pouring myself a little bourbon."

"Mariel."

"Oh, all right, Stuart! What is it you want to know?"

"How confused was Claire? More so than when I arrived?"

"*Much* more so. She was very confused, Stuart. Disoriented from the anesthetic... Oh, I see, you're wondering if that might be the case when she wakes up this time, as well."

"How did her disorientation manifest itself?"

"The usual way. She'd forget where she was and what had happened, and how to get from the neonatal ICU to the surgical one. She wasn't continually disoriented, though. There were times, most of the time actually, when she was fine. Completely together and in control. The disorientation happened primarily after dark—'sundowning' the doctors called it."

"Did she ever leave the hospital?"

"*Leave?* No. Of course—oh, well, she did wander outside one night. The night before you arrived, as I recall. She got lost between the ICUs, took a wrong turn, a few wrong turns, and was found in the visitors' parking lot."

"Do you know how long she was outside?"

"No. Until you arrived, she and I were almost never together. When I was with Paige, she was with Alan, and vice versa. I do know she was very wet. And cold. You remember the rainstorm. The doctors were pretty concerned. A private duty nurse was brought in to be with her that night. Once you arrived, the special nurse wasn't necessary anymore. You were there with her—and, with each passing day, she became less confused."

"Why didn't you tell me this?"

"Tell you what? You knew she was confused. Her wandering outside was just a symptom of that. There were enough things, more serious things, to tell you about

Alan. I don't understand why you're bringing this up.
Even if she becomes disoriented with the anesthetic
they've given her, we know the prognosis is good. The
confusion goes away. And I just don't think anyone's going
to lose track of her at the medical center. Do you?"

"No."

"So why are you bringing this up?"

"Because, Mariel, she's been having a memory of that
night when she was wandering in the rain. Wondering if
it was real."

"Oh. Well. It was."

"Tell me what happened at the crash site."

"*What?* Stuart. You *know* what happened."

"You're right. Tell me about Claire going into labor."

"There wasn't any warning. She just started to bleed.
Alan couldn't see the bleeding, but he could tell from her
expression that something was happening. She told him
she'd gone into labor, and that she could hear sirens,
which meant the medics were close by, and Alan told her
he loved her, and then blood gushed out of his mouth,
and... I hate you for making me re-live this, you know."

"I know. Just finish it, Mariel."

"Alan lost consciousness, and about a second later
Claire collapsed. I caught her, sort of, enough to break
her fall. The medics got there very soon after. Two of
them carried her up the cliff while several others started
attending to Alan."

"What did you do?"

"I stayed with Alan."

"And the ambulance took Claire to Monterey?"

"Yes. Almost immediately. They carried her up the cliff and then they were gone. *Why?*"

"Because I'd never asked before. And you're right, seeing Claire in the ICU brings back memories of that time. I'm sorry, Mariel. I just needed to know."

Beth and Dina had planned to spend the afternoon at the mansion with Claire. Jack's plan, as the end of the school day neared, was to ask his parents to meet the girls, tell them what had happened and walk them home instead. That way, Jack could remain in the SICU with Paige.

Who *wasn't* alone, as she pointed out. Stuart had returned. And it was clear that Cole wasn't leaving anytime soon—despite the assessment of Claire's progress by even the most dour of his consultants as "spectacularly" good.

Besides, Paige wasn't alone. Her mother was right here. And Paige looked forward to returning to Claire's bedside and listening to her breathe.

"Please go and be with your daughter," she said. "She might need you, Jack. She might have a day's worth of questions about Helen."

"Okay. I'll go."

"Thank you."

Jack grinned. "No problem."

34

"Mrs. Forrester's really going to be fine?"

"Yes, sweetheart," Jack reiterated to his worried Beth. "She really is."

"But what about Paige?"

"What about her, Beth?"

"She really needs to talk to her mom."

"And she will."

Just as Beth would talk to Helen, if she wanted to. Jack hadn't even contemplated that possibility for today. He hadn't been certain he'd make unprovoked mention of Helen at all.

But Jack saw his daughter's worry. What if the unspeakable happened and mother and daughter never had a chance to talk?

"It's such a nice day. Let's sit for a while and talk."

They found a sun-dried patch of grass on Marine View Academy's emerald lawn. Not surprisingly, there was a splendid marine view, too. The maritime vista was toward the west, a panorama of the Pacific, its deep-blue ruffles dappled gold.

"I have an update, if you'd like to hear it."

"An update on Helen?" Dina said enthusiastically.

"That's right." Jack tilted his head toward Beth. "But you don't need to hear it today."

"I'd like to, though. Did you find out where she lives?"

"I did. And something even more important—the reason the three of us weren't able to be a family. I didn't know the reason at the time, and it wouldn't have changed any of the decisions that she and I made. But I think it's something you should know."

"It's bad, isn't it?"

"Bad and good. What I learned—the facts I learned—are bad. But knowing them, understanding what happened, is good."

"What happened?"

"She had an unhappy childhood, I'm afraid. A bad one. Remember what you decided about the reason people hurt each other?"

"Because they hurt?"

"Yes. Because they hurt or have been hurt."

"But she never hurt *me*."

"No. That's right, sweetheart. As bad as her childhood was, and as much as she was hurt, she never hurt you.

Or anyone. And, Beth, she never would. The thing is, she didn't know that about herself at the time. Her own hurt was too fresh. She was afraid she might lash out."

"That's why she left?"

"That's why. Because she believed it was best for you. Safest for you. And happiest. That's what she wanted, Beth. For you to be safe and happy—the way she never was. I didn't know any of this until she and I talked today."

"You talked to her?"

"I did. We had a good talk."

"So you don't hate her."

"No, Beth. I don't. Not at all. But——" he cast a smiling but firm glance at both his daughter and Dina "——don't even *think* about a *Parent Trap* scenario."

The movie, in both its original and remake versions, was the girls' favorite to date. Jack didn't know its every line quite as well as Beth and Dina. But well enough.

"Of course not! I mean, what about——" Dina clamped her hands over her mouth.

"What about?"

"Paige," Beth said. "We thought… It seemed from the way you were talking to each other at the swim meet… You like her, don't you?"

"I like her a lot."

"And she likes you."

"Yes, sweetheart, she does. And she knows all about Helen."

"And doesn't hate her?"

"Nope. In fact, Paige thinks Helen sounds very nice." Jack almost didn't add Paige's assessment. His intent was to inform Beth without influencing her. But he couldn't let Beth worry about obstacles, such as Paige's disapproval, where there were none.

Jack looked from Beth's expressive face—in which he could see, so clearly, her every thought—to a fleecy cloud above the ocean.

The decision was Beth's alone.

Even Dina was silent.

"I wonder if she'd want to talk to me."

"I'm sure she would." The cloud reminded Jack of Claire's frolicking lamb. He turned to his daughter and saw that her decision had been made. "Very sure, Beth. But what matters most is whether you'd want to talk to her."

"I would." Beth spoke the assertion quietly, testing it, to see how it felt. Fine, apparently. She nodded decisively. "I would."

"That's settled then."

But, Beth's decision made, there were other issues to resolve.

"When should I talk to...my mother?"

"Whenever you like. Say the word and I'll give her a call."

"And set up a time when I'd phone her?"

"Sure. Or, if you like, a time when the two of you could meet."

"Meet?"

"She lives pretty close."

"I should probably think about what I'd want to ask her."

"Okay."

"Except…Paige said she wished she'd just talked to her mother when she was a girl. I think she meant without planning ahead. Maybe that would be better."

"Whatever you prefer, Beth. There's no hurry to decide."

But there was. The bond between mothers and daughters was that powerful. It could make even the most cautious of eleven-year-olds quite confident. And luminous.

"I've decided," Beth said. "I'd like to meet her as soon as she'd like to meet me."

Claire surfaced from her dreamless sleep as if she were a deep-sea diver startled by a shark—swiftly, gasping, afraid.

During her too-rapid ascent from slumber to wakefulness, she tried to make sense of her abdominal pain. It was different from what she'd recently known, but oddly familiar, strangely emotional. *Why?*

The answer caught up with her in the instants before she opened her eyes. She'd felt this way, her abdomen had, when she'd awakened in the hospital in Monterey, empty and aching, the little life, her dancing ballerina, no longer curled safe within.

It was a relief, for a moment, to open her eyes, to leave the aching sadness behind.

But the relief was short-lived as she realized she wasn't

in her bed at home, and something in her mouth, in her throat, was suffocating her. She wanted to reach for it, to pull it out. But she met resistance when she tried to lift her hands off the bed.

"Mother," Paige whispered, rising from her nearby chair. "You're awake. And you're fine. *Fine*. You're in the SICU, the one you designed. You've had surgery. You had an ulcer. But you sailed through. And your hands... Those are cloth restraints, at your wrists, so you don't accidentally disconnect the tubing."

Something had happened, though. Was happening. The slow, steady heartbeats had given way to racing, stumbling ones and the cardiac monitor was sounding its alarm.

The ventilator, too, signaled distress, no longer able to blow its precisely measured puffs into a compliant chest.

The response to the alarms was immediate. And impressive. Cole. Claire's nurse. The pulmonary specialist who'd been reviewing the most recent blood gas results.

And Stuart.

"She's awake," Paige informed them all, then spoke to Claire. "You're feeling a little panicky. That's understandable. But you're fine. Truly. Try to let the ventilator breathe for you. It's hard. It feels strange. But you're okay. Everything's okay. I know it's scary for you to be away from the mansion. But Jack's work crews are there. So even though you're here, if someone you've been

waiting for comes by, the crews will let them know—
him know—where you are…"

Paige's attempt to soothe wasn't working. Although it
did distract Claire from the medical assessment that was
taking place.

Panic attacks weren't fatal. Even though the afflicted
patient often felt she would die. But for a patient who'd
just undergone major surgery, the adrenaline rush posed
significant danger.

"She's bucking against the ventilator," the pulmonary
specialist said, stating the obvious. In an attempt to hy-
perventilate, Claire was working against the measured
puffs of the machine. The net effect was that she was getting very little air. "We're going to have to paralyze her,
Cole. We don't have a choice. She's going to get hypoxic
very soon."

Pharmacologic paralysis was easy. And, in some instances, it was a necessary emergency intervention. But
for a conscious patient, the sudden inability to move was
terrifying.

"I don't want to paralyze her. She's panicky enough
already."

"So what do you suggest?"

"That we extubate her. If she fatigues later on and has
to be reintubated, so be it. But maybe removing the
tube now will mean one less thing that's frightening
her."

"Okay. I'll call anesthesia."

Cole nodded, then joined Paige and Stuart by the bed.

Stuart was talking to Claire now. Whispering to her.

"Don't be afraid. We're here. Paige and I. And," he said as he removed the slender gold band from his pocket, "so is this. See? It's your wedding ring. I'll put it on your finger, and it'll be as if Alan's here with you, too. Okay?"

Stuart expected a frantic nod. *Yes, Stuart, hurry! I need Alan's ring. I need Alan.* But Claire looked straight at him. Held his gaze. And shook her head no.

"You don't want Alan's ring?"

She shook her head again. And in her eyes Stuart believed he saw the faintest smile. Of hope. Of courage.

Of the promise, he thought, to share her dream with him.

"Claire—"

"Stuart?" Cole interjected. "Anesthesia's here. We need to let them remove the endotracheal tube."

"Oh, yes. Of course."

Stuart withdrew, as did Paige. "She loves you, Stuart."

"And you, Paige. She's trying to stop her panic. Trying for both of us. But she can't."

"I'd always thought the reason for her agoraphobia was the fear of being away when my father came home. I know it wasn't *possible* for him to come home, of course. But there was no one else she would've been afraid to miss. Obviously, her agoraphobia is due to something else entirely."

"Maybe not," Stuart murmured. "Cole? I have a thought."

Cole joined them. "What thought?"

"Gwen," Stuart said. "Claire needs Gwen."

35

Mother and daughter walked in the fading sunlight on the emerald lawn above the ocean. A slow stroll around the academy grounds. And around again. And again. All the while, Jack kept Dina—champing at the bit to join the mother-daughter stroll—distracted if not entertained.

On their third lap, as twilight fell, Helen told Beth more—and less—than Jack had told their daughter about her childhood.

"It was always very hard for me to hear a baby cry," Helen said. "In many ways, including musically."

"Musically? *Oh*. I know why! Babies cry off-key, don't they? And it's so strident when they do." *Strident* was one of the academy orchestra director's favorite terms. As was... "*Discordant*. At least, it always has been for me... too."

"It has, Beth?"

"Yes! Maybe *all* babies don't cry off-key. But the baby brothers and sisters of my friends definitely do."

"What do you do when they cry?"

"I make them stop."

"How?"

"Oh, you know, first I ask them why they're crying. Why they're wasting time with tears. That doesn't usually work, though."

"Do you hold them?"

"You *have* to. And talk to them, and smile at them…and, what they seem to like best, you sing to them."

"It sounds as if you have a way with babies," Helen said. "Just like your dad."

"But not like you?"

"No, Beth." Helen smiled. "I wish I did."

"I could show you…if you want. There's a program at the medical center, in the neonatal ICU. Volunteers hold the babies who need holding. The ones whose mothers aren't there. Mrs. Forrester told us about it. I think it was her idea. Some babies need lots of holding, she says. Especially the babies born addicted to crack-cocaine. You have to be twelve to volunteer, so Dina and I won't begin until after my birthday next spring. But you could come with us, if you wanted to…if you're still here."

As fatigued as she was, Gwen hadn't expected to sleep. But, after a shower and with her face scrubbed clean, she'd curled into her bed, as she'd promised Cole she would do. Thinking of him, she drifted off to dreams.

Of him.

And awakened, at twilight, to her ringing phone and his gentle voice. "You were asleep."

"Yes. But...has something happened?"

"She's awake, Gwen. But she's having a panic attack. Stuart thinks that if you talk to her, it might calm her."

"*Stuart* thinks that? But this afternoon..."

"He didn't mention that she's been having memories of wandering and searching in the rain. At that point he wasn't certain the memories were real. But now he knows they are. According to Mariel, on the night which we know to have been the night you were left at the convent, your mother was found confused and disoriented in the hospital parking lot in Monterey."

"Does Paige know?"

"Stuart's telling her now."

"Do you think I should talk to...my mother?"

"Yes," Cole told the woman who trusted him. "I do."

"But..." Gwen felt panic of her own. "What if seeing me, learning about me, makes her panic attack even worse?"

"It won't." *It can't.* "Come now, Gwen. Your mother needs you."

"I can't believe she would've done such a thing."

"Nor can I, Paige," Stuart said. "But what if, in addition to everything else, she was experiencing postpartum psychosis?"

"I don't know. Yes, that could have made her give her baby, Gwen, away. But..."

"But what, Paige?"

"I'm not sure a diagnosis of postpartum psychosis would explain why she'd *forgotten* what she did. Even in the Yates case, as delusional as she was, the mother re-membered—in horrific detail—the murders of her five children. My understanding is that's typical of postpar-tum psychosis. Of many psychoses, for that matter. The disturbances are of thoughts, not memories. But," Paige murmured, "there *were* those other factors. The anes-thetic she was given. The emotional trauma she was going through. I guess we'll know when she talks to Gwen."

"I guess so," Stuart said softly. *I guess so.*

Paige met her twin in the elevator foyer.

"I knew," she whispered as they embraced. "Inside, I *knew.*"

"Me, too. Will you come with me? To talk to her?"

Paige hadn't considered it—but didn't question it.

"Of course. Stuart's with her now. The endotracheal tube is out, so she can talk, sort of, between gasps. She keeps saying she's sorry."

"For what?"

"The panic attack, she says. For not being able to make it stop."

Gwen had spent some time preparing herself to see Louise Johansson, so that she wouldn't recoil in horror no matter how deathlike Louise looked. And Gwen had also spent some time envisioning a first meeting with her mother.

But Gwen was quite unprepared for the first meeting with Claire to be exactly what she had feared with Louise.

Claire was dying. *Help her! Someone help her!* But no one was. Not Cole. Not Paige. Not Stuart. Yes, Stuart's hands were on Claire's shoulders, a tender caress. But beneath it her delicate shoulders heaved and fell.

It was only a matter of time—couldn't they *see* that?—before the effort of breathing became too great, and her racing heart took flight, and her eyes, downcast but darting, closed—forever—in surrender.

"Cole," Gwen whispered to the man she trusted, believed in...loved. "Do something. *Please.*"

"I will." Cole reached for Gwen's hand. "Come with me."

Maybe it was a leap of faith. But Cole had such faith. He'd missed Gwen all his life, after all, longed for her, but hadn't recognized that longing until she was found.

There was a missing piece, too, in Claire Forrester's life. A gaping wound that needed to heal. Cole believed Gwen was that balm—whether Claire knew what she'd been missing all her life or not.

"Mrs. Forrester?"

Claire looked up from her own hands, ringless and

knotted, but freed from their restraints when her lungs had been freed from the machine.

"Yes?"

"There's someone I'd like you to meet." Cole drew Gwen closer, supporting her, and bringing her in plain view of Claire. "This is—"

"*Gwennie*...I can't believe it's...you."

"You recognize me?"

"Yes! How can you...wonder?...You're my...sister. My *sister!*...I'm sorry...my breathing."

"It's okay," Gwen whispered. "My name *is* Gwen. But I'm afraid I'm not your sister."

"Oh? No. I see that...now. You're way too...young. You're Gwennie's...daughter, aren't you? Or...Becca's? Or...oh, you're *Robbie's* little girl."

No. I'm your little girl. "I...no."

"Robbie was Claire's twin," Stuart explained. "Claire? Gwen isn't your niece. But she is a twin. Like you. And the reason she looks so much like your sisters is that the two of you are related."

"How...lovely."

"It is lovely," Stuart said. "Gwen is Paige's sister, Claire. Paige's twin. She's the baby girl you've been searching for in your memory of that stormy night."

"*Oh.*" Claire's eyes closed, as if she was seeing a truth too bright to endure.

And, as if wishing they had a dagger to clutch, her ringless hands flew over her heart.

And then her breathing slowed.

And her heart no longer raced.

When her eyes opened they shimmered with love. It wasn't Alan she'd been waiting for all these years.

It was Gwen.

"I heard you cry," she whispered. "In the ambulance, at the crash site. I *did*. But I told myself it was impossible. Paige wasn't born until after we reached the hospital in Monterey, and I'd been unconscious in the ambulance. Unable to hear anything at all. And..."

"What, Claire?" Stuart asked.

"And Mariel told me that if I'd heard something, if my subconscious had, it must've been the wind. Or one of the sirens. There were so many sirens that day. But it was you, Gwen. *You*."

Claire reached to touch her daughter's unhidden cheek. "What's this? Oh, a birthmark." Which Claire caressed as if touching the most priceless of all treasures. And the most rare—a precious gem she'd never seen. "Where did you go? *Who stole you from me? From us?*"

Us. Claire. Paige. Stuart. Gwen. The family they could have been, and should have been, and would have been.

"Stuart?" Claire asked. "Do you know what happened?"

"Yes," he said quietly to the family that still could be. Should be. Would be. It was forming even now, healing as he spoke. Claire. Her long-lost daughters, both of them. And him. "I believe I do."

* * *

Mariel was smart enough to take a cab when she was drinking.

And she had been drinking.

Stuart opened the back seat door and paid the driver.

"Stuart! How gallant of you." She took his hand as he helped her out. "But what on earth are you doing camped on my doorstep at 3:00 a.m.?"

"We need to talk."

"Talk? Oh! *Claire.*"

"Claire's fine." Stuart didn't speak again until they were inside her home. "Tell me how a Main Line Philadelphia girl like you pretended to be a tourist from Iowa."

She hesitated a beat too long. "What are you talking about?"

"Or, just before that charade at the convent, how you passed yourself off as Claire at the newborn nursery in Carmel. We all know what you did. Gwen's the baby you gave away."

"Stuart, I have no idea——"

"What we don't know is why. Although I have my suspicions."

"Would you like something to drink?"

"No. You saw the birthmark, didn't you, Mariel? At the crash site when she was born. And you decided on the spot you weren't going to be godmother to such a blemished little girl."

"I would have been a *mother* to her."

"Claire was her mother."

"Yes. But Alan was going to get tired of Claire. He *had* to. It was just a matter of time before he and I would marry."

"And raise his daughters. The undamaged one, that is. How did you convince the ambulance to take Gwen to one hospital and Claire to another?"

"I *didn't*. It just...happened."

"And you seized the opportunity to get rid of the baby you didn't want."

"I gave her away for Alan, Stuart. *Because* of Alan. Not because of me."

"I don't believe it."

"I don't care! It's true. If you'd seen Rosalind's face at the crash site you might have done it, too."

"Never."

"You didn't see her face, Stuart. But Alan did. And I did. The birthmark...it looked *identical* to the way Rosalind's face was bloodied and torn. Do you know how hard it would've been for Alan—and, Stuart, how unspeakably sad—to spend every day of his life looking at a reminder of his mother's death? *Seeing* that reminder on the face of his child?"

"Hard for Alan, Mariel? Or for you?"

"For both of us, Stuart. Because of Rosalind. *Rosalind.* Not because of the birthmark itself. But it would've been hardest on Alan. Impossible. And I didn't want him to have that sadness. I *loved* him."

"You're the one who ended your relationship with Alan."

"I had to. It was the only way to show him how much he'd miss me, and want me, and need me. It would've worked, too. If not for Claire."

"Alan wasn't going to tire of Claire, Mariel. Ever. He'd never have gone back to you."

"Why are you being so cruel?"

"I'm just being honest. Claire was the love of Alan's life."

"I *know*. Don't you think I *know*?"

"But you gave his daughter away."

"I told you already. For Alan's sake. Because of Rosalind. You can believe that or not, Stuart. But it's true. Whether or not Alan and I got back together, I didn't want that sadness for him."

"But Alan died, Mariel. And you knew where the baby, *Claire's* baby, was. But you never said a word. And you could have. You know that. You could have told me at any time. I would've found a way to reunite Gwen with Claire and Paige without ever implicating you. But you didn't tell me. Why not?"

"*Because* Alan died, Stuart. Alan was dead. And I was dying, too. I *did* die. And for a very long time nothing mattered…still doesn't, not in the way things mattered when he was alive."

"Nothing," Stuart said quietly. "Including that little girl."

"I don't know. I…guess. I did think about her sometimes."

"Good for you," he muttered sarcastically.

"Oh, Stuart, please don't hate me! *Please.* Can't you please try to understand?"

"No, Mariel. I can't. But you know the hell of it? They will. Claire and Gwen and Paige. They'll try to understand. They *will* understand. And you know what else? They'll probably forgive you."

Epilogue

Pacific Heights Medical Center
Monday, November 10
One year later

It was the quiet time in the hospital cafeteria, when almost no one else was there, the same time Paige and Gwen had met for lattes last November.

A Monday afternoon latte, at a window table overlooking the bay, had become a weekly event for Claire and her daughters, a rendezvous so sacrosanct it was skipped only in the most extraordinary of circumstances.

Indeed, for each, only her own honeymoon had kept her away. On a Monday in January Claire had been sailing with Stuart aboard the QE2. And on the Monday following their Valentine's Day wedding, Paige and Jack had been in Paris. *Naturellement*. And in May, Cole had taken his bride to a secluded bungalow on Maui's northernmost shore.

It didn't matter how often Claire and her daughters had spoken during the week, or how many e-mails they'd exchanged, or even if there'd been a family dinner the night before. Each looked forward to their Monday afternoon as if it had been far too long since they'd seen each other last.

"Paige!" Claire rose to give her daughter a welcoming hug.

The mother-daughter embrace wasn't awkward, just as there was never any awkwardness, now, when Claire and Paige were alone...without any other daughters in sight.

Yes, Gwen had been the missing piece. The answer to the emptiness both Paige and Claire had felt, and the reason for the vast abyss between them. But, welcome though she always was, Gwen didn't have to be present to smooth the way.

"You're early," Claire said when the effortless hug ended and they sat.

"For once. You're early, too."

Always, Claire thought. Always early when it came to seeing her girls. Looking now at Paige, Claire saw rosy cheeks and eyes aglow. The daughter who'd been ill for so long, and lonely even longer, was the picture of health. And happiness. Except that... "You don't have a latte. Oh, darling, are you all right?"

"I'm fine!" Fine, fine, fine. A lie, a lie, a lie? No. Merely the wondrous truth. The HLA-match had been perfect.

Destiny would have it no other way. And Paige's immune system had welcomed her twin's kidney as if it were her own. "I was en route to get a latte, but I spotted you and came right over."

"Do you want one now?"

"Maybe in a while. I'm happily settled. And," Paige said softly, "I'm not really thirsty."

She wasn't on fluid restriction anymore. On *any* restrictions thanks to—

"Calm me down!" Gwen commanded as, flushed and breathless, she joined her mother and her twin.

She was smiling and, like Paige, rosy and aglow. Gwen's pinkness, the color of the cherry blossoms beneath which she and Cole had wed, came entirely from within. She wore no makeup and was blemish-free.

Gwen also wore a white coat. Hospital policy. It was imperative, the administrators concurred, that all medical center employees involved in patient care wear the readily identifiable garment embroidered with their names.

Admittedly, it was unlikely that someone pretending to be a makeup artist would enter a patient's room and start adorning a haggard face with color. But there were instances—none, thankfully at PHMC—of imposter physicians wandering onto hospital wards and performing physical exams. The hospital-issue coat, with the specially embroidered name, was one of many barriers to such an abuse.

"Why do you need to be calmed down?" Claire asked. "What happened?"

"I'll bet I know," Paige said. "Let me guess—the disaster-drill committee meeting?"

"*Yes.* It was very productive for the first, oh, forty minutes. They showed me photographs of the makeup done on mock patients in previous drills, and we discussed changes and improvements I'd make. Then, just when it seemed like the meeting was over, someone suggested throwing in a few diagnostic dilemmas."

"And it became a contest of which physician could think of the most obscure medical syndrome to portray?"

"You've been to such committee meetings," Gwen said.

"Worse." Paige smiled. "I've been to medical school."

"Well...it's *wonderful* that they know all the obscure syndromes, but when it became clear that no further decisions were going to be made, I told them I had an important engagement—and left."

"And here you are," Claire said. "Without a latte, either."

"I'll get one later. You said there's something you want to discuss?"

"There is. I'm thinking about orchestrating a little get-together."

The notion of Claire's arranging a get-together—a *party*—wasn't unusual. She did it all the time, loved doing it, especially for her family...which, even if the guest list only consisted of family members within a one-mile radius of where they now sat, couldn't be described as a *little* gathering. Nine adults counting Helen——who counted——and Beth. More often than not, Dina and Larry joined the party, too.

And if a call was placed to any of the frequently dialed numbers in Sarah's Orchard, the potential gathering was truly vast.

The MacKenzies had searched for their Claire. Her brothers and sisters had hitchhiked to San Francisco, when one of the boys was along, or, as Claire herself had done, they'd taken the bus. And they'd gone to the places where an impoverished street artist was likely to be. The Wharf. The Haight. The Park. Terrifying places, they thought…and where, they feared, their delicate sister couldn't possibly survive.

They'd even hired an investigator, despite the expense. But there'd been no computerized databases to examine three decades ago. No Internet to explore. And it wouldn't have occurred to any of them, ever, to search for her in a mansion in Pacific Heights.

They hadn't forgotten her, though. The holes in their hearts were as gaping as in hers. But when they heard her voice again, at last, Claire's family, like Claire, began to heal.

"A *little* get-together?" Gwen echoed.

"Actually, yes. Mariel's returned."

The Forrester women *had* forgiven Mariel, as Stuart had predicted they would. None understood what she'd done, the act itself. But each, in her own life, had experienced a sense of the world spinning out of control. And they felt so happy, and so whole, there wasn't room in their hearts for anything less.

Mariel had vanished within hours of her revelation to Stuart. She'd written, however, to Claire, to Paige, to Gwen. Anguished letters that had taken months to compose—and bore no return address to which to forward a reply.

And now Mariel was back.

"Have you spoken to her?"

"Not yet. She sent me a note. I wanted to talk it over with the two of you first. You'll probably want to think about it."

"Not really," Gwen said. "I always thought we'd see her one day." She looked at her twin. "Isn't that what you thought, too?"

"Absolutely. Let's do it. Just the four of us. *Soon*." Paige smiled at Claire, assuming she'd be relieved.

But Claire's attention was elsewhere, the latte bar—and Cole.

It was surprising that he was in the cafeteria at all, and a certainty he wouldn't join them. Or even let them know he was near. He, like Jack and Stuart, was protective of this special mother-daughter time—more protective, all three of them, than the wives themselves...so very protective of the women they loved.

They were dragon-slayers all, those loving men. Demon-slayers.

But the way Cole was looking at Gwen was something new.

A different fierceness.

A desperate tenderness.

"Gwen," Claire whispered. "You're pregnant?"

"Yes. How...?"

"I'm your mother. I can tell." *And I remember the way your father looked at me when I told him I was carrying his child.* His children. The twin daughters who glowed, on this day. *Both* of them. "Paige?"

"Yes," she said softly. "I'm pregnant, too."

"But..."

"It's okay. I'll be fine."

And she would be. Both twins would be.

In this, too, destiny would have it no other way.

Turn the page for a brief excerpt from
Katherine Stone's
moving and dramatic new book,

ANOTHER MAN'S SON.

Coming from MIRA Books in January 2004.

Sam Collier has always known he was abandoned by his father—the father he can't remember. He's felt a sense of homelessness all his life.

For years Sam was a drifter by choice, but now he's settled in a small Oregon town. In his travels, Sam enjoyed the company of dogs and he has just made the decision to get a dog of his own. He's recently called a woman named Marge Hathaway, a breeder of cocker spaniels. He realizes that "Marge might logically call some of the townspeople she knew," to be sure that her puppy's going to a good home, and imagines what those people might say....

And what would the good citizens of Sarah's Orchard, Oregon, say about Sam Collier?

That they'd all been pretty sure, when Sam had ridden into town on his Harley, that he was a Hell's Angel. The pieces all seemed to fit: long, black hair, black leather jacket, a fierce expression on his face.

Sam had been stopping for gas, that was all, a brief stop on his way to the coast. He'd felt the wary stares that greeted him and sensed the relief as he roared away.

The neglected apple orchard was two miles out of town. Its For Sale sign, like the trees themselves, slumped in despair.

Sam was traveling fast, speeding toward the sea, when the emotion—sadness—stole his breath.

Sadness, for the forsaken trees.

He skidded to a stop and waited until he could breathe. But intermingled with the sadness was that defiant emotion hope. Which was why Sam returned to town.

A dozen years of homelessness, combined with dangerous and lucrative work, enabled Sam to buy the abandoned orchard with money to spare for a haircut, a pickup truck and, most importantly, for the sad trees themselves.

Sarah's Orchard was known for its apples, just as nearby Medford was renowned for its pears. There wasn't a Harry and David equivalent in Sarah's Orchard, however, either in scope or in scale. Instead of one large enterprise, the Sarah's Orchard apple industry, such as it was, consisted of small-business owners, each with a particular type of apple-related produce.

When Sam arrived in Sarah's Orchard, the apple industry was in trouble. His orchard was by no means the town's only source of apples, but whatever had caused its trees to give up had affected, though less dramatically, other orchards, as well.

The townspeople seriously doubted that Sam's barren trees would ever produce again—specially since it was obvious, given the books he bought from the town's bookstore, that he knew nothing about the care and tending of fruit trees...or for that matter, *any* trees.

But Sam Collier was either a particularly good between-the-lines reader, or a grower with exceptional gifts. The town remained divided over which. There was no dispute, however, about the results—more apples than before and *better* apples, with a taste unlike any other.

Sam knew it had nothing to do with him. He'd merely followed the standard advice on pruning, fertilizing, watering, harvesting. The timing had been right, that was all. The ground had lain fallow, the trees in hibernation, long enough. Well rested, the orchard was ready and eager to be bountiful again.

Nonetheless, should Marge Hathaway happen to ask, any resident of Sarah's Orchard would insist that Sam Collier had both a green thumb and a golden touch. The town's economy had been revitalized, thanks to him. Sarah's Orchard was in his debt.

And if Marge happened to talk to one of the chattier

of the townspeople, she might hear that he wasn't a Hell's Angel, after all—though arguably a fallen one. Men admired him, Marge might be told. And women... Well, it was impossible to look at Sam—or hear his voice, or speak his name—without thinking about sex. It was a harmless fantasy. Sam was too private and too smart to become involved with any woman in Sarah's Orchard.

Sam guessed that Marge, fancying herself a "hip old gal," wouldn't be put off by such a report.

The trouble was, with only two possible exceptions, no one would say to Marge Hathaway what Sam most needed her to hear—that if there was ever a man who should have a dog, it was Sam Collier. And what a lucky dog it would be!

The conversation might not even get that far, however, for people would insist that Marge *must* be mistaken about the identity of the man who'd called her. It couldn't have been Sam. He wasn't even in town. In winter, while his apple trees slumbered, he always went away. No one knew where, but they all believed they knew why: to rendezvous with old lovers, perhaps meet new ones.

In the beginning, sex had been a major reason for leaving Sarah's Orchard every December first. Sex and the restless yearnings the Christmas holidays inevitably evoked. The restlessness hadn't diminished over time but more and more he chose to be alone.

And this year, despite the restlessness—or perhaps

because the restless yearning was as much about the wish for a dog as the remembrance of lonely Christmases as an unwanted boy—Sam had stayed home.

People might also tell Marge there was a second reason her caller couldn't have been Sam. If he ever did get a dog, it would be a creature like him—wild and dangerous, part wolf if not pure wolf. And it would be an adult dog, not a puppy. Oh, sure, Sam Collier had a gift for nurturing trees. But that was very different, wasn't it, from the care of a pup?

Whoever had called Marge, these people would say, it hadn't been Sam. No way. In fact, it was pointless for her to call him. He wouldn't be back in Sarah's Orchard until early March. And although quite expert when it came to computers, and most generous in offering his expertise to those who weren't, for some reason Sam employed neither a voice-messaging service nor an answering machine.

No one except Sam knew the reason. But it was simple. There'd never before been a phone call he'd regret having missed.

Sam wouldn't miss Marge's call. *If* she called.

And now, on December thirtieth, she had.

With a leftover puppy.

That was his if he wanted her.

"I do want her," he repeated. "I can come for her now if that's convenient."

"It *is* convenient, but why don't I tell you a little more about her first?"

Marge's question was a warning. There were things he needed to know before making the drive. Negative things that might make him change his mind.

Sam knew he wouldn't change his mind about the un-wanted puppy. But if Marge felt more comfortable re-vealing everything now... "All right."

"Well, she hasn't socialized. If anything, she's gotten worse. Mind you, she's a sweet-tempered little creature. A sensitive little creature. But, Sam, we'll keep her if you don't want her."

"I do want her."

"Well, great. I just had to be sure you knew she's going to need a lot of love and reassurance. Far more than the usual pup. But that's the way with problem children, isn't it? They turn out all right, though, if they get the love they need."

If. Sam felt a long-banished memory straining to be free. He knew what memory it was. The first clear mem-ory of his life. He was six. His baby brother, Billy, was due to be born in less than a month.

And Sam couldn't wait—until he overheard his mother and stepfather discussing him, *their* problem child.

I don't want Sam anywhere near my son, Vanessa.

Our son, Mason.

Yes, darling, our son. Our Billy. Who needs our protection from Sam.

You really think Sam might hurt Billy?

I have no idea. But it's not a risk I'm willing to take. There's something wrong with Sam. Very wrong. You know it and I know it. Maybe it's time to put him back on the medications.

He's calm now, Mason. Even off the Valium, he's calm. And we've never seen any violence in him.

Not yet. But the genes are there. I suppose you wouldn't consider shipping him off to his father?

Mason! You know what kind of man, what kind of monster, Ian Collier is. With luck, he's in prison by now...or dead.

"Sam?" Marge asked. "Are you there?"

"Right here, but leaving in about five minutes. I should be at your home by four."

If you enjoyed what you just read,
then we've got an offer you can't resist!

Take 2
bestselling novels FREE!
Plus get a FREE surprise gift!

KATHERINE STONE

66954   STAR LIGHT, STAR BRIGHT   ___ $6.99 U.S. ___ $8.50 CAN.

(limited quantities available)

TOTAL AMOUNT	$_____
POSTAGE & HANDLING	$_____
($1.00 for one book; 50¢ for each additional)	
APPLICABLE TAXES*	$_____
<u>TOTAL PAYABLE</u>	$_____

(check or money order—please do not send cash)

To order, complete this form and send it, along with a check or money order for the total above, payable to MIRA Books, to: **In the U.S.:** 3010 Walden Avenue, P.O. Box 9077, Buffalo, NY 14269-9077; **In Canada:** P.O. Box 636, Fort Erie, Ontario, L2A 5X3.

Name:_____

Address:_____ City:_____

State/Prov.:_____ Zip/Postal Code:_____

Account Number (if applicable):_____
075 CSAS

  *New York residents remit applicable sales taxes.
   Canadian residents remit applicable GST and provincial taxes.

MIRA®